ALWAYS YOURS

Emma Dunnill

Copyright © 2023 Emma Dunnill

All rights reserved.

The characters and events portrayed in this book are fictitious. Any similarity to real persons, living or dead, is coincidental and not intended by the author.

No part of this book may be reproduced, or stored in a retrieval system, or transmitted in any form or by any means, electronic, mechanical, photocopying, recording, or otherwise, without express written permission of the publisher.

ISBN: 9798865360391
Independently published.
Cover design by: Emma Dunnill

*For my family.
Thank you for everything.*

ACKNOWLEDGEMENTS

It has been an escape, a challenge, and a pleasure to write my first novel. I toyed with the basic themes of this book many years ago, when I was starting to write, completing a few chapters. Years later, I decided to bite the bullet and complete my manuscript, whilst working full-time and studying for a professional certificate. Well, I do like a challenge! To say I have a published novel, sitting alongside my favourite authors is something I would never have imagined. Thank you to all the publishing houses I spoke to, that gave me the confidence to proceed. Thank you to Diane Hall of The Writing Hall, for meeting with me and explaining everything about the world of publishing! Thank you to my boyfriend who has had to spend many hours alone, barred to the other room as I requested privacy and silence to write. Thank you to my family for not laughing in my face when I told them I had drafted a book! Also, Mum, all those photos of the US men's Olympic swim team that plastered my bedroom wall was most definitely research... honest!

I hope you enjoy my first novel and stick around for the next one. I am incredibly grateful to everyone who takes the time to read it.

PROLOGUE

Looking up at Jake on the stage, despite his sweat soaked face and hair; Jessica felt an overwhelming sense of love for him. The intense passion with which he strummed his guitar, with his strong arms made teenage fans swoon over him as he performed. Just as she did too. All she could think was 'he's mine!', as she continued to gaze at him with adoration.
Selfies weren't really a thing when they were at university, so many of the fan girls relied on their friends taking photos of them with the band. Jessica couldn't judge, she did exactly the same when she went to gigs. The difference was, Jake went home with her at the end of the night. There had been girls who had tried it on with Jake, right in front of Jessica's eyes, but he would quickly step away and make it clear to them that he had a girlfriend. Worryingly, that would sometimes encourage them more. At that point, he would just walk away.

One night, Jake's band, Juniper, had been scheduled to perform at a small venue owned by Leeds Metropolitan University. The band were both delighted and honoured to be supporting another local band who were starting to hit the big time. Her brother's band, Lateral Divide, were also supporting the main

band. The two groups did a few gigs together over the years. This certainly killed two birds with one stone for Jessica; only having to go to one gig to see both. She still found it weird that younger girls were lusting after her brother, as well as her boyfriend.
Jessica had a late lecture that day so instead of being backstage like usual, she arrived at the same time as all the other gig-goers. Part of her wanted to push her way to the front of the stage, where she could cheer them on. She decided instead, to hover near the sides. Cheap beer in hand, she got herself comfortable, leaning against the wall and waited for them to take to the stage.

It was certainly one of the best gigs that Lateral Divide had played; so much so, that she got out her phone to text her brother to congratulate him. After a short break, Juniper took to the stage, greeted by cheers from teenage boys and screams from teenage girls alike. Everyone in the crowd seemed to be having a good time. Jessica watched in amusement as she saw younger girls lining up their digital cameras to snap zoomed in photos of Jake.

'Oh my god, he was definitely looking at me. Did you see him? He was staring right at me!'
Jessica found herself eavesdropping into a conversation between two girls stood next to her. Both of them looked about her age or even older; it was hard to say.

'You should hang around near the door afterwards. See if you can get his number,' the girl's friend suggested. Jessica couldn't help wondering who they were talking about. The lead singer of Juniper, Tom, was a good looking guy, if not just a bit on the short side.

'Actually, I'm pretty sure he's in one of my seminar groups,' the girl's friend offered.

'What? Why didn't you say sooner?! Get me his number!'

Jessica smiled as she texted Jake to tell him the show was great. She decided to hang around to watch the main band. However, the band were yet to come on, when of the girls beside Jessica gasped loudly, startling her.

'Oh my god, there he is! He's over at the merch tables!' she squealed, pointing for her friend.

'Right, I'm off over. Wish me luck!' the second girl said, downing the rest of her drink.

Jessica still couldn't see who the girl had been pointing at. She hoped it wouldn't be her brother, the thought of him getting with random girls made her feel queasy. Then she saw the girl cornering Jake. Now she really did feel queasy. *Why wasn't he pushing her away? Hang on, was he about to... what? Why was he hugging her?* Jessica's mind was racing, and she could feel her stomach contents gurgling around. If she hadn't overheard the conversation prior, she would've just assumed they were old friends. She decided that enough was enough, downed her drink and was about to march over. She stopped when she saw Jake take out his phone as the girl was still talking.

Oh my god, he was going to exchange numbers with her, Jessica thought, raging inside. Just as her blood had reached boiling point, her phone buzzed in her pocket. It was a message from Jake. She looked up to see he was still cornered by the girl, but trying desperately to show her some of the merch on the table. Jessica opened the message.

HELP! MERCH. NOW.

Looking back up in Jake's direction, Jessica smiled, feeling her blood returning to normal temperature. She wandered over to where they were stood, and she saw the look of relief on his face as he clocked her. She politely but purposefully squeezed past the girl that was cornering him. She then dramatically threw her arms round him. She had to be honest and say that it did feel good that when girls were throwing themselves at him, she had the power to make it very clear that he was not available.

'Amazing show as always babe,' Jessica said, giving him a long kiss on the lips. She'd never called him *'babe'* in his life, but it felt like she had to make her point clear. He didn't say anything in reply. He simply put his arm round her and squeezed her tight to his body, smiling cheesily at the girl in front of him. Jessica heard the girl scowl as she stormed off, aware that the game was up. She grabbed her friend and they headed nearer to the stage as the final band started up.

'Thank you for that,' he laughed, giving Jessica a kiss on the cheek. 'Also, *babe*?' he said, pulling a face.

'Yeah, never again,' Jessica laughed, cringing at the word of supposed affection.

'Are you desperate to watch the group, or do you want to get out of here?' he said, gently pushing a strand of her hair behind her ear.

'Pizza and film?' Jessica posed, eyebrows raised.

'Sounds perfect. Lads?' he raised his hand to his fellow bandmates to show them that he was headed off. Tom rolled his eyes humorously; as he knew this was the standard protocol these days.

Jessica first met Jake at university when they were studying in Sheffield. They quite literally bumped into each other outside a seminar room. He was in a hurry and ran into Jessica, sending her flying through a door into another group's room. While she lay on the floor, utterly mortified and face the colour of beetroot, he scooped her up, whilst apologising to the group they had accidentally interrupted. He asked her out for a drink to make it up to her, to which she agreed. This was where they discovered just how much they had in common. From then on, they were practically glued to each other. His friends became her friends and vice versa, forming a tight knit group. When Jake and his friends first started the band, Jessica spent more of her time at the small, dingy rehearsal room they were renting from a friend. Whilst they thrashed out new music, she wrote up lecture notes. They'd often get mocked and jeered by their friends; for being so besotted with each other. Everyone said they'd be the first to get married and start a family. At the time, this seemed a million miles away for the pair; who were still technically teenagers, despite being considered adults by society.

One Thursday afternoon, writing up her notes and forgetting she was amongst company, Jessica nonchalantly joined in singing along to the songs she had begun to know well from the repeated rehearsals. Suddenly, the music came to a gradual stop, and she felt everyone's eyes on her as she put her pen down.

Oops. She'd been confidently singing away and harmonising with the lead singer, Tom, without realising anyone could actually hear her.

'Wow! Jessica, you have an amazing voice!' Tom called out, making her blush even more than she already was.

'Incredible...' Luke, the drummer noted while the other members of the band were nodding approvingly. She was trying to utter some words apologetically for interrupting their rehearsals, when Jake approached her with his guitar swung round to his back. He smiled gently in a way that always made Jessica melt inside, and then kissed her. That was when he said it for the first time.

'I love you.'

A matter of weeks after Jessica's harmonic outburst in the rehearsal room, she found herself rehearsing for a gig in Leadmill. The small venue was predominantly a student club, but had a stage to host up and coming artists. Tom, and the rest of Juniper were performing that night. When another band had pulled out of the line up; Tom had suggested Jessica's name to the venue. She'd spent a lot of her spare time writing poetry in between lectures, then decided to somewhat wing it by adding a melody to the verses with her old keyboard. Thus, providing her with her own songs to throw into the mix along with a few covers she'd got lined up. Feeling beyond amateur, Jessica outright refused to let Jake or anyone in the room while she rehearsed and sound-checked. She felt extremely out of her depth, but before she knew it, the hours had passed, and she suddenly found herself stood on stage in front of a full crowd. Granted, it was only about fifty people, but to her, it felt like

Wembley. She nervously sat down at the piano that Tom had arranged for her, and took a deep breath. Next thing she could recall was everyone cheering. She never imagined she could sing in front of anyone, let alone a room packed with people. She shyly raised her hand to the crowd, in thanks for their support, before leaving the stage for Juniper to set up.

'Jess, you were amazing' Jake said, holding her in his strong, safe arms. Smiling, she gazed back into his dreamy eyes.

'That was the scariest thing I've ever done!' she laughed, as he pulled her close for a long hug.

Over the next few months, Jessica was starting to become a bit of a local celebrity. People would recognise her in the street, mainly students, but it was more than she had ever known before. She'd been uploading recordings to a YouTube channel that she'd been talked into setting up, by Tom and Jake. She'd performed at assorted student unions round the UK. Even the university had clocked on and taken advantage of her growing popularity. They shamelessly used her for advertising purposes; to get more students to pick Sheffield Hallam University as their first choice.

Despite being smack bang in the middle of her business degree, she was being offered various short term music contracts with local producers who were trying to make names for themselves. As she was actively turning them down, she couldn't help but feel sorry for Jake and the rest of the group. They'd been working so hard to get themselves on the map. They'd only ever got as far as repeatedly touring a few small clubs in the UK. *They* deserved these offers, not her. She ultimately just wanted to finish her degree; she'd kind of fallen into this whole industry. Even her dad was referring to her as a 'pop star', which made her both laugh and cringe every time he said it.

One evening in late spring of their final year, Jessica was

out for dinner with the boys from Juniper, and a few of their girlfriends. The topic was raised of the most recent contract Jessica had been offered. She'd ruled it out instantaneously, as it would mean she had to move to Los Angeles. She hadn't actually told any of them this part though.

'We totally think you should go for it!' Lucy confidently said, with the rest of the group nodding along. Jessica saw Jake tense up and adjust his position on his chair, saying nothing.

'I really just want to finish my degree. I was just filling in for that band, when they pulled out at the last minute. It was just a bit of fun!' Jessica protested.

Even though she'd been uploading songs online, encouraged by great feedback, she still felt it was just a hobby more than anything else. She wanted to go into business management, not become the next Britney! After they'd finished eating and a few cocktails had been hammered, Tom came and plonked himself down next to her.

'Okay, look, I can understand you not taking those amateur contracts; those terms are shit. But why aren't you taking the other one? Am I missing something?'

'I'd have to move to LA,' she whispered so no-one else could hear.

Tom's eyes widened with excitement before he pulled a face and shrugged. 'So...?'

He noticed her eyes dart over to Jake, who was sat talking to Luke and Georgia.

'Ah,' he simply replied, nodding.

◆ ◆ ◆

'Are you kidding me?' Jake was shell-shocked. Jessica had just told him that she was going to accept the contract, meaning she was leaving for LA in a matter of weeks. She'd bartered with them as much as she could, to allow them to sign her after she graduated. For weeks, she'd been trying to find ways to tell Jake the news but couldn't find the right time. Whether it was the pressing time or the celebratory mood everyone was in, but for some reason this felt the right time.

'Jess... I can't lose you.'

'Come with me,' she stuttered.

'You know I can't do that... I've got this grad job signed and sealed.'

Standing outside City Hall in Sheffield, despite it being packed with graduates and their families, it felt like it was just Jessica and Jake, silence in the air. They'd both said goodbye to their parents shortly after the ceremony and photos. They'd arranged to go for celebratory drinks, just the two of them. In a sudden change of mood, everything suddenly went on fast forward and next thing she knew, Jake's face crumbled with a mixture of anger and hurt. He ripped off his gown and mortar board, throwing them on the floor. He was marching off, ruffling his hair as he did so. Fortunately, everyone else was in their own world with their families so no-one witnessed his dramatic outburst. He was heading towards Devonshire Green. Jessica calmly signed their rented gowns back in and headed in the same direction shortly afterwards. As she got closer, Jessica could see him sat under a large tree on the green, knees up with his head leant back against the trunk of the tree with his eyes closed. As she stood before him, she opened her mouth to speak but changed her mind, instead choosing to sit down next to him and take his hand. He must've felt her presence because he didn't flinch when she took his hand in hers.

'Jake...' she prompted, longing for him to open his eyes and look into hers. He granted Jessica half her wish, opening his eyes but staring down at the grass between his legs instead. Something inside him suddenly switched as he stood up and looked down at her.

'Come on,' he bluntly instructed after rubbing his face. His tone was one that Jessica had never heard before, so she held his gaze as she stood up to join him. She prompted him to lead the way, and that he did. He was clearly taking them back to his flat on Portland Lane. As they entered the building and took the lift up to the 8th floor, neither of them spoke. Jake unlocked the door to his flat, stood aside to let Jessica in and then closed the door behind them. He stood fidgeting with his keys for a few seconds, before making eye contact again and holding her gaze. This time though, instead of the dreamy eyes he usually made at her, his eyes looked more glazed and glossier, as if he was about to cry. Slamming his keys down on the kitchen worktop, he stepped forward and nestled his hands into her hair, lowering himself to kiss her. After a long, intense kiss, he retreated and looked at Jessica longingly, almost as if he was asking permission to kiss her so forcefully. She gave him a look of approval that caused him to lunge forward again to meet her mouth. This time he lifted her up to perch on the kitchen worktop, so she was equal height with him. As things began to intensify, he lifted her down and then led her to his bedroom. A room she'd been in so many times suddenly felt odd and cold. Jessica felt like a stranger. Before she knew it, they were intertwined with each other, her legs wrapping round his waist, never breaking eye contact. When they both climaxed, they just lay there in silence, holding hands. Tears began to fall down Jessica's cheeks and past her ears, onto the pillow underneath her head. Then, she started to sob uncontrollably. Usually, if she was crying, Jake would take her in his arms and hold her tightly. Not this time. He just lay there, even removing his hand from hers.

After half an hour of silence and sobs, she knew she had to leave. She quietly got dressed and stood at the door, looking back at Jake. He was still lying there just staring at the ceiling.

'I love you. I always have, I always will. I'm sorry,' she managed to whisper.

He blinked at the ceiling before bluntly saying, 'Bye Jess, best of luck with everything.'

A part of her wanted to jump back on the bed and never let him go, but she went with what she thought was the easier choice. She broke his heart and broke her own at the same time.

ONE

Jessica had been in LA for two years now and performing to 20,000 people had become the norm, despite still feeling somewhat bizarre to her. She'd met Daniel about a year ago when they were both on a Saturday night chat show. He'd represented Team USA in the Olympics, so he was showing off his medals with other Olympians. Jessica was promoting her new album. She was undeniably reluctant to accept his number at first; knowing he was a sportsman, as they don't have the best reputation. However, he completely shattered her reservations and she fell for him within a matter of months. She'd not heard from Jake since that fateful night, but speaking to Lucy and Georgia, she knew that he was doing okay. He was even dating again. Nothing of any significance though, apparently. She did of course have the occasional social media stalk too which revealed little in the way of romance.

'My mom's coming over this weekend; I'd love you to meet her,' Daniel said out the blue.

'Ooh, you want me to meet your mum?' Jessica mockingly asked.

'Of course, it's been long enough now!' he pulled her closer, kissing her forehead.

'Oh and just so you know, I've never introduced a girl to Mom before,' he added with a smile.

'Hmm, what does that say about me then? Clearly a keeper,' she mocked again.

'Definitely,' he paused, 'although I should probably tell you it isn't just my mom, my brothers and sister are coming over to hers too.'

Jessica nearly spat out the coffee she'd just made as he awkwardly smirked at her. 'Whoa! Way to spring that upon me Dan!' she spluttered. 'But, gets it all over with in one go I suppose.' She'd only heard stories of Daniel's family and they certainly seemed a lively bunch. Some of the stories she'd heard; they were quite a formidable group. Like most girls meeting the family, she was most nervous to meet his mother and sister.

The two most important females to him, and then me, Jessica thought. She needn't have worried about meeting the Brown clan; she was welcomed with open arms by each one. Daniel's sister, Hannah took Jessica to one side and told her how delighted she was that her brother had finally settled down with someone. Jessica raised her eyebrows at this point and Hannah quickly reassured her that simply meant 'someone normal.' Jessica decided to accept that as a compliment; the way it was intended. She thought.

The family spent a lot of the afternoon in the back yard and Jessica politely answered all the questions she was asked about her job, her family, and her blossoming relationship with Daniel. Fortunately, due to the number of siblings, there was never an awkward silence to be had. Jessica offered to help his mum do the dishes after they'd eaten. As they were doing their washing and drying production line, his mum paused and looked thoughtfully out the window.

'He was always such a quiet little guy when he was younger. It was as if he was living in the shadows of his older brothers.'

Jessica carried on drying the plate she'd been passed and remained silent, knowing his mum was going to continue her thought.

'I'm so pleased you bring him out of his shell. He's clearly so much more confident these days.'

'I think that may be in part to the Olympic gold medals he won…' Jessica offered.

She laughed and added, 'Perhaps. But I've never seen him this happy. Thank you.' She briefly looked to Jessica with a tiny smile, before plunging her hands back into the soapy water and continuing her task. A few minutes later, Daniel came bounding in, ducking under the door frame due to his height.

'Whatever she's told you, don't believe her,' he said with a laugh.

Both women looked at each other and Daniel's mum said, 'To which one of us are you referring to, my dear?'

'Both of you!' he laughed.

'Jessica's just invited us all to one of her concerts!' his mum beamed.

'Is that so? Maybe leave 'Your Body' off the set list for that one,' he whispered in Jessica's ear through a smirk.

'*Your Body*' was one of Jessica's most recent chart-topping hits. She had to be honest and say it was probably her least favourite song to record and perform. Yet, she had a contract with her management team that meant she had to go along with things like this. She had to prance around on stage trying to convey a sexy and alluring ambiance. Anyone who knew her understood this was entirely not her forte. She imagined Jake *et al* would be howling with laughter at some of the moves she was pulling on stage. Her second album didn't do as well as they'd hoped so her team decided to send her in a different direction. The second album was a lot softer and more acoustic. Her third album was set to be released in the next month and it had a more seductive vibe to it. Not really her thing, but Jessica did as she was told to bring in the big bucks!

The pair got into his car and when they were safely round the corner of the block, Jessica exhaled with a loud sigh. Daniel squeezed her knee as he was driving and said, 'Well done babe. I told you they'd love you.'

She looked over at him, smiling and admiring how handsome he looked with his ruffled hair and sunglasses. The sun was beginning to set so there was a beautiful orange glow, highlighting the contours of his face.

'What?' he asked, noticing her staring.

'Nothing!' she protested innocently, smiling.

The next morning, they were both up early as Jessica had press to promote the new single and Daniel was always up early for training. She got up to make a coffee for them both, choosing to enjoy hers on the balcony, watching the sun come up. Daniel appeared behind her, resting his cup on the balcony ledge as he wrapped his arms round her. He was resting his chin on her head, which still meant that at six foot five, he had to bend down a fair way in doing so. 'Beautiful view,' he said, swaying her gently from side to side.

'Mmm, I know,' Jessica sighed, taking a sip of her coffee.

'I wasn't talking about that view,' he muttered, spinning her round so she was facing him. He took the cup she was cradling in her hands and placed it down next to his on the ledge, then began running his hand down her back. She was only wearing a loose, silk dressing gown and she could feel his hands moving towards the knot at the front.

'Woah!' she grabbed his hands, laughing.

'C'mon...' he said, trying for a second time.

'Firstly, not on the balcony and secondly, you've got training,' Jessica smiled.

'Pfft,' he exhaled and laughed gently, giving up and grabbing his coffee. As he grabbed his coffee from the ledge, he managed to knock Jessica's cup with his hand. It crashed to the ground below with a dramatic smash, just missing a man rollerblading. As he spun round to look up, voicing assorted profanities, Jessica pushed Daniel back and out of sight.

'Sorry!' she shouted down as Daniel headed back into the kitchen, laughing.

TWO

'What's going on?' Jessica asked Daniel as he was storming round the apartment, slamming any cupboards he opened.

'Crap session,' he scowled.

'Oh, right,' she replied.

She knew she couldn't say anything to make him feel better; it was always the same. He sulked for a few hours, then came round to the idea that tomorrow was a new day.

'Do you want to grab some lunch?' she suggested.

'No.'

'There's a new place opened up just down…'

'I said no,' he interrupted sharply.

Jessica sighed and put her hands up to show defeat. She grabbed her book and headed out to the lounger on the balcony to enjoy the afternoon sun. She read her crime thriller for twenty minutes before the effects of the baking hot sun caused her to drift off into a snooze. She was awoken by something touching her leg which made her jump with a start. Opening her eyes and sitting herself up, she could see Daniel sat with her legs over his knees.

'Sorry,' he said with a sheepish half-smile. He reached down to the side of the lounger and presented her with a large plastic bowl full of greens. 'From that new place,' he said as he lifted his own bowl up.

She smiled and pretended to give him a gentle kick. She'd become used to his mini tantrums over the recent months, when he had bad training sessions. He'd been recovering from a rotator cuff injury and whilst getting back to his top form, he occasionally had off days. Unfortunately, he didn't deal with them particularly well. Jessica knew to just leave him to it, and he'd come crawling back with his tail between his legs. She tried to swing her legs round so she was sat up next to him to eat, but he kept hold of her legs and plonked his salad bowl on her shins. 'Nope,' he said before shoving a forkful of spinach, chicken, and pasta in his mouth, then looking up to meet her eye and giving her a wink. Jessica smiled in return and felt relieved that the tantrum was over, but also that she'd got some sustenance to fill her grumbling stomach.

'So, what went down today?' she asked, stabbing a tomato with her fork. He sighed heavily and shook his head.

'I just felt really heavy in the water and then my shoulder was playing up, so coach pulled me out and told me to go do some leg work in the gym,' he said with a mouthful of salad. Jessica furrowed her brow slightly, wondering what the issue was with that, surely his coach knew best. However, she also knew best in the way of not voicing her confusion about his upset. She just nodded in acknowledgement.

Daniel made his Olympic debut at the London 2012 Olympics, after years of dedication to his training throughout his college years and going professional. At London, he'd been lucky enough to race alongside the great Michael Phelps, a man he'd looked up to when he was a rookie in college, yet to discover his potential. They'd raced together in the 4x200m freestyle, with Daniel's third leg gaining Team USA a three second advantage on the French team, allowing them to swim to gold victory. They finished the race with a 6:50.70 time, with France coming second at 6:53.50 and Team GB coming a solid third with a time of 6:55.83. Jessica of course celebrated Team GB's win at the time, as she wasn't aware of Daniel's existence at that point. When Daniel met Jessica on the chat show, he was in awe of her voice and felt intimidated by her flowing blonde hair and icy blue eyes, paired with a bright red lipstick. Jessica was in awe of his achievements, his humble modesty and of course, his height and sculpted jaw. They were chatting backstage, both before and after the show, after discovering how close they lived to each other in LA, Daniel asked for her number.

They dated for several months in private, hiding out at each other's places, small restaurants and even at the pool sometimes. Daniel came to Jessica's gigs whenever he could, and she would go to his swim meets when she could. They wanted to keep their relationship between just the two of them for as long as they could, but after their debut red carpet walk at the Brit Awards back in the UK, word was out, and the news hit the Daily Mail and TMZ within hours. Jessica had to admit herself that they looked rather good together at these events. At the Brits, she was wearing a stunning lilac coloured Alexander McQueen gown that nipped her in at the waist with a white, jewel encrusted belt, then flowed out in a loose, angelic way. Meanwhile, Daniel was sporting a dark navy Dior suit, with a crisp white shirt, open at the collar. His hair was gently held down with product, but still looked modern and tousled. Jessica had to catch her breath when she saw him. Before they got out the car at the O2 in London, Daniel turned in his seat to admire Jessica in her glammed-up manner.

'You look sensational,' he'd said, lifting her hand and kissing it so as not to ruin her makeup. Jessica simply replied with, 'I could say the same about you.'

Later that night, back at the hotel, it turned into a scene from a romantic comedy movie, charging in the door and ripping each other's clothes off in an overly dramatic and unrealistic fashion. Jessica felt incredibly sore the next day, and it wasn't for the reasons people may think. Daniel had picked her up to carry her over to the bed and managed to bang her head on the low ceiling of the hotel. The first red carpet event that Jessica did, she was terrified as a young twenty-year-old girl. She thought Daniel would feel the same at his first, being so out of his comfort zone, but he was enjoying every minute. He had no problems posing for photos either with Jessica or by himself. After the 2012 Olympics, he'd become more well known in the world, not just the swimming community, so he'd had to deal with a certain level of increased fame. However, add on a famous singer on his arm, he was certainly up there with a valuable shot for paparazzi folk.

'So is the shoulder giving you bother again then?' Jessica asked after they'd polished off their lunch.

'I mean, not massively. It just twinged when I was doing drills and I just thought, *Ah, not again!*' Coach is gonna get the physio to have a look just to make sure everything's okay,' Daniel replied, leaning back on the seat to bask his face in the afternoon sun.

He was blessed with naturally olive toned skin that tanned incredibly easily, unlike Jessica who was a typical 'English Rose' colouration; relying heavily on fake tan to make her look less like a corpse that had been pulled from the sea.

Daniel sighed heavily before adding, 'As long as it's all okay for the championships, that's all I care about.'

The FINA World Championships had become Daniel's second primary focus, following the Olympics success. He was a certified Olympian now and he wanted that World title too before the next Summer Olympics.

'I'm sure it'll be fine, just see what the physio says, but I'm sure it's nothing to worry about,' Jessica tried to rationalise.

Days later and Daniel's shoulder had been thoroughly checked by the specialist physiotherapists and he'd been assured that there was no damage. It was just a twinge from an earlier injury. With that confirmation, he threw himself into training, deciding to train harder and longer and he'd joined a new gym opened up by his friend. The gym had really taken off and it was now a known haunt of people like Henry Cavill, Zac Efron,

Khloe Kardashian, Karlie Kloss, the list went on. Daniel would regularly come back with stories of the elite clientele, showering Jessica with names and anecdotes.

◆ ◆ ◆

The World Championships had come around quickly, and Jessica had already said goodbye to Daniel before he headed over to the training camp for intensive preparation with the team. Jessica certainly missed him when he was away for training and meets, but she often spent time away from home too, so it was easy to keep busy. This time, Jessica had already made plans to attend and surprise him at the meet in Barcelona. When she'd met his family a few months ago, they were all planning to do the same, so they'd invited her to join them, with Daniel being entirely unaware about the scheming plan that was afoot. His family were flying out a few days earlier so they'd be there to watch the prelims and semifinals, so Jessica would meet them there for the finals. The only downsides were that if there were any paparazzi there, she didn't want her cover being blown and the surprise being ruined. Also, there was a chance that Daniel didn't make it into the finals, but that was an exceptionally low chance going on his performance at the moment. Jessica had been in constant communication with Daniel's younger sister, Hannah, who had formed a close bond with Jessica even before they'd met in person. Both were the only sister in large families dominated by brothers, so they bonded simply on this fact alone.

It was one evening, as Jessica had received a message from Hannah, asking about her own family back in England, that Jessica had the bright idea to invite them over to Barcelona too. Unfortunately, her brothers had all declined due to work commitments, except Henry who said he would 100% be there and would fly out with their dad. It wasn't quite the full family reunion that Jessica had been hoping for, but two were better than none, Jessica thought.

After arriving in Spain less than a week later, Jessica had taken a car to her hotel, and she was just settling in when her phone started pinging with messages. She dug it out from her bag and saw messages from Henry explaining that their plane had been slightly delayed from Leeds Bradford airport, but they'd just landed in Barcelona and would be joining her at the hotel later that evening. Jessica sent back lots of excited, smiley face emojis in response. She'd not seen any of her family in person for over a year now and despite the fact she'd only been seeing less than half of them even now, she couldn't wait.

She'd always had a close bond with her dad, being the only girl in the family and everyone always said that Jessica and Henry were like twins that were separated at birth. She was close with the rest of her brothers but her and Henry were always referred to as 'the duo;' doing everything together. Jessica was adopted at just seven years old, and it was only a year after that when her mum died. She'd been placed into the care system when her biological Mother and Father were killed in a car accident. She was in the back and remained completely unharmed from the accident. When people hear about the accident, they often tell her how tragic it is and how tough it must have been for her. It's not that Jessica didn't want sympathy; the reality is, she had no real memories of her biological parents. She didn't even really have any photographs, so weirdly, she never thought of them as her parents. It really gets people going when Jessica would then tell them that her adoptive mum died of cancer. People tell her that a film could be made from her life. She just nods and smiles politely. Jessica's dad was truly her entire world; he took her in with his wife and raised her as one of his own, encouraging lasting relationships with their biological sons. Jessica felt so lucky in that sense; her brothers truly embraced her as their sister, despite sharing no blood relation at all.

A few hours later, there was a musical knock at Jessica's hotel door, and she grinned, jumping up knowing who was on the other side of the door. She screamed as Henry flung himself into her arms and nearly knocked her over.

'Henry, you fool!' a familiar voice said from outside the door and Jessica pushed Henry aside to be met with her dad, practically jumping into his arms to hug him like Henry had with her.

'Come in, come in!' Jessica beckoned as she ushered them into her room.

'Jesus, where's our suite?' Henry said as he surveyed the room of the executive suite in the hotel. Jessica just stuck out her tongue at him.

'Sorry, peasants are down the hall,' she said mockingly to Henry.

Jessica had offered to pay for their rooms, but her dad has insisted that all they needed was a bed for sleeping in and a bathroom to…well, you know. Much to Henry's annoyance, who would have jumped at the chance of having his sister pay for a fancy hotel suite for him.

'I can't believe you're here; this is so exciting! I can't wait for you to meet Daniel and his family,' Jessica said, clapping her hands together like a giddy child.

'The others told me I needed to give him a warning,' Henry said, throwing some popcorn up in air and catching it in his mouth, resulting in Jessica looking at him quizzically.

'Y'know, like warn him that if he does anything to hurt you, your brothers will come after him. That kind of thing,' Henry confirmed, firing another piece of popcorn above his head, mouth agape.

'You are aware he's six foot five?' Jessica cocked her head to one side.

'Oh,' Henry stopped, making Jessica laugh. 'Looks like that one's on you then dad!' he said, leading their dad to roll his eyes.

Jessica was struggling to keep her eyes open by 9pm so they left her to it and headed back to their own rooms. Daniel's family were staying in a different hotel, about a five-minute walk away, so they'd all meet up tomorrow morning and head to the pool. She'd just managed to nod off, when a loud vibration woke Jessica from her slumber with a start. It took a few minutes for her brain to process her surroundings. She grabbed her phone to see a message from Daniel. It was a photo of him pretending to look scared, biting his nails.

'Wish me luck! I love you. Xxx'

Jessica smiled through sleepy eyes and messaged back, minus a photo.

You'll smash it. I love you too! Xxx

You're up late! Sorry if I woke you! Xxx

Jessica paused and kicked herself for the rookie mistake. He thought she was still in LA where it was about 1am. She'd forgotten about the time difference.

Can't sleep! Too nervous for you. Xxx

She'd fallen straight back to sleep as she awoke the next morning with her phone still in her hand. Jessica rubbed her eyes, stretching and enjoying the 10am lie in she so rarely got these days. They were all meeting at the pool at about 1pm so she had plenty of time to get ready. Needless to say, it wasn't like she was getting fully glammed up; all she needed to do was slip on a pair of jeans and a T-shirt and do her make up.

A temporary pool had been set up in the arena at Palau Sant Jordi so as it was indoor, Jessica knew how humid it would be, especially with it being in the middle of August. She decided to tie her hair up to avoid any frizz from the humidity. She met her dad and brother in the hotel lobby, and they got a taxi to the venue. Jessica could see Daniel's family straight away; they were clad in an assortment of Team USA merchandise, all bearing Daniel's surname.

'Fucking hell,' Henry muttered under his breath when Jessica pointed them out.

She kicked him and warned him not to embarrass her.

'I think you've got the embarrassment factor already set,' he smirked, nodding towards the group, Jessica kicking him again as they stepped out the car.

'Stop it you two!' their dad hissed; fully aware they'd been spotted by the group who were waving towards Jessica.

'Jessica! Hello sweetheart!' Linda said as she threw her arms round her in a large embrace.

'Hi! this is my dad, Kevin and this is my brother, Henry,' Jessica introduced them to the group. They both took turns shaking hands with Daniel's family.

'Christ, there's hundreds of them,' Henry muttered, making Jessica give him yet another subtle kick.

As they took their seats in the arena, Jessica plonked herself in Daniel's mum and her brother.

'How's he been doing?' she asked Linda.

'He's got the 200 and the 4x100 today. He would've had the 4x200 tomorrow but…you know…' she replied, pulling a face.

Jessica did know. There was some controversy late yesterday evening at the men's 200 relay semifinal when Team USA got disqualified due to a false start from a rookie. His teammates didn't exactly hide their disappointment and frustration at the poor young swimmer.

As they took their places in the arena and sat through some of the other finals, such as the 400IM and the 100m backstroke, Jessica felt herself getting increasingly anxious, waiting for Daniel's first final of the day. After the 100-butterfly final, it was time for Daniel's 200m free. The arena announcer introduced each swimmer to the crowd, and all were met with enormous cheers of support. A few of them glanced around and put their hands in acknowledgment of the cheers, but the majority of them, like Daniel, kept their heads bowed to remain focused and in the zone. As the men mounted the blocks, Jessica saw that Daniel was in lane 4, in between swimmers from China and France. The arena went silent as they all arched their backs on the first count. The klaxon sounded and instantaneously the men flew forward and into the water, with the crowd erupting in cheers and yells of support. Daniel's family were shouting and clapping, yelling his name. Jessica couldn't help but join in with the excitement. At the split, Daniel kicked off the wall and he was in fourth place. Jessica held her breath as she watched him slowly but surely gaining on his competitors. One by one, he overtook them, and it looked like he touched the wall at the same time as the Chinese swimmer. Jessica felt sick as she watched the results board, waiting for the list to appear. Her eyes kept flicking back to Daniel who was treading water, pulling his goggles and cap off, breathing heavily with his chest.

'Yes!!' Daniel's family yelled and Jessica turned to see the board.

'First!' she screamed, throwing her hands up in the air and hugging Henry.

Daniel had just managed to touch the wall just before the Chinese swimmer, with a time of 47.32. As the swimmers were heaving themselves out of the pool, they were all congratulating the medal winners who were making their way towards the press. As Daniel was stood chatting to the American commentator for the event, he obviously heard familiar shouts and looked up to see his family trying to get his attention. His face broke into a soft smile, and he put his hand up to wave back at them. Then his eyes flicked over to Jessica, and he held her gaze briefly before beaming from ear to ear. All she wanted to do was run down and kiss him, but he had another final to get ready for in a few hours.

As Jessica watched Daniel finish answering the interviewer's questions, she felt utterly besotted with him; plus, he looked incredible, she thought. Her first thought was *'I want to rip his clothes off him'* then she remembered that wouldn't take long due to him only wearing his swimming shorts. With that being said, she'd seen Daniel getting his swimming trunks on and it was certainly a remarkable sight. It reminded her of when she fought with a pair of tights to yank them up her legs. There was nothing gracious or remotely attractive about the experience.

The next few hours seemed to drag as the two families were waiting for the next final. They'd managed to slip out and get something to eat and drink during their wait, but Jessica was starting to get fidgety again with the waiting, so she just found herself picking at a club sandwich and sipping a Diet Pepsi. When they were in the arena, they became acclimatised to the hot temperature and humid conditions. Jessica commented to her dad that it reminded her of the butterfly enclosure at Tropical World in Leeds, where the heat takes your breath away. They'd spent many a carefree day during school holidays at places like Tropical World. If it wasn't there, it was Temple Newsam, Newby Hall, Castle Howard; all the major tourist places surrounding York and Leeds. Memories like that made Jessica ache with homesickness, however this time, she'd got her dad here with her, so the feeling subsided very quickly.

Finally, 8pm rolled around and the stewards were milling around, getting ready for the next final. This was it. Team USA were top favourites to win, however the disqualification in the last team relay had sent shockwaves through everyone; nothing was guaranteed. Daniel was leading the team off this time with the first leg. This wasn't his usual leg but with the rookie who made the mistake in the other relay also in the lineup, it was clear they didn't want him making the same mistake again. They needed a safe pair of hands (and legs) to lead the team off safely. As Daniel took to the blocks, Linda took Jessica's hand in hers and gripped it tightly, squeezing harder when the klaxon sounded, and the race had begun. As each swimmer reached for the wall, the next in line flew from the blocks, launching themselves over their predecessor, just as they touched the wall. It was like carefully constructed choreography.

Jessica had started to lose feeling in her hand by this point due to Linda's grip, both of them shouting and cheering. Clear as day, Team USA were the gold medal winners. Linda gasped then screamed, pointing to the results screen.

Oh god, not another disqualification, Jessica thought, but as she turned, the screen was flashing with 'New world record!'

After a slight delay, Daniel and his teammates turned to see the screen and they saw the update to their gold medal win. They flung their arms round each other into a four-man huddle, clearly elated. The atmosphere was euphoric in the arena. The most senior and decorated swimmer of the group, Adrian Matthews jogged away from the group and up towards the stands, finding his wife and two kids. The stands were quite high up, so he had to reach up and clamber on some benches to get to them. Following suit, the others tried similar, finding their family and friends in the crowd. Daniel jumped up onto a bench and managed to haul himself up onto a small platform, reaching up and giving his mum a hug.

'I can't believe you're all here!' he said as he stepped back to acknowledge his family. He then did a little hop over to another platform, leaning up to take Jessica's hands.

'And you! What are you doing here?' he said with a look of amazement. Jessica smiled in return at the stupid question rather than giving him a stupid answer.

'I'm so proud of you,' she managed, feeling teary eyed with pride.

'I love you,' he said, reaching up and bringing her down to kiss him, causing the women in his family to sigh with adoration, and Henry to groan and fake gag.

'I love you too, umm, by the way, this is my dad and one of my brothers,' Jessica said, suddenly pulling away from Daniel's lips, remembering who else was present.

Daniel looked taken aback and a bit bemused.

'Oh, right, hi,' he shook their hands, 'I've got to go now but I'm sure we'll catch up and get to know each other later?' he said, looking at Jessica for confirmation.

She nodded and congratulated him again on his incredible win. As Daniel and his teammates stood atop of the podium, they all lay their hand on their heart ready for the national anthem. As the anthem ended, cheers erupted once again, as they had done when Daniel was collecting his individual gold medal. Looking round the arena, Jessica felt like she wanted to cry tears of joy and pride. Her incredible boyfriend was a World Champion.

THREE

'I still can't believe that idiot cost us a medal,' Daniel said as the families were sat having brunch in a local café.

Jessica rested her hand atop of his, understanding his frustration but also getting a little bit bored of hearing about it. This was about the seventh time he'd brought it up. She was very much of the mindset that everyone is human, everyone makes mistakes, and the poor guy was probably beating himself up more than anyone else could.

'Absolutely ridiculous. How he got on the team, I'll never know,' he concluded.

'So,' Jessica said, trying to change the subject. 'What are you guys up to today?' she addressed Daniel's family.

'Well actually, we've got to head on back home today. Our flight is this evening, so we thought we'd leave you four to spend some time together,' Linda said, gesturing towards Jessica, Henry, their dad, and Daniel.

Daniel looked up and smiled politely, 'Yeah, if that's okay with you guys?' he asked in the direction of Jessica.

'That sounds lovely,' Jessica admitted.

Daniel's family were wonderful, but they could be a bit intense, mainly because there was just so many of them. Jessica wanted her dad and brother to get to know Daniel primarily.

They spent the day exploring the tourist sights of Barcelona, spending the majority of the afternoon queuing to get into the Sagrada Família in the Summer heat. Jessica and Daniel were stopped a few times for photos with fans as they ambled around, hand in hand in the beautiful city. Jessica still found it bizarre that people knew who she was. Equally, Daniel was stopped by young fans of his; which seemed to faze him less than it did Jessica.

As they were making their way back to the hotel, Jessica and Henry hung back from their dad and Daniel, who had found common ground with their love of tennis.

'So, what do you think?' Jessica asked her brother expectantly.

'He seems nice,' Henry replied.

'Is that it?' Jessica laughed.

'Sorry, I mean, he's a hunk of a man with a body carved by the gods and a personality that could rival even...'

'Shut up!' Jessica cut him off, rolling her eyes.

'Seriously, I wouldn't have put his down as your type that's all. He seems like a nice guy, although he was going in a bit hard on that poor lad on his team,' Henry raised an eyebrow.

Ah, he'd noted it too, Jessica thought.

'He's just passionate. They all are, especially at events like this,' Jessica tried to defend Daniel.

'Yeah, I guess you're right.'

'Do you ever hear from Jake?' Jessica asked out the blue, taking Henry by surprise.

'Jake? Erm, yeah, I mean, no, but...' Henry stuttered, trying to find the right words.

He was torn between telling his sister what she wanted to hear or telling her the truth. In reality, he wasn't really sure what she wanted to hear.

'He's…he's married now,' he finished, causing Jessica stopped in her tracks and stared ahead, feeling like she was going to faint.

'Are you okay?' Henry grabbed her arm.

'Married?' she repeated, checking if she had heard her brother correctly.

'Yeah, and he's got a kid too…' Henry added.

'Married? To who?' she demanded, her eyelids fluttering as she tried to focus.

'Some girl from university I think,' Henry said, still holding her arm.

'He's got a kid too? Wow,' Jessica pushed her hair back, feeling sticky and faint.

She felt like throwing up; she had no right to be upset. She was the one who ended things and moved to another country, but she felt as heartbroken as she had when she said goodbye to Jake. Also, who was this girl from university? Had there been someone else he'd got his eye on? Maybe she was romanticising things more than reality. Her thoughts raced.

'Jess?' Daniel's voice suddenly broke Jessica's racing mind and startled her back into reality. 'Jess? Babe? Are you okay?' his hands had replaced Henry's on her arm, and he was trying to get her eyes to meet his.

'Sweetheart?' her dad asked, concerned look on his face.

'Oh, sorry,' Jessica half laughed, 'I think it's just the heat. I'm fine, sorry, just felt a bit woozy. I think I'll just get my head down for a bit when we get back to the hotel if that's okay?'

'Of course, but are you sure you're okay? Here, have some water,' Daniel offered her his bottle.

She slowly took a sip of the tepid water from the plastic bottle that Daniel had been carting around all day. The bland liquid coated her dry throat, helping with the retching feeling she'd been trying to suppress. She saw Henry raising his eyebrows, knowing the real reason behind her sudden change in mood.

When they reached the hotel, Jessica gave her apologies and insisted that the three of them went for dinner as planned, she'd be fine. Reluctantly, they all agreed, with Daniel promising that he'd be up to the room in a few hours to check on her.

Jessica kicked off her shoes and flopped onto the enormous bed. She plugged her phone in to charge and without a minute's hesitation, she opened Instagram and searched Jake's name. His profile was there, but it hadn't been updated for over a year. She clicked on the tagged photos, sucking in air with a sharp gasp as she saw masses of little squares, showing her ex-boyfriend in a suit, stood next to a petite blonde woman wearing a gorgeous white gown. Few people could pull off wearing white for their wedding as it often washed them out, however this girl looked stunning. Jessica felt a pang of jealousy mixed with regret and self-loathing. Again, she had to remind herself that *she* ended things with Jake. He was bound to move on at some point. She'd moved on. Why was it bothering her so much?

She spent the next hour and a half scrolling through the Instagram feed of Jake's wife. There was a lot of content to go through. Jessica didn't remember her from Uni...then again, she kept her circle of friends very tight. As she thought Jake had too, but evidently not.

When she heard the door key beep, she quickly closed the app and put her phone down on the bedside table.

'Hey, how are you feeling? Oh, you're up and about, that's good,' Daniel said, pushing her hair behind her ear.

'Feeling a little better thanks,' Jessica smiled lightly.

'So, your dad headed off to bed, saying he wanted to finish his book,' Daniel shrugged, making Jessica laugh as she knew her dad was looking forward to meeting Daniel, but realistically, he was a homebody who liked his routines. Ultimately meaning, he was in his slippers for 8pm, scanning through his Tom Clancy book with a cup of hot chocolate in hand.

'And Henry?' Jessica asked.

'He just said he was tired too,' Daniel said, playing with a small piece of Jessica's sweeping side fringe that was too short to go behind her ear.

Jessica nodded in response, wondering why Henry didn't hang around and get to know him. She made a mental note to question him tomorrow.

'So, just exactly how much *'better'* are you feeling?' Daniel asked with a slight smirk.

Jessica rolled her eyes and sighed with a smile, causing him to pull a faux shock face. He leant forward and planted his lips on hers, putting his hand behind her head and slowly guiding her down so she was lying flat. His hands started manoeuvring her dress up her thigh until he reached her underwear. Wearing a thong with a summer dress was an innovative idea; there was no obvious VPL on show and it felt cooler and freer. However, despite being considered slim, Jessica's thighs were always insistent on being together. She'd bought a pair of thin, silky cycling type shorts, colloquially referred to as *'chub rub pants,'* which stopped any form of chafing. Needless to say, she hadn't worn them yet as they weren't particularly flattering, and she was still in the *'trying to impress'* stage of her relationship. This meant under garments in the form of thin pieces of string or anything with lace, i.e., the most uncomfortable items. Daniel gently kissed her neck.

'I love you,' he murmured, planting kisses along her body as he moved his way down the bed as Jessica groaned in delight.

They must've fallen asleep afterwards as Jessica woke naturally at 6am thanks to the European sun blazing in through the window. As she adjusted her position to face Daniel, she watched as his toned, tanned chest moved up and down with every breath he took. She wriggled forward to snuggle into him and he was obviously awake enough to realise this, putting his arm round her to encase her into his chest.

'Good morning beautiful,' he whispered, kissing her head.

'Good morning, my handsome World Champion,' Jessica kissed his chest, feeling him gently chuckle at her remark.

Their flight back to LA was later that afternoon and while Jessica had managed to get a direct flight to Barcelona on the way out, heading back they had to go via Charles de Gaulle in Paris. Fortunately, they'd only need to kill about an hour in the airport before their connecting flight back to the States.

After washing off last night's antics, Jessica and Daniel headed down to meet the other two for breakfast at 8:30am. As Jessica and her dad came back from their second round at the continental buffet, Henry was prodding at his cooked breakfast, nodding along to whatever Daniel was saying. Jessica wondered why Henry was being so dismissive and rude.

'...so basically, that gold medal would've been ours for the taking if he'd have just practiced his block starts.'

Ah. Jessica only caught the end of Daniel's sentence, but she needed no context. She sat down opposite Henry and pulled a face at him, showing that she too was getting sick of Daniel's rants about the rookie who cost them the medal. Henry rolled his eyes in return, luckily Daniel didn't notice this.

So that all parties had time to pack up their things, they said their goodbyes after breakfast. Henry was flying back to Manchester Airport to see some friends in Oldham for a few days, meaning their dad was flying back to Leeds Bradford by himself, with her brother Chris waiting at the other end to pick him up from the airport. Jessica was secretly jealous that her dad would be back home in about three hours, compared to her thirteen hours including layover time.

'How are you feeling today about the whole...Jake thing?' Henry whispered as he hugged Jessica goodbye, dramatically enunciating Jake's name in a whisper, like parents do with swear words when kids are present.

Jessica shrugged and mumbled something about being fine, it just being a shock. She sure as hell wasn't going to tell him that she'd excused herself from the family dinner to stalk Jake and his wife on social media for hours on end. Then again, he knew his sister well enough to come to that summation by himself. Waving her dad and brother off from the hotel restaurant, Jessica heaved a sigh and mentally prepared herself for the thirteen hour journey home.

FOUR

'What have I done now?' Jessica asked whilst sobbing.
'Nothing,' Daniel replied curtly.
'Well clearly it's something!'
'Just forget it,'
'But...'
'I said forget it! I'm off to the gym. I'll see you later,' Daniel said, grabbing his rucksack and slamming the door.

For the last few months, since they got back from Barcelona, Jessica and Daniel had been having more arguments than they'd ever had. Usually, they had minor disagreements then made up, but recently, everything felt like it was spiralling. Daniel's tantrums were becoming more like personal attacks, and they weren't just when he'd had a bad training session either. The last thing they'd had a fight about was how Jessica was feeling pushed in a certain direction with her management team. Daniel previously would've been comforting, understanding and practical, trying to think of solutions. The Daniel now was unsympathetic and useless, saying if she wasn't happy, to quit music. As someone who was always so supportive of her career, Jessica couldn't quite believe Daniel when he'd suggested that as a solution to the problems. When she asked if he would just quit swimming, he flew off the handle, saying it wasn't the same.

Jessica noticed a change in him too after he'd signed on some major brand deals. He was now one of the brand faces for Speedo and Arena, two significant brands in the swimming world. After his further success at the World Championships, he was becoming a well-known face. The sweet, kind, charming man she had fallen in love with was now turning into the stereotypical athlete that she'd been cautious of.

A few weeks ago, Jessica had been invited to attend a film premiere and when she politely declined, Daniel was raging. He argued that he wanted to go as it was all exposure for him, then when Jessica pointed out that technically, he hadn't been invited - it was Jessica and another, he flipped and started screaming at her; asking why she was trying to dim his limelight. She'd never heard him speak like this and it inwardly made her cringe. She'd lie awake at night, trying to decipher when he became a fame hungry creature. Jessica had confided in friends about his behaviour, but they just brushed it off as him gaining confidence being in the limelight. He had confidence before, Jessica thought, but it was a kind of suave, charming confidence as opposed to outright *'look at me!'* arrogance.

The only friends who had her back were Ellie and Alison; they were spoiling for a fight to defend her honour. Christie was less enthusiastic and agreed about him just gaining confidence, but quickly changed her views when Ellie and Alison started listing off reasons on their fingers why his behaviour was not okay.

Jessica was really struggling to cope with everything that life was throwing at her. She felt stuck on a rollercoaster, and she just wanted to get off. Life wasn't fun anymore; she wanted her boyfriend back, her career back and well, her independence and dignity. The final straw for Jessica was when her team actually called a meeting about her weight.

'It's just not a good look for the record. You're supposed to be portraying this strong, powerful, sexy female and honestly, it's hard to find outfits in your size these days,' her manager, Michael commented.

If it wasn't for the fact that she'd been having similarly bizarre conversations with her team over recent months, she would've laughed, thinking it was a joke. Yet, not one person in this room was laughing or joking. They were deadly serious. It might be a suitable time to point out that Jessica was a healthy UK size 12. She went to the gym regularly and ate well. So, whilst she wasn't stick thin like a runway model, she was toned and fit. Jessica went home that evening and cried until her eyes were sore and her cheeks were red raw.

When Daniel had got back, he seemed genuinely concerned and held her as she sat on the bathroom floor, weeping. He was appalled that this had even been a conversation and started yelling that he was going to ring her manager and give him a piece of his mind. Knowing that wouldn't help anything, Jessica managed to talk him out of this. Unfortunately, talking him out of it meant that Daniel quickly lost interest in the topic of conversation and suggested that perhaps Jessica play them at their own game and work out harder at the gym.

A few days later, Daniel had to go to New York to film a brand commercial and Jessica had taken up a friend's offer of heading out to a party downtown. Her and Daniel had left on bad terms; Jessica had seen photos of Daniel with a svelte young woman at the gym, with his arm round her in seemingly more than a friendly way. It turned out she was a new up and coming model who had just been gifted her wings by Victoria Secret. Jessica didn't usually get jealous, but something about that photo (and the others that followed) made her question Daniel's loyalty. She'd asked him about it, very casually, but he became extremely angry, claiming he would never cheat on her. He was a little too defensive…guilty conscience perhaps, she thought.

The party Jessica and her friend were heading to was at some young actor's house, a movie star that Jessica had never heard of, and it seems she wasn't alone. Needless to say, Jessica and her friend Darcy headed out to the party to see what it was about. The pair had met when Darcy was signed not long after Jessica by the same label; bonding over their love for song writing.

Darcy's career had been somewhat turbulent from the get-go; she'd been a recovering addict and recently, she'd found her way back into that lifestyle. Jessica had tried to take her under her wing somewhat, looking out for her like an older sister. Tonight, it felt like Jessica would be the one who needed looking after.

Lounging on some chairs by the pool, Darcy presented a small packet containing an unknown white powder. She wiped the table with her hand, then poured the powder out, before expertly dragging it into small lines with a credit card. She got out a rolled up dollar bill with a tatty elastic band wrapped round it tightly, then raised it to Jessica in offering. Jessica shrugged her shoulders and said, 'I don't know how to!'

Without saying anything, Darcy leant forward and put the makeshift tube to her nose, snorting up two of the lines before collapsing back into her chair and exhaling loudly. She offered the bill to Jessica again, who this time took it from her. Part of her wanted to blow to lines away into the breeze to stop Darcy taking anymore, but then something in her brain clicked and she leant forward and mimicked Darcy's technique with one of the lines. It made Jessica splutter and cough, her eyes stinging and watering, her nose the same.

Why the hell did people do that for fun? Jessica thought. *Yuck!* Fifteen minutes later, she could see exactly why people did this for fun.

◆ ◆ ◆

All sense of Jessica's reality had been thoroughly twisted by this point. She wasn't even mentally aware of anyone around her as she looked round the room, despite her eyes showing her people stood there. She bent forward and knowledgeably held her left nostril closed, while snorting the white powder through a straw with her right nostril. The bitter chemical always made her cough as it entered her body, as if trying to reject a foreign object it knew shouldn't be in there. She sat back on the couch and looked round the room again; people were shouting and dancing. Here she was at another party of some unknown soul, except this time she was by herself. Give it fifteen minutes and she'd be right there with them. The high was usually short lived so she'd soak it up with assorted spirits to prolong the effects. As she sat there waiting patiently to feel more animated and happier, she felt the couch cushions give slightly to her right. She'd been joined by a tall, dark blonde haired man. He nodded towards the white lines on the table and pointed at himself, asking permission. Jessica waved her hands in a way which acknowledged, and he leant forward and followed the same routine she just had.

'Ah! Not my usual but it'll hit the spot for now,' he said, and Jessica just glazed over while he continued talking.

'The name's Mike,' he offered a handshake and Jessica lamely took it.

'Jessica,' she slurred.

'You seem set, but after this I'm heading out to meet my dealer for some H. You're welcome to join,' he laughed raucously, the sudden volume causing Jessica to flinch.

'H?' she questioned.

'Smack? Gear? Heroin?' he added as if she was some sort of expert who knew all the terminology.

'New to the scene, huh?'

Jessica continued staring at him; he was slowly going in and out of focus.

'Suit yourself,' he said and stood up, dancing his way over to some girls who were drinking in the corner of the room.

As he stood up, Jessica launched herself upright and felt a new lease of life. She grabbed her cup and swerved her way to what had become the dance floor. She dropped the cup and starting manically laughing, kicking it out the way.

'Watch it!' a girl scorned her as the cup and its remaining contents hit the girl's Jimmy Choos. Jessica yelled back some profanities and continued dancing; she was starting to feel on top of the world. She was throwing her body around and singing at the top of her lungs, only stopping to laugh. She was just scouting for another drink when she felt a hand on her arm, causing her to jump and scream loudly.

'Jessica, for God sake, it's me!' Daniel's hazel eyes tried to get Jessica's to focus on them.

'Ooh!! Hello you,' she said, throwing her arms round his neck.

'Come on, I'm taking you home. What have you taken this time?'

'I've not taken anything, I've chosen happiness!' Jessica slurred, laughing again.

'Jesus. Come on,' he tugged her arm.

'Excuse me! She clearly doesn't want to go with you. Leave her alone!' a girl from across the room shouted.

'I'll call the cops if you don't let her go!' another girl shouted.

'It's fine, I'm her boyfriend!' Daniel shouted back, then hissed at Jessica, 'What kind of fucking situations are you getting me into?'

He pulled her out of the house and towards his car, trying to keep her upright as she was stumbling and laughing at her complete lack of co-ordination.

'In,' he said firmly.

Jessica liked this side of him, and she made what she thought were bedroom eyes but from his reaction, she guessed he wasn't impressed. He drove her back to the apartment, muttering about how lucky she was that there were no paparazzi hanging around. He pulled into the garage and switched the engine off. He stayed still and stared ahead.

'How long are we gonna keep doing this?' he asked.

'I'm just trying to have some fun!' Jessica protested.

'At what cost?'

'What do you mean?'

He just shook his head in response and got out the car.

Jessica stumbled up to the apartment behind him, where he'd left the door open for her. She threw her bag down in the hall and shouted at Alexa to play some music. She started dancing round the room and suddenly the music stopped. Daniel had pulled the plug, quite literally.

'Go to bed,' he ordered.

Jessica scoffed and swaggered past him towards the bedroom, intentionally shoulder barging into him as she did so.

'You need help, Jess.'

'Oh piss off.'

'I love you, but I can't keep doing this.'

'Lighten up!'

'I'm serious, Jess. This can't continue. You need to get help.'

Jessica felt a strange wet feeling on her chin and realised she'd started crying.

'You don't get it!' she sobbed.

'Jess,' Daniel softened. 'Then talk to me…why are you doing this to yourself? To us?'

'I can't cope with all this! I'm supposed to parade around on stage pretending to be all sexy and provocative, but I feel disgusting! I've got my team telling me I can't eat this and I can't eat that; telling me I've put on some weight and it's not good for the image! I've got you constantly picking fights with me and potentially cheating on me!'

'What?!' Daniel snapped.

'You're fucking joking? Not this again. I AM NOT CHEATING ON YOU!' he enunciated every word angrily, with purpose.

'And about your team, I've told you, just ditch them,' he softened again, sweeping her hair behind her ears.

'It's not as simple as that! I signed a contract with them for another year,' Jessica wept. 'I just hate myself. When I take drugs, I can forget about everything, and it makes me feel alive again. It's the only thing that can get me on stage these days!'

'Do they know?'

'What do you mean?'

'Do they know you take something before you go on stage?'

Jessica nodded.

'Fucking unbelievable…I'm gonna call them. Give me your phone.'

'Daniel, no! Don't you dare!' Jessica begged.

'They can't treat you like that. It's fucking disgusting! How can they sit back and do nothing?! Do they not have some kind of duty of care? Do they not realise how shit it looks for your image?'

She frowned as he got his phone out and started typing.

'Who are you calling?'

'No-one, I'm looking at facilities we can get you into.'

'No! I don't need to go anywhere!'

'Yes, you do!' Daniel shouted, scrolling on his phone.

Jessica didn't reply, she simply heaved with sobs as Daniel held her hand, rubbing his thumb gently on hers.

'Okay, there's a place here in LA. I'm gonna call them in the morning,' he said.

Jessica knew there was no point arguing anymore. He was right…she was just in denial.

'For now, let's get you in the shower and then to bed, okay?'

FIVE

As she sobered up and came round from her antics, Jessica and Daniel went back and forth arguing about her going into a facility. Daniel wasn't giving in, and neither was she. At 11am, she finally buckled and agreed for Daniel to drive her to what she now knew to be 'Crossing Bridge Support and Rehabilitation Centre'. They had some cheesy slogan about crossing the bridge into a new and healthier life. Daniel helped Jessica pack a bag of essentials, constantly telling her how much he loved her and how proud he was of her decision. Jessica blankly nodded, knowing full well that it wasn't her decision at all.

The drive was about forty-five minutes on the Pacific Coast Highway and Jessica couldn't hold back tears as they got closer. It was located just over twenty miles away, up in between Topanga and Malibu.

'I don't want to do this,' Jessica sobbed.

Daniel inhaled deeply and squeezed her thigh with his right hand, promising her it was for the best and it would all be okay. Pulling into the grounds, Daniel was looking around at the greenery and the aesthetic beauty of their surroundings. Meanwhile, Jessica just stared ahead. As they came to a stop, a middle-aged, brown-haired woman came down the steps to greet them. Daniel jumped out the driver's side and went to shake her hand. They began talking and gesturing about something, then both turned to look at Jessica. Daniel walked to the car and opened the passenger door, closely followed by the woman. He knelt and took Jessica's hands.

'This is the best thing for you right now, okay? I promise you, it will all be worth it. This is Elaine,' he turned to gesture at the lady in her maroon-coloured turtleneck and denim jeans.

Jessica couldn't even concentrate on what Daniel was saying and let tears fall from her eyes as she swung her legs round to get out the car.

'Show me the way then,' she said to Elaine without looking at her.

'Perhaps you'd like a moment to say goodbye to your boyfriend?' Elaine said, kindly.

Jessica grunted and turned to Daniel without looking at him. He noted this and lifted her chin to point her face towards his. She couldn't meet his eyes though.

'I love you,' he said. 'I'm gonna come and see you when I'm allowed. I'll be right here rooting for you, okay?'

Jessica nodded and collapsed into the embrace he gave her. She felt sad but numb at the same time. She'd had to give up her phone, her vices, her friends, her boyfriend, and her career; to name a few. This was supposed to be a good thing, but Jessica just felt like she was entering a prison.

'Alright, if you want to come with me then Jessica and I'll give you the grand tour?' Elaine smiled, taking Jessica's bag.

She then smiled and nodded at Daniel, which was clearly a signal for him to leave, as he nodded back and got into the car. He gave a weak wave at Jessica, then drove back out, away from her. Elaine was talking and pointing at things, but Jessica wasn't taking anything in. She just followed her around like a lost puppy dog, nodding at the right moments.

'I'm afraid this is the awkward part,' Elaine began. 'We need to check your bag just to make sure you're not bringing any contraband in.'

Contraband. This really was a prison, Jessica thought. Elaine and another man began rifling through Jessica's belongings, making her feel like a school child who had gotten into trouble. She felt her dignity slowly ebbing away.

'Okay, all good!' Elaine said spritely and handed Jessica her neatly re-packed bag back.

'Now to your room. Every resident has their own room, with an ensuite bathroom. There's a beautiful view from your window too!' Elaine added this last part as if she was giving a tour of an exclusive Airbnb.

Reaching the bedroom, even in her zombie like state, Jessica could appreciate that the view from the room was beautiful. The grounds were lush green and perfectly manicured, with enormous trees towering high. Jessica noticed that the window had an extender lock on it.

'Really?' she pointed, with a sarcastic look on her face.

'Ah yes, well I'm afraid we can't take any risks. We house a lot of extremely vulnerable residents,' Elaine sympathised.

'Anyway!' She clapped her hands together, making Jessica start. 'I'll let you get settled in for an hour and I will see you later this afternoon for our first session. Then you'll have the opportunity to meet some of the other residents for dinner, then it's group art therapy, then anger management therapy, then meditation, then bed!' Elaine smiled sweetly.

'Umm... that seems awfully busy. When will I get some time to myself?' Jessica asked.

'Well, we like to keep residents occupied with a structured day so they can focus on recovery better. We find that if they are left to spend too much time in solitude, this hinders recovery and can actually increase their risk of relapse. When the mind is left to wander too much, it can become difficult to stamp out those negative thoughts.'

Jessica nodded in response. There wasn't a great deal to unpack as she wasn't allowed to bring too many personal items. She placed her toiletries in the bathroom and hung up some of the clothes she had brought. Anything with laces, tie cords, belts or basically anything that could be used to hang oneself, was banned. Jessica was increasingly feeling like a prisoner. Even her room in halls at university was better. When the thought of university entered her mind, so did Jake. Jessica wondered what he would think if he could see her now. She settled on the thought that he would be appalled, worried and angry. Basically, exactly the same as Daniel felt now. Jessica felt guilty thinking about Jake and instantly tried to think of Daniel instead, as if trying to cleanse her thoughts. She instantly felt like she wanted to scream and cry but didn't want to draw any attention to herself. Just as it all felt like it was getting too much to handle, Jessica's thoughts were interrupted by a knock on the door.

Okay, maybe Elaine had a point about keeping busy to keep negative thoughts at bay, Jessica conceded.

Speak of the devil.

'Jessica, are you all unpacked? Would you like to follow me for our first session together?' Elaine asked, but Jessica knew this wasn't really a question, more of an order.

She obeyed by nodding and following Elaine out the room and down the stairs. They came to a large, light filled room with large windows from the ceiling to the floor. The warm glow of the sun was flooding the room.

'Take a seat, Jessica.'

'Where?'

'Anywhere that you'd like.'

Jessica seriously debated hopping onto one of the enormous beanbags in the corner to see if Elaine would pounce onto one too, but instead opted for one of the chairs near the window. Elaine waited for Jessica to sit and then sat in the chair opposite and crossed her legs.

'So, I want to start by introducing myself and then find out a bit about you,' Elaine said in her posh American accent. 'My name is Elaine and I'm the lead Psychologist here at Crossing Bridge. I'm married with two children. I've been at Crossing Bridge for eight years now; before that I was a Psychological Therapist at another facility in Arizona. I like hiking with my husband and children and we also like going on road trips in our

RV.'

Jessica's eyes rolled in a *'Are we really doing this?'* gesture.

'Now tell me about you,' Elaine beamed, getting her pen and paper ready for notes.

'Umm... I'm Jessica and...' she hesitated, 'and...I'm a singer. I live with my boyfriend. I'm originally from the UK.' Elaine nodded as if encouraging her to continue, but realised Jessica had nothing else to say.

'It seems like your boyfriend is very supportive, what about your family?'

'I don't really see them much since I moved to the States.'

'Why is that?'

'Erm... because it's far away?' Jessica answered, mockingly.

Elaine spent the next hour desperately trying to get Jessica to open up about everything from her family to her career.

'Okay, thank you for that Jessica. I think it's important to find out about our residents when they first arrive; the only way we can help them recover is by understanding them and seeing them as individuals. I'll show you to the canteen now and you can meet some of the other residents while you have dinner.'

Jessica followed her into an equally beautiful room, bathed in sunlight with an airy and open feel to it.

'If you have a look at the menu and then let the cook know what you'd like. Also, if there's anything that you would really like to eat while you're here, please do let us know and we can arrange this for you,' Elaine said as she guided her towards a table where two other girls sat talking. Both looked similar age to Jessica.

'Ladies, this is Jessica,' Elaine said before smiling and leaving.

'Hi Jessica!' The blonde girl said. 'I'm Caitlin and this is Jamie,' she motioned to the other girl with jet black hair, scraped up into a tight ponytail. Jessica noted that both were completely 'normal' looking girls, whatever normal may be anyway. She wondered what brought them to this place.

'Hi,' Jessica smiled weakly. 'So, what are you guys in here for?' Both laughed and Caitlin said, 'It's not prison!'

'You sure about that?' Jessica said, looking around.

'Trust me, it gets easier. The first day is always the worst,' Caitlin replied.

'I'd say the first week is the worst to be honest,' Jamie said, sipping her drink.

'Have you had a look at the menu for today? We've not ordered yet but we're thinking the creamy garlic chicken.'

'Erm…I'll just have that too,' Jessica said, still with a feeble smile.

Once orders were placed, Caitlin went on to explain that she was currently in recovery for an eating disorder after an abusive relationship, while Jamie explained she was receiving treatment for cocaine and alcohol abuse after her boyfriend was killed in a hit and run. Now it was Jessica's turn and she felt embarrassed that her situation was almost self-inflicted.

'I've been struggling to cope without cocaine; I think it's because I've been under pressure my manager to be perfect at my job, I suppose.'

'Ugh, I hate that!' both nodded in agreement.

Jessica decided to leave it there so no further questions were asked. Food was served and she noticed that Caitlin's serving was significantly smaller than anyone else's and this must have been part of her recovery. Jessica wasn't massively hungry either so just picked at her food, eating just enough for sustenance.

'Are you both part of the group art therapy now?' Jessica asked.

'I am,' said Jamie. 'But Caitlin's got her session with Doctor Elaine now. Come on, I'll show you the way.'

Starting to feel like the new girl at school, Jessica followed Jamie down the corridor. The art group consisted of turning all the lights off, drawing the blackout blinds, and trying to draw a portrait of the group leader. The idea was that everyone sees you differently and everyone will remember different things about you. Looking around at some of the contributions in the room, it was a clever idea using the member of staff as the subject as opposed to other group members; the results were certainly self-conscious inducing, Jessica thought. The only part of the militantly structured day that Jessica liked was the meditation at the end of the day. It allowed her to sit and relax, knowing she was in a safe place, however in line with the structured element of the rehabilitation, the meditation was guided by a member of staff as opposed to anyone outside. It was clear they weren't a professional instructor by some of the things they'd come out with. Jessica had taken up yoga several months ago and she'd fallen in love with it. It gave her time to reflect on each day, whilst also stretching her increasingly tired body.

SIX

After the first three weeks of being a resident, visitors were allowed. It felt like a punishment that others who had been here longer were allowed visits from loved ones, yet as Jessica was still in the induction phase, she had to sit them out. Jessica did however feel slightly fortunate that Daniel had been here to witness her withdrawal from the cocaine. She hadn't realised she'd become so reliant on it; in her head she just used it at parties, before events, before gigs, before interviews, before... okay, maybe she was quite dependant on it.

She'd spent many a nights in the first few days, shaking uncontrollably and sweating profusely. It was certainly a sight for her to see in the mirror, so felt relieved that her loved ones didn't have to see her in this state. Then the stomach cramps and nausea began; Jessica rolling around in agony on her bed as a staff member held her hand and accepted all the abuse that Jessica was throwing in their direction. She truly didn't recognise herself anymore. Daniel had arranged to come and visit as soon as he could, just like he'd promised, so when Jessica came into the lounge room and saw him, she burst into tears and jumped into his arms.

'Hey, it's okay. I told you I'd come and visit, didn't I?'

'I've missed you so much. I'm so sorry for everything. I just want to come home. Please, can we just go?' Jessica begged.

Daniel hesitated and peeled her from his body.

'Jess, no-one is forcing you to stay. You can leave anytime you want, but I genuinely think this is the best place for you. You've done three weeks. You've got three more to go. You can do this!'

Jessica silently nodded and dropped her arms from his shoulders, admitting defeat.

'Now, I've got some news which I've been debating whether to share or not. Your team contacted me when they'd not heard from you, so I told them you'd come here. Then they seemed to turn nasty and started hounding me for details. They put out a statement on social media from your accounts saying this.'

He read from his phone.

'After some personal issues worsened, Jessica has made the decision to seek help. We kindly ask that Jessica's privacy is respected during this challenging time. Her health and recovery remain the utmost importance to us. Jessica would like to say thank you for all the love and support from her fans.'

Jessica saw Daniel roll his eyes, making her smile.

'Can you comment back and tell them it's their fault I'm in here?'

Daniel laughed and took her hand.

'So yeah, they were ringing me and demanding to know which facility you were at and trying to get an appointment to see you. I just shut them down. I've also told that lady Elaine not to allow them any visits. It's not a conversation for now, but they really are vile…we need to get you away from them.'

'I wish it was that easy…I've got a contract and who's going to want to sign a risk like me anyway?'

'Don't worry about the contract, that's what lawyers are for.'

'I think I've lost my passion for this whole industry anyway…'

'As I said, not a conversation for now anyway!'

Jessica proceeded to give him the grand tour of the centre; showing him her basic room and walking round the grounds, showing him where they did meditation each day. Daniel stopped to look at his phone, opening a message before abruptly saying, 'I'm going to get off okay. But just hang on in there, I promise you it's gonna be so worth it in the end.'

Thus, concluding their tour. They hugged and said their goodbyes but as they were at the door, Jessica could see a small group of people pointing and whispering. Daniel didn't notice and as he trotted down the steps, he was swarmed upon by a group of middle aged woman.

'Hi, sorry, but can we get a photo?' they asked pointlessly as they were already holding up their phones for selfies. Daniel caught Jessica's eye and shrugged with a smile. Jessica smiled back, but she knew he was in his element, devouring the attention.

'Who on earth is that then?' Jamie's familiar voice perked up behind Jessica, making her jump.

'Is that really Daniel Brown, the swimmer? Please tell me that's your brother...' Caitlin piped up. Jessica suddenly felt shy.

'Yes, it is, but he's my boyfriend not my brother.'

'Holy shit! How did you meet him?!' Jamie squeaked.

'We met on a TV show,' Jessica said as she waved Daniel off and turned back inside.

'Wait a minute...' Caitlin put her hand to her mouth. 'You're...'

Oh god, Jessica thought.

'You're that singer, aren't you? Jessica! I knew I recognised you! This is insane!'

'Holy shit,' Jamie interjected, causing Jessica to awkwardly shuffle and try to hush them both.

'Please, I really just want to get this all over with and go home. Please can you just forget about it?'

Both stood up straight and nodded.

'Oh my god, of course. We weren't going to say anything...it's just a bit bizarre that's all.

We're your friends, we won't say anything, isn't that right Jamie?'

'Of course! Sorry Jessica!'

Jessica smiled uncomfortably but weirdly trusted their word. Also, it felt reassuring that they'd bonded for weeks before they even knew who she was. There was a moment of silence as they all struggled what to say next.

'Does he have a brother that's single?' Jamie asked bluntly and they all burst into laughter.

'He's got four so you can take your pick!' Jessica giggled.

◆ ◆ ◆

Jessica had suddenly had an epiphany one night that she didn't want to live like this any longer. In the past, when she'd had thoughts like this it was when she was feeling depressed and thinking of other ways out. However, this time she felt inspired and ready to take anything on. She'd felt this before, when she was using, but this time it was a natural high. She acknowledged how hard it would be when she got out of here, but she was determined to make it work.

The next two weeks seemed to sail by; Jamie had left the week before and Caitlin was due to leave this week. They'd all promised to keep in touch and even guaranteed to be each other's sober buddies. In her sessions with Doctor Elaine, Jessica had concluded that despite having a happy childhood and being raised by a loving parent, the trauma of losing her biological parents and then her mum was enough to make anyone struggle. They spoke of how honest conversations were needed with her management team; explaining how she felt about certain situations, even if they didn't intend for it to be taken that way. Jessica even found herself talking about university and her relationship with Jake. She acknowledged she was carrying some guilt and trauma about abandoning him like she'd felt abandoned at times in her life.

After 180 days as an inpatient, Jessica's time to leave had come. Daniel was picking her up at 10am to take her home. Jessica found herself emotional at the thought of leaving, completely opposite to her feelings upon arrival. She thanked Doctor Elaine for all her help and nodded along when she was given all the information about continued outpatient support. As she sat in the car, donning her grey sweatshirt and black sweatpants, she felt like she was being released from prison. As they pulled out the long drive of the grounds, Daniel put his hand on her right knee as he had done when they'd arrived.

'I'm so proud of you,' he said, sniffing back tears.

Jessica didn't say anything, she simply placed her hand atop of his and stroked it gently with her thumb. Nothing could have prepared Jessica for the carnage outside their apartment block. As their car entered the street, cameras were flashing, and men were shouting.

'Oh my god, hurry!' Jessica panicked.

'What the fuck are they playing at?' Daniel said as he honked at the paparazzi to move.

Jessica held her bag up to cover her face as they swung into the private garage. The car stopped and everything went quiet.

'Wow...okay...' Daniel exhaled as Jessica started crying.

'Come on, let's get you inside. We'll go in through the back stairs so they can't see us, okay?'

No matter how much Daniel reassured her, she couldn't help thinking that someone close to her must have told them that she was coming home that day. She suddenly felt bitter about Jamie and Caitlin, wondering if it was one of them. After all, they knew when she was leaving.

Could it have been Daniel? No, definitely not, it must have been someone else from the facility. She scolded herself for even thinking it could be Daniel. *It must have been Caitlin or Jamie*, she conceded.

Daniel convinced her to let it go and focus on getting better. He cooked her spaghetti meatballs that night. Usually, her favourite; his speciality.

'What's wrong with it?'

'Nothing. It's just not as good as what they serve back there...' Jessica smirked.

'You cheeky...' he laughed.

As they headed to bed, Jessica decided to switch her phone

on. Without sounding big headed, she knew it would be full of notifications from assorted people, whether they genuinely cared or were just nosey, was for Jessica to decide. As the notification bell dinged continuously for five minutes, Daniel smiled and shook his head; Jessica switching it to silent. Once the phone had calmed down, she began scrolling through her messages to see if she recognised any names. Sure enough, family names and old friends popped up. She stopped scrolling and clicked on the first one – from her dad. She read through the lovely message which included a plea to come home, making her suddenly feel guilty for all the worry she caused. Part of her wanted to ring him and apologise for everything but the other half of her was terrified to do that.

'Daniel, did you tell my dad where I was?'

'Yeah, I messaged him on Facebook because I didn't have his number. I hope that's okay? I thought it best he heard it from me rather than read it online or something. I kept in touch and gave him regular updates on how you were getting on. He was obviously really concerned.'

'Thank you,' Jessica smiled, continuing to look through messages.

There were ones from her brothers, one from Tom, friends from university, assorted people she'd met throughout her career. All wishing her well and sending her love. She selected a few to reply to in a copy and paste fashion; thanking them for their well wishes and that she was ready to take on the world again, maybe just with a little bit of help this time. She knew she'd have to ring her management team tomorrow morning, so she took the opportunity to switch off her phone again and try to get a good night's sleep.

Jessica woke early the next morning and toyed with the idea of going for a walk on the beach. She quickly dismissed this idea at the fear of any paparazzi folk stalking around. She made a coffee and settled down with her Kindle, enjoying watching the sun come up and brighten the room with an orange glow. Daniel appeared an hour later and said his goodbyes as he headed out to swim practice. She decided to use this opportunity to make the inevitable call. She felt incredibly nervous to speak to the people who were partially to blame for her downfall. After two rings, the familiar authoritative voice of Michael appeared.

'Well, well, well, if it isn't my favourite struggling starlet.'

Jessica cringed at his manner.

'Hi Michael, I just wanted to let you know that I'm back...'

He interrupted, 'I know sweetheart, your endearing boyfriend told me he was picking you up yesterday.'

Jessica wondered if it was in fact someone in her team that had tipped off the paparazzi after Daniel had spoken to them. This was seemingly more likely than her new friends, she thought.

'Oh...okay. So, what happens now?'

'You tell me sweetheart; we are no longer representing you.'

'Wh...what?' Jessica spluttered.

'Sweetheart, we can't take the risk with you. We're not paid to be therapists. We need people who are going to make us money, not tarnish our reputation.'

'But we have a contract!'

'Look sweetheart, if you actually read your contract before you signed it like every other dumb blonde we represent, you would've seen the bit that states we can terminate the contract at any time without giving notice, if we see fit.'

Jessica's blood boiled.

'Excuse me? Fuck you, Michael! And fuck your team! I was looking for a get out clause from you anyway. You lot are the reason I ended up in that place!' Jessica heard Michael scoff and before he could reply, she hung up, bursting with anger.

Shortly afterwards she received an email titled *'Confirmation of ceased contract'* which she skim read but then slammed her phone down on the side. She took her pillow from the neatly made bed, held it to her face and screamed into it at the top of her voice. She stopped when her throat began to burn.

SEVEN

One year later

Since returning from the facility nearly a year ago, Jessica felt like a new woman. After being dumped by her earlier, toxic manager, Michael and his hareem of servants, Jessica had taken a break from music for several months to focus on herself. She felt like one of those Disney stars who found fame so young that they grew up in the limelight, allowing the world to see all their mistakes as they grew into an adult. She felt guilty for those who couldn't afford fancy inpatient treatment facilities. She thought of her cousin back home, who was struggling with depression and anxiety; at the bottom of a three year long NHS waiting list for CBT. At the time, Jessica had spoken to her dad about offering to pay for private treatment for her cousin, but her dad advised against it, for all sorts of reasons. Jessica was fortunate enough to have been admitted so quickly and begin treatment at once. Jessica had become distant with her family since returning from the facility, having not spoken to her dad or brothers in any great extent for months. She felt embarrassed about everything and ashamed; she knew they loved her, and they wouldn't judge her, but she just couldn't shake the feelings enough to pick up the phone or book a flight. Avoidance was the best medicine in this instance, or so she thought anyway.

Things had been better with Daniel, they still had arguments, but he was constantly telling her how proud he was of her for how far she'd come. His main focus now with training was the 2016 Olympics in Rio later this year. He'd been away for a few training camps for more focused sessions, and he seemed to be confident with how his preparation was going. As Olympic and World Champion, he'd automatically qualified for his events in Rio. Unfortunately, Jessica had to break the news to him at some point that she wouldn't be coming to Rio as she'd booked a tour to relaunch her career. She'd decided that today would be the day to reveal that news before it was announced to the public; she'd put it off long enough.

'Dan, can we talk?' Jessica said, leaning over the counter where he was washing up after dinner.

'Uh-oh, you breaking up with me?' he mocked, then paused to check this wasn't the case.

Jessica gave a soft smile to confirm that this was not the case and he carried on rinsing the soapy plates.

'What's up?' he asked.

'Okay…so, I've got some news which is good news, but it's kind of bad news too,' Jessica started.

'Right…'

'So, I've booked a tour later this year…'

'Oh brilliant!' Daniel interrupted.

'Wait,' Jessica said, stopping him going any further, 'It's in the Summer,' she finished.

'Okay?' Daniel replied, not getting it.

'This Summer, as in, July and August,' she prompted.

'Oh, right. Is this you saying that you won't be coming to support me in Rio?' he snarked.

'Yes, like you won't be able to come support me on tour,' she matched his tone, and he slammed a mug down.

'You know what a big deal this is for me! Plus, it'll be great for both our careers if we're seen together there! Why would you agree to that?' he asked, turning to face her as he dried his hands.

'What are you talking about? My life doesn't revolve around

following you around!' Jessica snapped, feeling anger bubbling inside her now, ready to explode like a volcano.

At times, Daniel did make her feel as if all he wanted in a partner was someone who would follow him around and worship him and his successes. That was never going to be Jessica.

'I'm not saying that, I'm saying that I can't believe you didn't even consider it,' he said.

'Firstly, I did consider it – I spent two weeks with my manager trying to work around it, but it just wouldn't fit in the schedule. It's not like I'm not going to support you. I'll be cheering you on, just from here instead of in Rio,' Jessica reasoned.

'Not good enough,' Daniel said to her like a disappointed parent would say to a child who was making excuses.

'Daniel, I'm sorry. I love you. I am your biggest cheerleader, you know that. I just can't change this, I'm sorry,' Jessica sighed, putting her arms round him.

He brushed her arms off and scoffed.

'Some cheerleader. Maybe I'll just ask one of the girls from the gym to come with me instead,' he said with a vicious tone.

'I beg your pardon?!' Jessica shrieked, both shocked and confused at what he had just said.

'Right now, they seem more supportive than you!' he snapped back.

'You're unbelievable!' Jessica tried to storm out, but Daniel grabbed her arm.

'Ow!' she yelled as he gripped her forearm tightly. He realised his own strength and quickly released her.

'I'm sorry! I'm sorry! I genuinely didn't mean to grab you that hard. Honestly, I'm sorry. I just didn't want you to storm out,' he held his hands up and seemed truly remorseful.

'It's fine,' Jessica conceded, realising it was an accident.

He could be a prick, but he certainly wasn't that guy, she reasoned.

'Jess, I just, I want you there cheering me on with my family. You are my family,' Daniel sighed.

'I want to be there cheering you on, but I honestly cannot change this. I tried, I really did,' she stepped forward to kiss him but couldn't reach him.

She had to put her arms round his neck and tried to pull him down to her. As she aimed for his lips, he turned his head, so her kiss planted on his cheek instead. She exhaled heavily and stepped back. Jessica went to sit on the balcony and enjoy the sunset, reclining on the chair. As she stared at the sky turning a beautiful red colour, she noticed that it all started to go blurry. She blinked and tears overflowed from her eyes, falling into her hairline as she remained reclined. She bit her lip, trying not to let loud sobs emerge from her throat, so much so that she began to feel a burning sensation in her chest and throat. It felt like she'd swallowed a large lump of dry bread that was forcing its way down her windpipe, slowly choking her. Every time she tried to take a deep breath, it hurt. She wasn't sure if this was worth it anymore; she loved Daniel so much, but she couldn't recall the last time they laughed and joked like they used to. Even when they had sex, it didn't feel remotely romantic or passionate. Jessica just put that down to the fact that they were in a long-term relationship now, and the passion and romance started to die down after the honeymoon period of dating each other.

Despite her concerns about the relationship, Jessica decided that she loved Daniel enough to try and work through their problems. She couldn't change the dates of the tour, but she would cheer him on from wherever she was during his swims.

As the Summer progressed, they were both starting to train harder for their individual tests, similar in some respects but miles apart in other ways. Daniel was starting to taper, meaning that his training was dramatically reduced in both quantity and intensity to allow for maximum rest and recovery before a major championship. Ultimately, it allowed swimmers to be at their peak before something like the Olympics; the idea being that they would be both mentally and physically prepared to ensure fast and powerful swims when it really mattered. Jessica meanwhile was increasing her stamina by having more regular sessions at the gym and running. Gone were the days where she would be expected to rehearse ridiculous dance routines for hours on end, with backing dancers that made her feel self-conscious about her own skills. All she needed to be able to do these days was move around the stage whilst singing and not getting out of breath. No-one wants to hear panting and gasping for air through a microphone. Well, some might.

Jessica had said goodbye to Daniel several weeks ago; before he set off to the holding camp – this is where athletes from the same country join together and stay before moving into the athlete village at the Olympic site. They were in touch every day, but Daniel still felt distant and withdrawn from their relationship. Jessica tried to put this to the back of her mind and focused solely on supplying an exceptional performance each night. She'd do several nights in a row in one vicinity, then have a couple of days off before doing it all again. Being on tour was stressful but Jessica thrived on the buzz she got when she came off stage. She no longer got nervous. Thinking back to her first 'gig' at Leadmill back in Sheffield, she was so terrified that she refused to let Jake or Tom even listen to her rehearse. It was comical really.

A month had gone by already and Jessica was just a few shows away from finishing her US tour, something she still couldn't quite comprehend. She'd managed to watch Daniel's 200m freestyle final on Facetime via his mum who had kindly called her and held the phone up. Jessica didn't have the heart to tell her that she was watching the race on her laptop as she couldn't see a thing on the blurry phone screen. Daniel won the race and Jessica proudly watched his medal ceremony. She was in Austin, Texas at this point so the time difference was only a few hours, meaning she could call Daniel and congratulate him on his win.

'Well done babe, I'm so, SO proud of you. I love you,' she'd told him.

'Thank you. I was starting to doubt it on that second turn, but I just felt this new burst of energy and went for it. I love you too. I wish you were here,' he said in return.

He'd managed to qualify for the 400IM final but ended up coming third – something which was by no means anything to be ashamed of, winning a bronze medal. However, he was peeved he'd missed out. He'd raced to victory with his teammates to win gold in the 4x200m and the 4x100m too. He was fast becoming a highly decorated Olympian. He'd already been home for three weeks when she'd finished her final show in New York, ready to fly back to LA the next day. She'd celebrated her *'win'* with her team by going to McDonalds. She didn't need any fancy restaurants; all she needed was a Big Mac that was guilt free thanks to her fantastic new team, who encouraged her to order more to celebrate. Daniel and his friends were planning a congratulatory party for his wins but he insisted on waiting until Jessica was back so she could join them. This was something that Jessica took as a huge compliment; he wanted to celebrate with her, he wanted her there with him and his friends.

When Jessica returned home, she was full of stories about the tour and Daniel was equally full of stories about Rio. They stayed up late into the night, taking it in turns to share anecdotes. It had been a long time since Jessica had seen Daniel so happy and he could arguably say the same about her.

They'd had a really rough couple of years, and it finally felt as if they were coming out the other side. The party was a few days after Jessica got home, so she had time to settle back in again. It was being held at a swish bar that Daniel and his friends had hired out for the private function. Daniel opted for a pair of stone coloured chinos with a crisp white shirt, unbuttoned at the top for a more casual look. As he knelt to slip his shoes on, Jessica looked at him with adoration.

'Are you trying to turn me on?' she said.

'No, happy accident I guess,' he replied, smirking before looking up and seeing Jessica in her figure hugging black jumpsuit.

'Wow,' he took a sharp intake of breath as if something was catching in his throat. He got up from his knee and took her hand above her head to spin her round, before kissing her.

'Come on, we're gonna be late!' she said, grabbing her clutch bag and leading him towards the door by his hand.

They took a cab to the bar and Daniel's phone was pinging away with notifications, presumably from his friends who were already there. They were slightly late after all. He unlocked the phone and smiled at something on the screen before it beeped again. His face went to steel and Jessica could've sworn she saw him blush as he quickly swiped up to close the messaging app before locking his phone again and putting it into his pocket. When they walked in, everyone was there and waiting for them. They all cheered and clapped for Daniel, congratulating him on his wins. One guy who Jessica had never seen before thrust a beer into his hand before knocking his own beer bottle against it to say 'cheers.' Another man that Jessica had met was now congratulating Daniel, slapping him on the back.

'Congrats buddy! We never doubted you!' the man guffawed.

'Congrats Dan,' a woman's voice said, causing both Jessica and Daniel to turn around.

'Hey Riley,' Daniel said smoothly, his face lighting up at the woman that stood before them. She lunged forward to embrace him with one arm, kissing him on both cheeks. How very European, Jessica thought. Riley had a smooth, velvety voice that wasn't like the usual LA girls; it was almost husky and deep as opposed to the often whiny, squeaky voices that some girls donned, elongating the ends of words. She extended her long, toned arm out to Jessica.

'I don't believe we've met. You must be Jennifer, I'm Riley,' she said with a sweet smile.

'Umm, it's Jessica and hi,' she replied feeling self-conscious as she reached out her significantly less toned arm to shake Riley's hand.

'How do you know Daniel?' Jessica asked, sipping her drink.

'I joined Phil's gym and when I was doing some weight training, Daniel here offered to spot for me,' she laughed, play punching Daniel's arm.

'Oh, haha, cool, cool,' Jessica mumbled, wondering why Daniel was willingly volunteering to basically hold this woman's arse while she bent over to lift weights. She eyed Daniel who was smiling nonchalantly at Riley. Jessica even noticed that he was eyeing Riley up and down, checking her out, right in front of her. *The audacity of it!*

EIGHT

Watching Daniel from the other side of the bar, Jessica knew. He wasn't exactly subtle with the hand on Riley's back, sliding down to her perfectly pert arse. Surely other people could see this? she thought as she looked around the room. Jessica debated what to do and decided to down her drink and leave rather than approaching the situation and making a scene. She wasn't entirely sure what was happening, but she didn't want to see it anymore. She felt so cross with Daniel for being so disrespectful to her; he'd not even introduced her to any of his friends. She didn't need to be ushered around with a chaperone, but she thought Daniel might have at least spoken to her since they arrived.

She'd been back at the apartment a few hours by the time Daniel rolled in looking somewhat dishevelled, clearly with lipstick on his mouth. At risk of paraphrasing Chandler Bing, could he *be* more cliché?

'What happened to you?' he asked with no genuine concern in his voice, just vague interest.

'I wasn't feeling too well so I thought I'd bow out. Plus, it looked like you had your hands full with your friends.' Jessica's dig went unnoticed in her drunken state.

'Fair enough,' he said as he rolled into bed whilst

simultaneously texting on his phone. They lay there in silence until he fell asleep, with Jessica drifting off about half an hour later.

She woke early the next morning to see Daniel still fast asleep, snoring. She'd been awoken by a strange, vicious buzzing noise as she began to get out of bed and quickly realised it was Daniel's phone vibrating on the floor. She glanced over to see Riley's name flashing up. Jessica had never been one to check boyfriend's phones; partly it wasn't her style and also, she felt that if the doubt is there then it usually means your gut feeling is right. When his phone didn't wake him, Jessica got up, brushed her teeth and on her return, slammed the bathroom door shut, knowing that would wake him with a start. As expected, his eyes shot open.

'Jesus, I was trying to have a lie in. What are you doing?' he snapped.

'Your phone was ringing,' she retorted, watching as he looked at her quizzically before tracking down his phone.

As he saw the name of the missed call, his face changed into a brief smile. Her doubts had been confirmed with that simple twitch of the corners of his mouth.

'So how long has it been going on with her?' she blurted out without thinking.

Whilst most men would look baffled and at least try to lie, Jessica had to respect the fact that he was either very brave to own up straight away, or perhaps he was just stupid. She decided to go with the latter.

'We met at the gym about a year ago. We started working out together and realised how much we had in common.'

At this point, Jessica wasn't even upset; he'd just proven everyone right. Everyone who told her she shouldn't have dated an athlete; they had a reputation for this kind of behaviour.

'Okay,' she whispered, 'So I was right, all those months ago. Before I went away, I thought you were cheating, and you were. I was right. I saw photos of you together looking cosy, you denied it, but I was right. I wasn't being paranoid, I was right. I assume you were hooking up the entire time I was at the facility? Of course you were,' Jessica said, answering her own questions.

'I'm sorry. I really am. I didn't expect anything to happen,' he explained.

It appeared as if he was waiting for Jessica to kick and scream, maybe even shed a tear. She knew full well she was certainly not going to give him that satisfaction.

'If you were with her, why did you convince me to get help? Why did you come track me down and pick me up from those parties? Why didn't you just break up with me?' Jessica asked.

'I still cared about you, Jess. I still do care about you...' Daniel said, reaching for her.

'I'll arrange for my stuff to be moved back to my place as soon as I can. I'm going to head back there today,' she said plainly, pulling back so he couldn't reach her.

It was at this point that Daniel began to look shifty and uncomfortable.

'I must say, you're taking this awfully well...' he said cautiously.

'I think I came to terms with it a while ago, y'know, when I first found out...months ago...I should've listened to everyone else. Even your brother said to keep an eye on you.'

He looked hurt by that comment more than anything else. Daniel's dad hadn't been on the scene since he was four years old; and he'd always looked up to his eldest brother as a father figure. No additional words parted either of their mouths. Jessica packed a bag with essentials in while Daniel sat and watched, awkwardly fiddling with the bed sheets.

Later that day, she'd already been avoiding calls from Daniel's mum and Sister. They'd both left messages of concern, asking what was going on and why their son's private Facebook relationship status had changed to 'Single.' Jessica had been subtle enough to hide hers from her timeline, but needless to say, Daniel didn't, thus inviting the obligatory shocked emoji faces in the comments underneath. *Ah, to be in a relationship in the modern era,* she mused. She looked at her phone with the missed calls, including five from her publicist. Weird. She listened to her messages.

'Jessica, call me now! What's going on?'

She didn't have to listen to any others. It was out in the world. Great. The phone barely rang for one ring before she picked up.

'Oh my god, where have you been? What is going on? TMZ have been hounding me for confirmation of your split with Daniel. I thought it was a load of shite until I went online.' She sounded genuinely panic stricken.

'Well, what can I say? He cheated, it's over. End of. No story,' Jessica said plainly.

'Are you joking? What a prick!' she said. 'How are you bearing up?' she added with concern to her voice.

Matter of fact, Jessica said, 'I mean, its fucking shit, but whatever. He's made his choice.'

Over the next few days, she tried to stay away from social media as much as she could. She couldn't help seeing stories here and there that she'd been tagged in. Headlines read; *'Heartbreak for Jessica!' 'End for Jessica!' 'Back to rehab for Jessica after heartbreak scandal?'*

She thought about the fact that whenever anything was reported to be slightly 'going wrong' in her life, people assumed she was going to go under again. Then again, she supposed history showed they would have good odds. Her manager always told her that she should never Google her own name. Technically, she followed his advice; she 'Twitter Googled.' *That's okay right?*

As she was scrolling through articles, she was only half paying attention to the nonsense written in front of her, when she accidentally swiped up to accept an incoming call from Daniel's mum.

'Shit!' Jessica muttered as she heard a concerned voice at the other end.

'Hello? Hello? Jessica? Can you hear me?'

Realising it was past the stage where she could easily hang up without his mum knowing she could most definitely hear her, Jessica raised the phone to her right ear.

'Hi Linda, how are you?'

Now she was the silent one. After what seemed like minutes but was probably in fact 5 seconds, she spoke frantically.

'I've been seeing lots of stuff online about you and Daniel. Have you broken up? Are you okay? Has something happened? Can I do anything?'

Fair play to the woman, she was clearly concerned, albeit a little bit nosy. The real question Jessica had was should she be honest and tell her that her beloved son is a lying, cheating wanker? She decided not to. Not yet anyway.

'We just drifted apart really. I'm fine. It's all fine.'

Jessica was quite proud of how convincing she sounded; she even fooled herself. She'd managed to end the call by saying just how busy she was with meetings, and she must get on. Again, quite pleased with how convincing she came across. With this in mind, she threw her phone onto the bed, slid out of her clothes, and plunged into the soapy, boiling bath. She even treated herself to a luxurious bath bomb from a PR package, which she could feel fizzing away near her toes. She closed her eyes and inhaled the soothing lavender scent, feeling the bubbles gently bursting on her shoulders that sat above the water line. The silence was simply fantastic. She opened her eyes and stared ahead, before bursting into uncontrollable sobbing. After a long hour in the bath that now felt tepid on her prune-like wrinkled skin, Jessica hauled herself out and slipped her dressing gown on. She picked up her phone to see assorted other missed calls, swiping to clear the notifications. She scrolled through her contacts and clicked.

'Hello?' a sleepy voice answered.

'Oh shit, I forgot what time it was there, sorry dad!'

'Is everything okay, sweetheart?'

Jessica paused then burst into tears again.

'No!'

'Oh sweetheart, what's happened?'

'Daniel is a cheating wanker and I feel so angry with myself that I've pushed him to do this!'

'Hey now, what on earth are you talking about? You've not pushed anyone to do anything!'

'I did! When I lost the plot, I put him through so much! No wonder he started to look elsewhere! I'm surprised he didn't wander sooner! To be honest, I don't know that he hadn't!'

'Now hang on one minute young lady,' the voice suddenly became stern.

'You stop blaming yourself right this second, especially when it comes to your health. I'm sorry that you're hurting sweetheart, I really am. I wish I could be there to give you a hug...' he sniffed, trying to stifle what sounded like a sob.

After a moment of silence, Jessica whispered, 'I'm sorry for causing you all to worry and I'm sorry for not getting in touch and screening your calls. I was just embarrassed and didn't know what to say.'

'Sweetheart, we're just pleased you're okay. I won't pretend it wasn't difficult to watch you struggling and knowing there was nothing we could do from so far away. Me and your brothers are just pleased that you stuck to the programme, and you've turned everything around. This is just a blip, okay?'

'I know...it doesn't make it any easier though.'

'I know, sweetheart.'

'I'll let you get back to sleep...sorry for waking you. I'll message you tomorrow.'

'No apologies needed; you need anything, you ring me right away, okay?'

'Okay.'

Jessica ended the call and rested her phone on the bed side table, but before the backlight had even gone off, her phone pinged with a message from Daniel. She debated deleting it right away, but curiosity got the better of her and she opened the message, to find it a lengthy essay.

Jess,

I've spoken to my mum, and I've seen some stories online with all sorts being said. I wanted to say I'm so sorry for the hurt I've caused you. I really am. I've known things haven't been right for a while and I should have just ended it back then. I met Riley at the gym, and she was just so energetic and fun. We became friends and began working out together. She started telling me about how her boyfriend broke up with her because she started focusing on her career more. I told her that I'd been struggling in our relationship due to the pressures you were under. We started going for coffee after the gym and that became increasingly regular. It became a lot flirtier, and we were texting pretty much every day. Then, one night she invited me round to hers. I naively assumed this was just a friendly offer to watch a film and eat take out. I'd barely been in the door five minutes, and she kissed me. First, I pushed her off and explained I was in a relationship, then when she asked me if I was actually happy, I stopped and thought. No, I wasn't. Something in my brain clicked that night, and after we'd had sex, I said I needed time to figure out how to end things with you. She was really patient and told me she would wait for me to do the right thing.

The thought of Daniel having sex with someone else made Jessica feel sick to her stomach. She also half laughed at the irony of Daniel trying to do the 'right thing' after sleeping with another girl. She continued reading the message.

Days became weeks and weeks became months. I just couldn't find the right time to tell you. So, we both agreed that we'd just carry on doing what we were doing as we couldn't be apart. Looking back, I should have just called it quits with you there and then. I'm sorry for stringing you along. I was just worried what you'd do to yourself and how you'd cope. I suppose really, I'm writing because I'm asking you not to share with anyone that I cheated. Riley's family are pretty conservative, and they'd be devastated to find out she'd been part of something like this. Thanks, x

Jessica's mouth fell open and she boiled with rage. How dare he ask her a favour for the girl he cheated on her with. She skim read the rest of the message, scrolling through endless pleading not to speak out and to move on. His mission wasn't to apologise, it was to beg Jessica not to ruin his public profile. She hit reply and typed angrily.

*I have nothing to say, except a big **FUCK YOU**!!!*

She pressed send and once it was gone, she deleted the messages and blocked his number. She blocked him across all social media accounts too, not actually feeling massively upset, just angry. She'd arrange for her stuff to be moved out of his apartment at some point; for the moment, she had everything she needed right here in the safety and comfort of her own home. Within these walls, she was safe, alone and content.

NINE

March 2008

'Bye Jake, see you tonight!'

Jessica turned round to get a better look at the girl who had just brushed past Jake. She looked familiar on first glance but she was still none the wiser. 'Who was that?' she asked him.

'Just a girl from one of my seminar groups. We've got to do a project together so I'm going round to hers tonight to work on it.'

'Oh okay,' Jessica nodded in understanding. She'd had to do some group work as part of her university course too. Personally, she loathed group work; there was always one person who never did any work towards it but received the same final grade as the others in the group. She much preferred solo work; being responsible for her own efforts. They were in their final year of university, so a lot of their spare time was taken up by working on assignments. The gigs and clubbing had become less frequent, however they still made time to have fun both with and without each other. Walking down Carver Street, Jessica thought about how different the street was depending on the time of day. During the hours of daylight, it was just a normal street that shoppers would use as a cut through in the city, students would walk to and from university, and buses would travel down. When the sun went down, the street was filled with drunken students and revellers. Some queued outside clubs, waiting to be allowed in after individually having their IDs checked, some poured out of the same clubs, drunken and looking for the nearest takeaway shop. In their first year, Jessica and Jake would head to Carver Street at least once a week with their friends. By the end of their second year, they had become regulars at places like Plug, Leadmill and Corporation. They quickly discovered that they preferred the music, atmosphere and people at the latter three. Although, anyone who has been to Corporation, more colloquially known as 'Corp', would have their own story about the floor there. It was unique mix of sticky, wet and slippy. Everyone had a pair of 'Corp' shoes – a cheap pair they didn't mind getting ruined. It was a great night out, but that floor was something to behold.

'So does that mean you aren't coming out tonight?' Jessica asked as they wandered back towards Portland Street, where Jake was living. They'd decided not to move in together, despite them spending every night together, switching between each other's places. Jake lived with Tom and crew, while Jessica lived with a group of girls from her course whom she became friendly with midway through first year.
'Nah, sorry. I really should crack on with it; been putting it off for a while and my partner was getting impatient,' he laughed.
'You are the kind of partner I hate working with...' she replied with a laugh.
'Hey!' he said with mock outrage.

At 8pm, Jessica rocked up at Portland Tower, Tom buzzing her in. He'd left the flat door on the latch so she could let herself in. They were having pre-drinks at their flat before heading out to Plug.

'Hellooo!' she called, as she closed the door behind her and wandered into the kitchen/living space, where the music was coming from. Jake was sat on the kitchen counter, finishing a can of Pepsi.

'Bloody hell!' he coughed, trying desperately to swallow the Pepsi he'd just guzzled. 'Look at you!' he said to Jessica, looking her up and down. She smiled in return and as she walked over to him, he stuck out his legs to wrap them behind her knees, holding her in front of him. 'You look insane,' he said, staring into her blue eyes. He found it hard to control himself; she looked sexy as hell. She was wearing a black bodycon dress that hugged every inch of her. Her legs looked even longer than usual thanks to the bright green heels she was donning. Her long blonde hair was poker straight and fell down her back. Tom walked past and wolf whistled, making her laugh but also making her feel self-conscious.

'Damn, I wish I was coming out with you now...' Jake admitted, gently playing with her hands.

'I can always come back here afterwards?' she suggested, raising her eyebrows.

'Yes please,' he said, widening his eyes and nodding. 'Ugh, I best be off. She lives on Eccy Road,' he said, hopping down from his seated position on the counter. He gave her a kiss goodbye, then headed out.

Jake knocked on the door to an old house along Ecclesall Road. A girl with brunette hair scraped back into a top knot, answered the door.

'Ah, project buddy, yes?' she said inquisitively.

'Um, yeah I guess so,' he said as she opened the door and let him in.

'That's her room,' she pointed towards one of the bedrooms just off the hallway. He thanked her and knocked gently on the bedroom door which swiftly flung open.

'Hey, come in,' she said, opening the door. As he walked in, he did the obligatory examination of the room. His eyes darted around from the photos of groups of girls, to the band posters on the wall. He noticed a Bullet For My Valentine poster hanging above her bed.

'I have to say, you don't look like a typical Bullet fan,' he laughed, looking at the dainty girl stood before him.

'What does a typical fan look like?' she protested.

'Good point. Sorry!' he laughed. 'Right, shall we crack on?' he said, taking his backpack off.

'Are you sure I can't get you a drink?'

'Go on then actually, just a glass of water is fine, thanks,' Jake said. While she was out the room, he took opportunity to look at his phone which had been buzzing with messages all evening. He didn't want to appear rude by getting his phone out when they were working on mind maps and bar charts.

He scrolled through the messages in the Facebook group chat, and he swallowed hard, suddenly feeling a lump forming in his dry throat. He looked through the messages and photos that Tom et al had sent with laughing face emojis.

Look out pal! Haha!

You've got competition here mate! :')

What? Jake opened a blurry, low quality video that accompanied the latter message. It showed Jessica dancing away, drink in hand. There was what looked like a fellow student, dancing behind her, faux grinding on her. *Was she aware? Did she know he was doing that behind her?* His questions were answered when the video showed her swivelling round and laughing, taking the boy's hand and continuing to dance with him. *Why was she encouraging him?* The video ended with Jessica falling into the boy's arms and laughing. He felt sick and all he wanted to do was head over to the club they were at, grab his girlfriend and take her home. As his mind debated what to do, the door opened, and he was handed a glass of water. 'Thanks,' he said, clearing his throat.

'Are you okay?'

'What? Yeah, I'm fine. Sorry. Just tired. Can we call it a night? I think we've got enough for the presentation, haven't we?'

'Oh, yeah, sure. Are you sure you're okay though?'

He felt a hand come to rest on his thigh and looked up, locking eyes with his study partner. She held his gaze for a few seconds, then eased towards him. He swallowed hard again, this time his throat felt like razor blades as his mind felt wuzzy.

It took him a good five seconds to realise that her lips had met his and he reacted by opening his mouth to kiss her back. As he thought of Jessica in the club, he adjusted his position, and the kissing became more passionate. He abruptly stopped, realising that if he cheated, he was no better than her. He mumbled apologies and got out of there.

Jessica arrived back at the flat with the rest of the hoard at about 1:30AM. She said goodnight to the other guys and crept into Jake's bedroom. The light was on, and he was sat up in bed on his phone, so she abruptly stopped tip-toeing and jumped onto the bed.

'Hello you,' she said, crawling towards him to kiss him. He turned his face, so her lips planted on his cheek instead. 'Is everything okay?' she said, pausing as he took a deep inhale and exhale.

'Mhm.'

'What's wrong?' she pushed, knowing something was up.

'Who was he?' he said without looking at her.

'Who was who?' she said, genuinely confused by his question.

'The guy on the video? The guy you were dancing with?'

'What guy? What video?' she said, furrowing her brow.

'Jess, don't,' he began.

'Don't what? I don't understand. What video?'

He thrust his phone in her hands and watched her as she watched the clip. He didn't say anything as she handed the phone back to him. 'That guy? I don't know, just some random student,' she said innocently. 'It was just dancing. Nothing happened. Honest! Ask the other guys. He just came up and starting dancing behind me, I was trying to dance out of his way, Tom thought it was hilarious and obviously started filming it. Then I thought it was easier to dance with him jokingly rather than get nasty.'

'It looked like you were egging him on,' he said, watching and waiting for her reaction.

'Egging him on? What are you on about? Sometimes it's just easier to dance and have fun than get mardy with a guy on a night out. You don't know how they'll react,' she protested. It wasn't the first time she'd been hit on by a guy on a night out and it certainly wouldn't be the last. Like many other girls, it was easier to be polite and have fun, rather than start a war with a stranger who you didn't know from Adam. 'Seriously Jake, I was with the others all night, ask them!' she said, feeling slightly hurt that he thought she'd ever cheat on him.

Realisation hit him that she was telling the truth and he heaved at the thought of what he'd done, knowing he had to tell her.

'Jess...I've done something really stupid...' he began, causing her to sit upright. 'I kissed someone else.'

'You...what?' she stuttered eventually.

'I'm so sorry. That girl from my course. I saw the messages from Tom and that video while I was over there. I thought you'd cheated on me, so when the opportunity came about, I took it, stupidly.'

'When the opportunity came about?' she repeated his words back to him as a question. 'What the hell does that mean? Did she make a move on you? What a bitch!'

'I mean, technically yes, but I didn't stop it. I kissed her back and well...'

Jessica felt like she was going to throw up. 'Well, what?' she said, her voice shaking.

'Well, that's it, I kissed her back,' he said, trying to take her hand in his. She pulled her hand away, sniffing back tears.

'How could you...?' she asked, getting up and grabbing her bag. 'I need to go,' she said as she fumbled with the door handle.

'Fancy a night cap?' Tom's voice came from the kitchen as he saw her in the hallway. Realising she was crying, his face changed, and he swiftly moved towards her, embracing her.

'What's wrong? What's happened?' he said as she sobbed into his shoulder.

'He fucking cheated!' she sobbed louder.

'He... what?' Tom pulled back and held her shoulders. He gently moved her to one side and rapped hard on Jake's bedroom door before bursting in without waiting for an invitation. 'Is that true?' he demanded. Jake simply nodded in response.

'What the fuck is wrong with you?' Tom yelled at his friend. Jake went on to explain how he thought Jessica had been unfaithful first, so he thought he'd do the same, before quickly changing his mind.

'It was just a kiss,' Jake began before Tom raised his hand to interrupt him.

'Don't you dare! What if she'd have kissed that guy tonight, just a kiss, would that have been, okay?' Tom argued.

'No, of course not,' he conceded.

'You're fucking unbelievable. Those messages were clearly a joke. Firstly, how could you even think she'd cheat on you. Secondly, how could you think we'd all send messages making light of it!' Tom yelled as he slammed the door, escorting Jessica back into the kitchen.

Deciding that she just wanted to go back to her own bed, Tom agreed to let her but insisted on walking her home. She lived near Bramall Lane and there was no way he was letting her walk through those underpasses on her own. Once he could see she was safely inside, he ambled back towards his own flat, still angry at his friend for hurting his other friend.

After a long lie in the next morning, Jessica rolled over and picked up her phone. She expected to have a message from Jake and there it was, waiting to be opened and read.

Jess, I don't know what to say except I'm so sorry and I love you so much. There are no excuses for what I did, but I completely misread a situation. I've spoken to the guys who have cleared everything up for me. Please can we talk? I love you. Xxxxx

Despite the hurt she felt from the betrayal, she knew Jake would be beating himself up about it. She loved him too and she didn't want things to end this way. She messaged him back to say she'd come over to his later that afternoon. The torrential rain outside seemed to match her mood perfectly. Throwing on her cagoule, she headed out, constantly reminding herself to buy a new umbrella to replace the one she broke the other week. By the time she arrived at Jake's flat, she was drenched and cold. Her cagoule put up a vague fight against the storm, but Mother Nature won, and she was shaking.

'Fuck, come in,' Jake said as he opened the door, seeing her shivering and her teeth chattering. He took her cagoule and hung it near the radiator to dry off. She followed him into his bedroom, where he opened a drawer and pulled out a T-shirt, hoody and jogging bottoms for her. 'Put those on, or you'll freeze.'

'Too late,' she said, peeling the clothes from her body.

'Come here,' he said, pulling her in for a hug and rubbing his hands over her limbs in an attempt to warm her up. He abruptly stopped, realising that physical contact was probably the last thing she wanted from him right now. 'Sorry,' he said, stepping back.

She got dressed in silence then stood, staring at him.

Was she waiting for him to say something? he thought as he opened his mouth to speak.

'I love you,' she said, getting in there first.

'I love you too, so much,' he replied quickly.

'It'll never happen again?' she asked, adjusting her stance.

'I swear. Once was too many,' he said, looking at her pale face. He mentally asked himself how he could be so stupid.

'Okay,' she said quietly.

'Okay?' he repeated back to her, to check. She nodded and shuffled forward, nestling into his chest. He enveloped her in his arms and sighed loudly. 'I love you so much, I'm so sorry,' he said, kissing her head.

TEN

A few months had passed, and Jessica found herself occasionally unblocking Daniel's Instagram page to see what he'd been up to and who with. Part of her was hurt by the constant feed of photos of Daniel and Riley, but another part of her felt satisfied with results from her stalking. The brain is a complex being. Amidst her stalking sessions, she always found her way back to Jake's feed too. He was rarely active on social media which frustrated her tirelessly; she was desperate to know what he was up to. That's how she always ended up on his tagged photos from his wife's account. She found out a few weeks ago via Jake's wife's page that he and his wife were expecting their second child together. Jessica's gut wrenched at this; whenever she thought of having a family, she had always pictured Jake as the father. Even when she was with Daniel, she couldn't remove that image from her mind. Your first love really does wreak havoc for the rest of your life.

One evening, Jessica was doing her usual online stalking when she suddenly realised all photos of Daniel and Riley had disappeared from his feed. Ha! They've broken up, she surmised. *That didn't last long,* she laughed to herself.

She found out later from mutual friends that he'd cheated on Riley with another underwear model. It became noticeably clear early on that Jessica's team were keeping a close eye on her and any potential reaction she would have to the heartache. Fortunately, she managed to cope in the normal way of crying, eating copious amounts of chocolate and ice cream and watching rom-coms.

It became evident that Daniel wanted fame so badly that he was posing on Instagram with expensive watches, tagging the company in so he'd get paid for advertising the brand. Half the PR stuff he was doing had nothing to do with swimming. It was vastly different from the Daniel that Jessica knew. A part of her questioned if that's why he was dating models, to try and raise his profile. Jessica had gone the opposite way and hidden herself away more. Not because of any significant issues, she quite simply couldn't be bothered having to get dolled up for events anymore. It was exhausting having to sit in hair and make up for three hours, only to stand on a red carpet for ninety seconds, and she never felt like herself at the end of it all.

About six months after their breakup, Jessica finally began to feel like she was healing from the experience. She had more up days than down days and she was even starting to casually date again on weekends. Most weekdays and evenings were spent holed up in the studio, using song writing as therapy. Everything just seemed easier with her new team; there was no pressure to release music by certain deadlines, no pressure to look a certain way or sound a certain way. Everyone seemed to simply love their job and focus on the enjoyment of that as opposed to the monetary value of things. Sure, it was always a bonus when the money came in, but Jessica finally felt like she was amongst friends and being supported to do what she loved. Her latest music felt more authentic to her; there was no more sexy, dance type music. Each lyric Jessica wrote had meaning, either obvious or subtle; everything was personal to her. Her team would celebrate successes and wins by ordering takeout pizza and desserts. Jessica would often note what a far cry this was from her previous team, who would actively try to limit her food intake to ensure she stayed toned and svelte. The main worry for this team was whether the food tasted nice or not.

As part of exposure for her new album, Jessica had agreed to go on a national radio station to promote it. She hated live interviews, but she knew her team only put her forward for things they knew she could handle. It was just a one on one interview with the radio presenter, so even she felt she could manage this. Despite being a radio show with no live audience per se, there were cameras in the studio so people could watch online. Sat in hair and make-up, Jessica kindly requested that her make-up artist, Fiona, add more dramatic contour to her naturally un-sculpted cheekbones in a bid to try and hide the McDonalds she had last night. A loud knock at the dressing room door caused Fiona to abruptly stop with her delicate application of mascara; ensuring she didn't make Jessica look like the guy from Clockwork Orange. As Fiona opened the door and gestured for the person to enter, a tall, clean shaven, dirty blonde haired man identified Jessica and pointed in her direction as he marched towards her with purpose, camera over his shoulder and phone in hand. Jessica shuffled in her seat, feeling a bit wary of this man who had suddenly come to dominate the room.

'Hello, I'm Ryan and you must be Jessica,' he said in a Northern sounding British accent, whilst flicking through sheets on a clipboard. Jessica made a murmur of approval as Fiona resumed with the mascara.

'Where are you from in the UK?' Jessica asked through a half closed mouth, trying not to move her face too much for Fiona's sake.

'Leeds. I'm here to take some exclusive backstage footage.'

'Leeds?! No way! I'm from Yorkshire too! Not far from York itself!'

'Okay. Please can you just act natural, and I'll film while you're getting *'glammed up'*?'

He used air quotes as he replied in an entirely uninterested tone. Jessica was beginning to feel a little bit put out by this guy. She wondered what would happen if she outright refused to participate, then realised it would probably cost her the job so smiled and nodded at him to go ahead. While Fiona applied blusher to her newly carved out cheekbones, Jessica picked nervously at her fingers.

'I said act natural, not twitchy.'

Jeez. What was his problem.

'Erm, sorry. It's just hard to act natural when there's a camera two inches from your face.'

'If you think that's two inches then your boyfriend must love you,' Ryan said bluntly, rolling his eyes obviously at her.

'Excuse me?' Jessica's eyes widened.

'Just chat with her,' he gestured rudely to Fiona, 'or look at your phone or something!'

Jessica could feel herself getting moodier and Ryan was seemingly irater too. Suddenly, a gruff Boston accent boomed through the door.

'Ryan! Have you got it yet?'

'Fuck off,' Ryan muttered in response, heading towards the door, and opening it, causing Fiona to raise her eyebrows at Jessica in astonishment. Jessica shook her head disbelievingly.

'Well? Have you got the footage?' the Boston man scathed.

'Not quite. I'm just working on a few angles.'

'Fuck angles, we need this on socials now! She's going to be live soon and I told you we need this on before that! Just get it done for fuck sake!'

A sheepish and blushed looking Ryan appeared again, nodding at Jessica and gesturing for her to carry on pretending to be on her phone or mid conversation with Fiona. Jessica swiftly started to feel a bit sorry for Ryan; she assumed the Boston man was his boss.

Thinking back to her earlier manager, Michael, she had a lot of sympathy for Ryan and decided to make the job easier for him. Fiona muttered something under her breath which caused Jessica to break into a natural snigger and laugh. Ryan flicked the camera up and managed to get a shot of her mid-laugh. He looked at her, then the camera and then back at her, meeting her eyes.

'Oh God, is it really bad? If it's really ugly, please delete it!' she panicked.

'No, no. It's...' he paused as he continued to examine her with his piercing blue eyes. 'It's fine.'

Fine. Jessica thought about how she'd been called worse and with the attitude he'd started with, she took it as a compliment.

'Thanks. Have you got everything you need for your boss?'

'Umm, yeah, I think so. Thanks. Sorry about him, he's a bit of a despot.'

Jessica smiled kindly in response to his sincerity.

'A despot is a...'

Jessica sat back, looking baffled and raised her hand to shut him up.

'I know what a despot is, thank you! Give me some credit!' she said.

'Sorry, you just never know with celebs,' he said as he headed out the door, leaving Jessica and Fiona laughing in disbelief.

The half hour interview flew by and after Jessica had performed her new single, she hung back in the studio until a commercial break to thank the presenter. Fortunately, there were no nasty surprises with the interview and any questions remained light hearted and standard. There was pretty much a bunch of set questions that were asked when any singer had a new single or album being released. This meant you could rehearse the answers and just reel them off. There was often the odd curveball thrown in, but on the whole, nothing too controversial. As she walked back towards the dressing room to get sorted, a familiar British voice called after Jessica, causing her to turn in her tracks.

'Hey, umm...I just wanted to apologise for my behaviour earlier.'

'That's okay. Like you say, your boss seemed a bit of a tyrant!'

'Hey, shh!' Ryan awkwardly chuckled, looking around to make sure no-one heard.

'Oops, sorry! But anyway, it's fine.'

'Sorry, a tyrant is...' Jessica began, sarcastically.

'Ha-ha. I have to say, you're not really what I expected.' Ryan looked at his feet and shuffled them around on the spot.

'And what did you expect?'

'A blonde airhead.' Ryan said so bluntly that it made Jessica laugh out loud.

'Gee thanks!' she managed.

'Let's just say, you get used to a certain type of person in this industry...'

Thinking about some of the crap that was on TV these days, Jessica was inclined to agree. Anything passed for reality these days and she could certainly see why he would have presumptions.

'I actually studied Economics at Manchester University.'

'And you ended up filming social media content for a radio show?'

'Ouch!' Ryan grabbed his chest in a dramatic fashion, smiling.

'I moved out here with my ex three years ago and I needed work. I really want to do photography, but this pays the bills, unlike that,' he explained.

Jessica realised that they were still stood in the corridor and their increasingly personal conversation was open for anyone. She turned and began walking back towards her dressing room, signalling for him to follow as they continued their conversation.

'What kind of photography do you do?' Jessica asked, genuinely interested.

'Nature stuff really but I'll try my hand at anything. I got some really cool ones the other week actually,' he reached into his pocket for his phone.

As he scrolled through his phone, trying to find the photos, he abruptly stopped and looked at Jessica again with those blue eyes.

'Sorry, assuming you want to see them of course,' he awkwardly laughed.

'Sure!' Jessica said enthusiastically.

He proceeded to swipe through various close up shots of several types of birds that were mid-flight, some even mid-feed to their young. Jessica looked in awe, noting his talent.

'Wow. How they are not making you money is beyond me...' Jessica meant this seriously.

'Thanks, you're kind. Maybe it's just meant to be a hobby!' he smiled.

The Boston accent broke the sound barrier for the second time. 'Ryan!' Ryan rolled his eyes and fake smiled at Jessica.

'I'd better go...'

'Of course. Thanks again,' she replied as he headed for the door.

A few nights later, Jessica was scrolling through Instagram and her direct messages. Most were either young girls telling her how much they loved her or weird men sending questionable photos. With that being said, there was also a number of men telling her how much they loved her and weird women sending questionable photos. Social media was a wonderful thing, but it had its flaws too. Some of the things that Jessica came across were quite frankly haunting. She spotted one message from a familiar name as she scrolled down the list.

Hey, not sure if you'll even see this...just wanted to say it was great meeting you today. Sorry again for misjudging you. I feel awful! Ryan.

Jessica sat with it for a few minutes, debating what to write back. She decided to keep it polite and simple.

Nice to meet you too. No need to apologise! :) Jess.

She wasn't expecting a reply back but waited to see the message show as read. She then clicked the profile to do a bit of social stalking. There were various artsy photos of animals, buildings and even food. Scattered amongst them were occasional photos of Ryan, either posing with a camera or posing sarcastically in a dramatic way. Jessica liked one of him pretending to pose like a model, pouting at the camera with a cheeky look in his eyes. Double clicking the photo, she thought how times have changed; this was considered flirting in this modern age. As a TV ending theme tune broke her train of thought, she switched it off and headed for bed. She reopened Instagram and noticed a notification of one of her photos being liked by Ryan. He'd scrolled right back and liked one of Jessica stood covered head to toe in mud after a walk in the Peak District back in her university days. Her hair was wet and knotty, and she'd got a massive cheesy grin spread across her face. Living in Sheffield at the time, the Peak District was so nearby, that she'd often spend Saturdays there, walking with friends. She opened her messages and started typing.

Can't work out if you're a fan of the natural look or if you just like the Peak District. ;)

Well, being a Northern lad, I most definitely appreciate the beauty of the Peak District.

Still can't believe the chances of running into a Yorkshireman in LA!

Right back at you! The Yorkshire part, not the man part…

Speaking of man parts, I think you're the only guy in my DM's that hasn't sent me a photo of your bits!

Is that you asking…?

NO!!! haha!

Just kidding! Not my style, I must say.

Thank God for that.

The brief conversation came to a natural end and Jessica realised she'd got a smile on her face as she rested her head on her pillow.

ELEVEN

Two weeks had gone by with Jessica and Ryan chatting daily, moving their conversation from Instagram to WhatsApp after exchanging numbers. He'd asked if Jessica wanted to meet for a coffee at the weekend and with a rare weekend free, she'd agreed. As she was getting ready, she had butterflies in her stomach, a feeling she hadn't felt for a long time. She assessed her appearance in the mirror and decided to accept what she saw. She'd tied her long blonde hair up in a high ponytail and chose to keep her make up looking natural with no heavy eyes or lips. With it being a relatively casual place, Jessica opted for skinny jeans and a nice top, the standard dress code for girls who had no idea whether the event was formal or informal. She spent enough time getting dolled up with three layers of make-up and squeezing into tight dresses during the week, so weekends were the time to let both her skin and body breathe. She got an Uber to drop her off near the restaurant on Beverly Boulevard and made her way on foot down the street. She clocked a few photographers hanging outside another restaurant nearby but kept her head down. In the grand scheme of things, Jessica was considered a minor celebrity, yet there were always paparazzi trying to snap a photo of her, good or bad, to sell on. She had significant sympathy for celebrities such as Beyonce and Adele; how they coped with this but ten times worse was beyond Jessica's imagination. She felt relatively grateful of the comparatively modest interest she fetched. As she skirted round some lost looking tourists, one of the regular photographers shouted to his fellow paparazzo's.

'Jessica! How are you today?'

This was then followed by more shouts and clicking of cameras.

'Are you doing better?' 'Are you moving on from Daniel?' 'Love the new song, Jessica! Can we get a smile?'

Jessica tucked her chin, kept her eyes down and powered through the crowd, into the restaurant. She scoured the room and her eyes landed on Ryan. He was thankfully also dressed casually, in jeans and a black tee, which revealed a tattoo on his right upper arm. Jessica watched him seemingly nervously dart his eyes round the room, tapping his fingers on the table. His eyes locked onto hers and his face melted into a smile. She smiled back, making her way round other tables to reach him.

'Hey, sorry I'm a bit late,' she offered as she took her jacket off and sat down.

'No worries at all. I got here a bit early anyway,' he smiled, ostensibly settling down from the nerves.

'Can I get you a drink?' he gestured to the wine list.

'Just the house red please,' she smiled. Ryan gestured to a waiter to come over and placed the order, Jessica noticing his polite manner to the service staff. She'd been on a few dates in the past where her date had been outright rude and condescending to the staff – a major red flag in her eyes. When the waiter brought a glass of wine back for Jessica, they placed their food orders and decided this was the time to start their conversation before they both had mouthfuls of pasta. Jessica asked him how work was going with his boss and Ryan explained once again that it simply paid the bills, and it did mean he got to meet a range of people. He pointed out that many of the celebrities he met were rude to him, hence why he had pre-judged Jessica. She did think about the first time she met him and if he was as rude to others as he was to her from the offset, she could see why they'd respond in the same manner.

'Some just treat you like shit, honestly. I often wonder whether they'd have the same attitude if they were in my job, or if they suddenly wake up one day after some success and turn into wankers!'

Jessica laughed and agreed that it must come with the success, thinking you're better than everyone else. She agreed that it was probably also because they were surrounded by a team of people who were constantly bigging them up and inflating their ego even more.

'Is that your experience of the industry? I'm fascinated.'

'Ermm…Not quite…' Jessica hesitated, debating how much to share.

'Do tell.'

At this point, the waiter arrived with two plates. Great timing, Jessica thought. After a few mouthfuls and agreeing that the food was delicious, Ryan gestured to Jessica to continue her story.

'Sorry, you were saying about your experience of the industry.'

'Yeah…erm, just that my previous management weren't the most supportive; they were very selfish and were only concerned about making money for themselves.'

'That's shit. Is that why you ended up in rehab?'

Jessica coughed, half choking on a mouthful of pasta in response to Ryan's bluntness. Obviously, it was public knowledge to anyone who simply Googled her name, but even then, it took her by surprise.

'Yeah, kind of,' she nodded. Ryan paused and put his cutlery down, examining Jessica's face.

'Sorry, that sounded a bit abrupt, didn't it?' Jessica awkwardly laughed.

'A little, perhaps!'

'Sorry, I read it online when I was Google stalking you when we were first messaging…guilty as charged!'

'It's fine. Just a bit heavy for a first date!' Jessica smiled.

'Sorry,' Ryan offered sincerely.

'It's fine, really,' Jessica smiled, equally as sincerely.

They finished their meal and declined dessert due to the amount of pasta they'd both just filled their stomachs with. She started to regret wearing skinny jeans and she felt the zipper and button starting to bulge under pressure. She thought about how hard she was going to have to work at the gym tomorrow to burn off all the carbs and parmesan she'd consumed.

'I've got this,' Ryan took the bill.

'Are you sure? I really don't mind going halves!' Jessica suggested, reaching for her bag.

'Nope, really. It's my pleasure,' Ryan insisted, giving the waiter his credit card. The waiter gave Jessica that look as if to say *'ooh, you've got a good one here.'* Jessica thanked Ryan for paying, reiterating again that he really didn't need to. They exited the restaurant and were met by the same paparazzo, shouting.

'Jessica! Who's the new man?' 'Are you moving on from Daniel?' 'Jessica! Jessica! Jessica!'

'Sir! Are you Jessica's new boyfriend?'

Ryan looked slightly bemused and as if he was about to open his mouth to say something, so Jessica grabbed his arm and dragged him away quickly. She managed to drag him into a small boutique store to get away from those that were chasing with their cameras. The woman behind the counter of the store looked equally bemused as she eyed the pair of them over her trendy red glasses.

'Can I help you?' she asked, her eyes flicking between them and the flashing cameras from outside.

'Oh, just browsing, thanks!' Jessica said cheerfully.

'Ugh! I'm so sorry about that!' Jessica whispered to Ryan as she pretended to admire some small handbags that were on display.

'Comes with the territory I guess,' Ryan said matter of fact, seemingly unbothered by the repetitive flashes from the cameras.

'So, why'd you drag me into this delightful little shop?' he asked.

'Just to get away from those poachers,' she whispered again, not wanting to offend the store owner.

'Right, but we have to go back out there at some point you know...why not decide and let's just get it over with. Any shops with shoes and handbags give me hives if I stay in them too long,' Ryan joked.

Jessica smiled and nodded, planning to catch an Uber to his apartment as it was nearer than her place. When the car arrived nearby, they nodded and made a run for it, only stopping to thank the store owner before sprinting from her store. They skirted round those gathered outside the store and into the back of the Honda. They'd lost the paparazzi as the car drove off; they'd probably found another celebrity to harass; someone more famous. Ryan put his arm round Jessica in the back of the car.

'I should probably tell you that I do live with a few other people...You know what rent is like in these parts,' he confessed, looking a bit sheepish.

'But don't worry, they'll probably be out anyway. Just wanted to warn you it's a similar get up to university halls...'

'Jesus,' Jessica muttered under her breath, making Ryan laugh and squeeze her shoulder.

Despite her reservations after Ryan's confession, Jessica was pleasantly surprised when they pulled up to the apartment block. It was relatively modern looking and seemed perfectly nice from the outside. On inspection, the inside turned out to be equally as nice - pieces of modern artwork hung in the communal halls and on the face of it, the building was exceptionally clean and well kept, unlike any University halls that Jessica had been in. Unlocking the door, Jessica heard voices in the apartment and Ryan seemingly cringed, turning to Jessica, and whispering an apology. He ambled his way into the open plan kitchen-diner, with Jessica closely following behind, starting to feel anxious about who would be there to greet her.

'Hey Ry, who's your friend?' a skinny girl with bright pink hair asked, causing two other men and another girl to turn round from the sofas. Ryan shuffled on his feet and mumbled something about a work colleague. Jessica had to admit she felt a little sting at being referred to as a work colleague.

'I don't know about you guys, but I don't often bring my work colleagues home,' the second girl said with a smirk, flicking her chocolate brown hair over her shoulder.

'What do they call you then?' one of the men piped up, taking out his earphones.

'Jessica,' she meekly replied.

'I'm Paul and when this one ditches you,' he pointed at Ryan, 'I'll look after you,' he said with a wink that made Jessica's skin crawl slightly.

'Yeah, yeah. Right, we've got Daisy, Laura, Paul, and Dominic,' Ryan said as he pointed them out individually.

'Nice to meet you all,' Jessica smiled as the man she now knew to be Dominic stood up and sidled past her, acknowledging her with a brief smile and nod.

'What do you do then Jessica?' Paul asked.

'Oh erm, I'm a singer,' Jessica said, suddenly feeling quite embarrassed. The pink haired girl, Daisy, gasped and clapped her hands together, bursting into laughter. She was swiftly followed by the other girl, Laura.

'Hey, shut up,' Ryan said.

'Ryan, you…with a famous singer…stop! I think that's your best one yet!' Daisy was still laughing.

'Shut up,' Ryan repeated and steered Jessica away from the kitchen, towards his room, leaving her feeling confused about what just happened. He shut the door and stood in front of it, facing Jessica.

'Sorry about that…' he sighed, ruffling his hair.

'What did they mean about being the best one yet?'

'Oh, ignore that. Daisy thinks she's being funny. Just because I spend half my day moaning about celebs and singers who I work with. They'll just think it's ironic that I'm actually enjoying the company of one!' he smiled, edging towards her, and gently touching her arm.

Jessica relaxed and fell into a smile. She was looking round his room and admiring the old CD's he'd kept, the posters and photos stuck on the walls. His room did remind her of a student flat, it must be said. Ryan plonked himself down on the small green sofa and gently tugged her arm to join him. He put his hand on her knee, gently making patterns with his thumb. They sat in silence briefly and just as Jessica was about to ask him something, he looked up to meet her eyes and then gently leant forward, meeting her lips with his. He leant backwards and ran his hand down her long ponytail, bring his hand back round to lift her chin.

'You're beautiful,' he whispered, and Jessica felt the butterflies in her stomach fluttering around at high speed as if they'd had a shot of caffeine. He kissed her harder this time, pulling her closer to him as he moved his hands over her body. She felt like a giddy teenager, making out with a boyfriend in the confines of his bedroom, trying to remain quiet. His hand caressed her body, and he moved down to lift her shirt up. He lifted her shirt over her head, then followed suit, pulling his black tee over his head so she could now see the large Māori style tattoo spreading from his upper bicep and over his shoulder. He gently but purposefully pushed her down onto the sofa and climbed atop her. Reminding her humorously of a horny teenager, he scrambled around in his bedside drawer for a condom, briefly pausing kissing her to put it on.

TWELVE

'Well, that was a nice surprise,' Ryan said as they lay on the sofa in the most unnatural of angles.

Jessica didn't find the experience quite as satisfying as she felt ridiculously full of pasta still; feeling very self-conscious about the little pot belly she'd gained since eating. She was also very aware that there was a room full of people just metres away.

'So do you have plans for the rest of the day?' Ryan asked and Jessica replied with something non-committal to leave her with some options, depending on what he suggested.

'Feel free to take a quick shower if you want. You can use my towel. It is a shared bathroom though I'm afraid – just down the hall on the left.'

'Oh, could I? Thanks, I'll be 5 mins!' Jessica said, grabbing the slightly damp towel from the chair and wrapping it round her.

The bonus of Ryan living with girls was that there was a broad selection of women's toiletries to choose from, rather than the standard 'wash and go' all-in-one that most men used. She rinsed the coconut scented suds from her body and combed her hair through, before shoving it into a towel dried, messy bun. Grabbing the slightly damp towel, she wrapped it round her body, instantly regretting not bringing her clothes into the bathroom with her. Post-sex she felt relatively confident and carefree marching down the hall just wrapped in a towel. Now she'd washed the sex off her, she felt a little more cautious. She peeked out the bathroom door to check the coast was clear and sprinted for Ryan's room. Fortunately, it seemed that the others had taken to their rooms, so she knew there was less risk of her bumping into anyone. She grabbed the handle to Ryan's room, but it wouldn't budge. Lightly knocking on the door, she whispered, 'Ryan!' to get his attention, but not that of the others.

Silence.

She heard a door close behind her and pressed herself into the wall round the corner so she wouldn't be seen. She heard the shower start up again and realised she was truly trapped now. She tapped a little louder on the door and hissed, 'Ryan! Let me in!' Still no answer.

'Fuck,' she muttered, starting to feel panicky.

'Are you okay?' a man's voice said from nowhere, making Jessica jump.

'Erm, hi, do you know where Ryan is?' Jessica asked the man she recognised to be Dominic.

Dominic paused and then sighed heavily, rolling his eyes.

'Yeah…he'll have scarpered,' he said.

'Pardon?' Jessica replied, confused.

'This is kind of his thing I'm afraid. He'll charm a girl just enough to bring her over here, sleep with her, then pisses off,' Dominic said very matter of fact.

Jessica stared at him, stunned.

'Is this a joke…?' she half laughed. 'I just need to get in his room…My clothes are in there…'

Dominic puffed his cheeks in an exhale.

'Jesus, that's a new one. Right, okay. Let me think. He won't be back anytime soon until he knows the coast is clear. Let me see if the girls have anything you can borrow.'

'No!' Jessica hissed and waved her hands to stop him in his tracks.

'Please, this is confusing and mortifying enough! I don't need more people involved!'

'I hate to tell you, but unless you're going to step outside in that towel, I don't think you have many other options.'

'I'll think of something. Please…' Jessica begged.

Dominic held his hands up in defeat and seemed to pause to think for a second. Jessica interrupted his thoughts.

'Just how many girls has she brought back here?' she asked.

'Honestly? You probably don't want to know,' he pulled a face.

She openly gagged at the thought and thanked God in her head that he was most definitely wearing protection.

'Okay,' he sighed again, 'you can borrow a top of mine and some shorts or something. You can change in here, come on,' he beckoned to his room.

Jessica eyed him as if to say, *'nice try pal.'*

'I won't be in the room at the same time, obviously,' he clarified, rolling his eyes at her.

'Urgh, fine!' Jessica snapped.

'Thank you!'

'Bottom drawer on the right,' he muttered as he held the door open for her.

There was a stark contrast between Ryan and Dominic's bedrooms. Whereas Ryan's felt like a student flat, this was definitely a young professional's flat. It was very basic, and everything had a place. Rifling through the drawer, she found a baggy white T-shirt and a pair of Nike shorts, equally as baggy. She turned to check that the door was firmly shut, then dropped the towel and slipped into the clothes. They looked clean but they had a pleasant smell of aftershave embedded in them. Before opening the door, she paused to think about what had just happened. She looked in the mirror at her sorry state and felt embarrassed and ashamed. It wasn't as if she felt used for sex, she just felt embarrassed that she'd not noticed it and how suave he was, getting away with it. She was awoken from her anger by a faint tap on the door.

'Hey, you've been a while. Are you okay?' Dominic said in hushed tones from the other side of the door.

Jessica wiped tears that had fallen without her realising and cleared her throat.

'Yeah, sorry, come in.' Dominic lingered in the doorway, watching her roughly wipe her eyes with her hands.

'You okay?' he repeated, awkwardly hovering near the door.

'Mhm! Just trying to fathom what's just happened, that's all. Thank you for this,' she tugged at the clothes.

'You're welcome. I knew he was a prick, but this,' he gestured at the clothes, 'is certainly a new one!'

'I'm so embarrassed!' Jessica sobbed.

'What was your name again?' Dominic asked.

'Jessica,' she sobbed.

'Listen, he's really not worth your tears or energy. I promise you. He's a grade A asshole and always will be.'

'I'm surprised you're so critical of your friend.'

'Friend? Christ, no way. He's just a roommate until I move. I'm waiting for my house to be completed and I had to move in somewhere while I waited. The rent was very favourable and with it being temporary, I wasn't overly bothered.'

'Oh okay, I thought it was a bit weird. You seem quite different from the others.'

'Yeah, let's just say they aren't my type of people, but as I say, it's a means to an end so...' he tailed off.

'Can I call you a cab or anything?'

'It's fine, thanks. Now I'm clothed, I feel a little happier venturing outside,' she laughed, wiping her eyes.

'Okay, well here's my number just in case it doesn't turn up or if you get in any trouble or anything. I can run down,' he handed her a business card.

'Thank you,' she sniffed. Fortunately, she was able to hail a cab a little further down the street which took her back to her place.

She suddenly realised she'd left her bag and phone in Ryan's room, meaning she had to politely ask/beg the driver to wait so she could run in and get some money. She managed to track down enough cash to pay the driver, as he sat huffing and puffing while waiting for her to reappear. Once settled and in her own clothes again, she opened the fridge and poured herself a generous sized glass of white wine. It's a good job she didn't have her phone as she would've sent Ryan some unwarranted, and slightly called for abusive messages. Instead, gulping down the wine, she reached for her laptop and Dominic's business card. The card told her that he was a personal injury lawyer based in Beverly Hills. She tapped out a new email.

Hi Dominic,
Just back at mine now. Sorry to catch you on your work email, but I've just realised I left my bag and phone in Ryan's room. Thank God my place is all pin codes rather than keys! Can I be really cheeky and ask you to get them for me...? It also means I can return your clothes.
Thanks, Jessica.

She hit send and topped up her wine, held the cool glass to her forehead and closed her eyes. She sat thinking about what the last few hours. She'd laugh about it one day, for sure, but today was not that day. She was more worried about her phone, which was pathetic but true. A ping from her laptop brought her back in the room.

Glad you got home safe. Sure. Meet at my office tomorrow? I'm there all day. It's on California Boulevard.
Dom.
That would be great, thank you so much! I can't do the morning but would 2pm be okay? Thanks, Jessica.

Sure. See you then.

THIRTEEN

Jessica had fired off another brief email to her team, explaining she'd left her phone at a friend's so would be out of contact until tomorrow afternoon. She confirmed that she would be attending the photoshoot in the morning and that she'd see them all there without fail, explaining that if any vital details were to be shared, to please email her. The high-pitched ringing of the traditional alarm clock caused Jessica to flinch when it announced the time at 5am. Usually using her phone as an alarm, she found the old school analogue clock in a cupboard. The sound of the bells on the top being rung by the little instrument was piercing as she scrambled to try to make it stop. She had to make it across town for a photoshoot with 'Life' magazine; they were making her the cover star for the month featuring an 'in-depth' interview. It was all part of her so-called comeback. She jumped in the shower and washed her hair, leaving it wet so they could style it for her. Likewise, she would be having her make-up done for her too so that saved time. She forced some dry toast down, as this was all she could stomach, still cringing at the thought of last night. Realising she couldn't book an Uber on her phone, she had to wander down the street with her wet hair, to hail a cab, then she'd have to collar one of her team to foot the bill. Needless to say, on arrival, the driver was a lot nicer than the one from last night. She swore she'd be two minutes and ran into the offices to track down her publicist, explained the situation and managed to scrounge what she needed to pay the driver. Her publicist was appalled and shed concerns about whether Ryan would try to sell a story about it. Jessica hadn't even thought about that, but for some reason she felt he wouldn't. She had no idea why she held this faith in him as his behaviour was nothing to go by, but she just felt that he was literally in it for the sex and that was it. He was just an expert player.

The morning raced by, and it was soon becoming one of Jessica's favourite shoots that she'd done. Having to pose for photos was one of her least favourite things; it just felt awkward, forced, and unnatural. However, the photographer was so lovely, and the staff were all incredibly friendly, so this put her at ease. Fortunately, there was no 'sexy' style shots which she loathed posing for. The food was fantastic too. Jessica thought about how her earlier team would've kept her away from the buffet table and given her a pre-made, portioned out protein salad. Nowadays she had to fight off her team to get to the table first, like something from The Hunger Games, quite literally. She wolfed down a warm BLT and a flaky pastry then it was time for the interview. She was introduced to the magazine's senior editor called Jane, a middle aged woman with dark grey hair and thick black rimmed glasses. She'd perfected that look of aging gracefully but still being still trendy and cool. She greeted Jessica with a formal handshake and then a friendly hug, assuring her that she'd see everything in full before going to print so she could make any amends she wished. Jane asked about Jessica's family and how she ended up in Los Angeles. Jessica explained, carefully omitting certain details about certain people, that she'd been at university when offered the chance of a lifetime. She spoke about how she desperately missed her dad and her brothers. Jane asked about relationships and Jessica had flashbacks to last night, having to change into a stranger's comfy clothes to get home. Of course, she omitted this part and simply said something relatively profound about how when you find love, don't let it go. In other words, thinking about what she could have had with Jake.

Jessica had definitely become more infrequent with her social media stalking of Jake, but he was still always a thought in the back of her mind, occasionally even at the forefront of her mind. With Jake not really posting much on social media, it was more his tagged photos that she was interested in. His wife consistently posted photos of happy, family life and the exciting adventures they were embarking on. There were times when Jessica would give anything to be her. Last time she'd checked, they were announcing news of their second baby, due in the Summer. When she saw this, Jessica nearly threw up; she felt a pain in her stomach of loss and definitive conclusion. She only wished that she could find some absolute closure on the whole ordeal, but that seemed a million miles away. She wasn't even sure why she kept looking at the photos; it was like picking at a scab, so it never healed. Yet, for some reason she liked seeing recent photos of him. He was considered extremely attractive when they were younger, with other girls lusting after him and trying to tempt him away from Jessica. Now, he'd grown into a handsome man, sure he didn't have a six pack and bulging biceps, but he was still toned, just in a more padded way...

Little did she know, despite Jake not actively posting on social media, he too constantly found himself on Jessica's pages. He would scroll through the images of her latest posts that were promoting new tracks or interviews. He had to fight hard not to comment or message her directly. When he heard that she'd entered treatment, he locked himself in the bathroom and cried. He was not a particularly emotional man in that sense usually, but he was gutted for her. All he wanted to do was hold her and tell her everything would be okay. He knew Tom had messaged her and received replies when she was out, so he got vague updates from him, but it took all his strength not to message her directly. Plus, he was married, and she was with some US swimmer at that point anyway, so he felt it wouldn't be right to be sending heartfelt messages to his ex-girlfriend. He'd seen online that Jessica and her Olympic beau had parted ways as there was already photos of her going on what seemed like dates with other men. He was secretly pleased when he found she was no longer with Daniel; Jake didn't know the guy, but he felt just by looking at his Instagram, that he wasn't the man for Jess.

Dominic's office was pretty easy for Jessica to track down; it had enormous silver signage that shone blindingly bright in the afternoon sun, reading 'Paxton and co.' It was quite different from the family run solicitors in Jessica's hometown, 'Smith and Sons.' Jessica recalled it had a horrid lime green shop front with a rotting wooden sign hanging above the door, which looked ready to fall and take out any customers. Still wearing the flawless make-up from the photoshoot, Jessica certainly looked the part as she strutted into the building towards the arc shaped reception desk. If the make-up from photoshoots was extravagant, she would remove it before leaving, but this was a nice natural look that looked like her skin, but better. She certainly wasn't going to waste it! She waited for the receptionist to finish her call and was met with a bright, luminous white smile. Why did everyone in LA have these ridiculously white veneers? Jessica thought to herself.

'Hi, I'm here to see Dominic...' Jessica suddenly realised she didn't know his surname so tailed off.

'Do you have an appointment?' The receptionist looked Jessica up and down.

'Umm...kind of.'

'Right... he doesn't take walks ins, so you either have an appointment or you don't.'

'Okay, I have an appointment.'

'What's your reference number?'

'Eh? I don't have one. Look, please can you just call him and tell him I'm here to collect my things? He is expecting me.'

The receptionist eyed Jessica, trying to figure out what to do next.

'I'm afraid if you don't have an appointment...' she started before Jessica interrupted her.

'Look, I'm really sorry but he asked me to stop by, look I've got the emails to prove it!'

Jessica reached in her pocket for her phone, then groaned as she remembered why she was there.

'Okay, so I can't actually show you because he's got my phone. That's why I'm here.'

She looked at Jessica with a look of pity and contempt, then picked up the phone, rolling her eyes and tutting at Jessica.

'Mr Paxton, hello, I'm sorry to bother you but there's a woman in Reception who doesn't have an appointment but is asking to see you. She has no reference number either,' she added with a sickly smile to Jessica.

'He's coming down and he didn't sound happy...' she said with another sickly-sweet smile.

'If you'd like to take a seat,' she pointed towards the corporate looking grey sofas. For a front of house member of staff, Jessica couldn't quite believe how rude she was and sat scowling at her as she waited for Dominic to materialise.

A few minutes later, Dominic appeared, walking towards the reception desk. Jessica was taken aback by how different he looked to the other day when she first met him. The receptionist muttered something to him and made a motion towards Jessica, to which his eyes followed. She couldn't be certain, but Jessica swore that his mouth fell slightly open before his jaw re-clenched as he made his way over.

'Ah, you should've said it was you, I'd have had you sent straight up to my office,' Dominic said with his hands shoved in his trouser pockets.

'I tried, but she wasn't having any of it!' Jessica muttered, nodding towards the receptionist who was tapping away at the computer.

'Ah, okay. Yeah, Kelsie is great at admin and all the rest of it, but she can be a bit of a gatekeeper. Usually, that's a good thing! Sorry. Come on, I've got your stuff in my office.'

As Dominic led the way, Jessica felt like sticking her tongue out to Kelsie as if to say *'told you so!'* but refrained from being so petty. The building was only a few stories, so they took the stairs, much to Jessica's dismay in her Louis Vuitton heels and figure hugging bodycon dress. She considered herself fit, but stairs were always a sure fire way to make her pant! She followed Dominic past an open plan office with lots of both men and women in suits, on the phone or typing away at speed on computers. Some looked up briefly from their work, spotting her but then quickly returned to whatever they were doing. She followed Dominic to a large glass walled office, with stunning views of the city.

'Wow...' it took Jessica's breath away again as she tried to gasp in air after the stair climb.

'Can I get you a coffee?' Dominic offered as he unbuttoned his suit jacket to sit down behind the desk.

'I'm fine thank you.'

He pulled out an Armani gift bag from behind his desk and handed it to Jessica.

'I believe everything's in there,' he handed her the bag for her inspection, 'all laundered too.' She peeked inside to see her clothes neatly folded and her phone on top. She prodded it but it was out of battery, then she felt herself blush at the sight of her neatly folded, freshly washed thong. She snapped the bag shut and looked at Dominic who was looking at something on his desk.

'Thanks!' she said, eager to leave to spare any further embarrassment. Dominic picked up a pen from his desk and fidget clicked it.

'Sorry again about Ryan. He really does make my skin crawl. He treats women like absolute shit.'

'Meh, I'm partly to blame; I chose to sleep with him,' she half laughed. Dominic adjusted his position on the chair and clenched his jaw again. Jessica still couldn't believe just how different he looked compared to their first meeting. When she first saw him at the apartment, he had a navy-blue tee on and some jogging bottoms, with slightly ruffled hair. He was most definitely handsome but now, sat in front of her, he was wearing a tailored slim fit suit with a light blue shirt with a dark grey tie.

His mahogany brown hair was styled into an ivy league style cut, neat but still a bit textured. She noticed his jaw was still clenched as he clicked the pen, gazing at her.

'Yeah, he has that effect on women. They always blame themselves...'

'Look, he's a prick but we were both consenting adults, so it is what it is. He's just a "fuckboy," as they say!' she air-quoted.

'I guess...as long as you're okay,' he said, still staring at her.

'Oh fuck!' she clapped her hands to her mouth, causing Dominic to start, his eyes widening at her profane outburst.

'Sorry, potty mouth. I was meant to bring your clothes back and I completely forgot!' she confessed.

'Ah I see, no bother. Just drop them in anytime, whenever you're passing. No rush.'

'Sorry,' she said again and Dominic shook his head, saying there was no need to apologise.

'I'll leave you to it then, but thank you again for doing this. I really appreciate it! Sorry to have got you involved in my drama!'

'I suppose a socialite needs her phone!' he joked as he stood up, re-fastening his jacket buttons.

This took Jessica aback slightly.

'I wouldn't describe myself as a socialite...' she said, with a tone to her voice.

'Sorry, a singer was it?'

'Erm, yeah...thanks again.'

As she was walking away, Jessica clocked the sign again and realised 'Paxton' was 'Dominic Paxton'.

Wow, he was certainly doing well for himself, she thought, wondering why on earth he was sharing an apartment in the city with someone like Ryan. She remembered him saying the rent was cheap while waiting for his house renovations to be completed. Surely he could afford something better than that, the money he must be raking in.

FOURTEEN

Once all the new album promo had been done, Jessica's schedule was pretty freed up for some time off. There had been discussions about a tour, but Jessica and her team made the decision not to go ahead with that for this record. She was still technically in recovery and both her and her team didn't want to jeopardise her health. Again, Jessica thought back to her previous team who would've dolled her up, thrown her on stage and expected a performance of a lifetime every night, regardless of the consequences, like some kind of performing chimp. She decided to use this time off to catch up with friends and she briefly considered flying home to see her family, then decided against it. She still felt somewhat embarrassed that she'd ended up in rehab; no doubt this would've been the hot topic of the village. She just couldn't face her dad or brothers in person at the moment; speaking to them on the phone was hard enough. She'd not heard anything from Ryan since that night, which was no surprise as she'd blocked him on all accounts. Her publicist had informed her that there didn't seem to be any potential stories doing the rounds in the press, something which didn't surprise Jessica, but she still felt relieved about. Ryan had no doubt moved on and was probably onto his fifth hookup of the month by now anyway. She'd emailed Dominic a few weeks ago to ask when was convenient to drop his clothes round, but she'd not heard back so decided to locate his business card and call him directly. After just one ring, the memorable, assertive voice flowed down the phone.

'Dominic Paxton, hi there.'

'Hi, it's Jessica. I dropped you an email but didn't hear back so thought I'd give you a quick call to check when I can drop your clothes off? Don't worry, I've washed my shame off them!' she cackled.

There was a brief pause and a click, and Dominic cleared his throat.

'Can I call you back? I'm just in a meeting at the moment. Give me an hour or so.'

'Oh, sure, sorry!' she said, wondering why he even picked up the phone if he was in a meeting.

The phone cut out almost instantly and she was left feeling very confused. She used the time to give her house a once over. Most people on her income would probably hire a cleaner or two without any hesitation, but Jessica was one of the oddballs who actually enjoyed cleaning. There was a certain satisfaction about it, even scrubbing a toilet. Not that her toilet was particularly in need of a deep clean, of course. About forty five minutes into scrubbing the bathroom tiles, her phone pinged with a message.

Hey, sorry about earlier. All done now. I've got a bit of time before my next appointment and I'm starving! Do you want to meet at the little bistro near my office? Dom.

Jessica looked at herself in the bathroom mirror and winced. Her hair was lank and scraped into a messy bun atop her head. She'd got no make up on with a bright red spot coming up on her nose.

Sure. Can you give me half an hour?

She assessed herself in the mirror again as she waited for a reply.

Cool, see you there.

Jessica hopped in the half cleaned shower and quickly washed her hair, yanking out the knots with a wide tooth comb. There wasn't time to dry and style her hair, so she'd have to be content with a slicked back bun. She stuck a pimple patch on the ever-growing spot on her nose and just enough makeup to look human. It was a pretty sweltering day in LA, so denim shorts and a band t-shirt had to do. She grabbed her phone and booked an Uber to the bistro. The traffic was surprisingly light for the middle of the day so despite initially running late, she managed to make it there in record time. Then it hit her, she'd left the bag of clothes by the door.

'Fuck!' she said from the backseat, causing the driver to catch her eye in the rear view mirror.

'Everything okay miss?' he asked.

'Yes, sorry. Just remembered something,' she garbled.

She thanked and paid the driver, then sheepishly ambled into the bistro, spotting Dominic in a sharp suit but open collared and minus the tie today. He stood up as she approached the table and pulled out her chair for her. The only man who had ever done this for her previously was her dad. As he took his seat again, she placed her hands on the table and pulled a face.

'I've got a confession to make…' she hesitated.

'Go on.'

'I've left your clothes again! I left them by the door so I wouldn't forget them, and I was in such a hurry to get here, I walked right past them. I'm so sorry. I'll mail them to you as soon as I get back.'

His face broke into a smile and a laugh with her confession.

'If I didn't know better, I'd say you were just using the same excuse to try and see me,' he smiled gently.

'Christ no! Not at all!' she said a little too defensively. His smile settled into a solemn line and his jaw clenched again as he fingered the salt and pepper shakers on the table.

'Sorry, I didn't mean it like that, I just meant it's genuinely because I was in a hurry to get ready. When you messaged asking to meet, I was in full flow cleaning mode and looked a complete state!'

'Well you certainly pull yourself together well. I must say, you look very different from when I saw you in my office the other day.'

'Ah, I'd come straight from a photoshoot so I was a bit more dolled up than usual,' she gestured at her current attire, wondering if she should've dressed up a little more today as he sat there in his business attire.

'So are you a fan or are you one of these women who just buys a band shirt because it's trendy?'

'How very dare you,' she mocked in response, 'I am most definitely a fan!'

'Okay, name five of their songs,' he said, locking his fingers as if waiting for an answer in a job interview.

Jessica began to reel off some of the lesser known Fall Out Boy songs she liked.

'Okay, fair enough,' Dominic laughed, 'Although I've not even heard of some of them so you could be lying for all I know.'

After they'd placed an order, Dominic leant back and seemed to relax more into the conversation.

'Sorry if I was a bit rude on the phone when you rang. I was in a meeting and we were waiting for a call from another lawyer in New York. So, I'd put the phone on loud speaker before answering it...'

'Oh my God!' Jessica interrupted, clapping her hand to her mouth.

Dominic nodded and raised his eyebrows.

'Yup, so there I was in the boardroom with the company partners, with a woman on the other end of the phone saying she'd washed herself out of my clothes...'

'I'm so sorry!' Jessica said as she laughed at the second hand embarrassment she felt.

Dominic laughed and his entire face lit up. He had the most gorgeous blue eyes.

'It's fine, I just told them you were my over familiar cleaner,' he winked.

Dominic couldn't fathom that the stunning girl sat in front of him was the same girl who was sobbing in a towel just days ago. He felt angry that Ryan had found her first; not that it would've been likely that he met her by chance otherwise. He'd been trying to shake this feeling since he saw her in his room, almost a feeling of protectiveness. Then, when he saw her in his office all glammed up, he had to really control himself from saying anything that could be considered inappropriate. She looked charming in the towel, stunning in her dress and today, she looked beautiful. *How could one girl pull off such an assortment of looks?* he thought to himself.

While they were waiting for the bill, a teenage girl approached their table cautiously.

'I'm really sorry to interrupt, but please can I get a photo with you? I'm a huge fan...I waited until you'd finished eating. I hope that's okay?'

Dominic blinked and looked from the girl to Jessica. Semi-used to approaches like this, Jessica smiled and obliged. She smiled for the photo that the teenage girl took in selfie mode and then spent some time talking to her – how old she was, where she was from. All the while, Dominic was just staring at Jessica, watching her every interaction. He couldn't take his eyes off her, watching her face light up as she laughed, listening to her British accent as she spoke.

'Thank you again!' the young blonde girl called as she excitedly skipped off back to her family.

The waiter came back with the bill and Dominic offered his card, all the while continuing to eye Jessica.

'Oh, thank you for paying. Do you want me to pay you half back?' Jessica asked.

Dominic shook his head and raised his hand. 'It's fine. You can get the next one...so, when you said you're a singer...just how famous are you?'

He played with the salt and pepper shakers again.

'Bleurgh, my most hated question!' Jessica winced. 'It's fine if you've never heard of me,' she continued.

'Wait a minute...' he got out his phone and googled, then opened a page and pointed at the screen.

'That's you?' Jessica looked at a heavily photoshopped photo of her on a magazine cover.

'Argh! Yes, that's me!' she said as she batted his phone down with embarrassment, making him laugh.

'I knew I recognised you! When you came to the apartment, I thought you looked familiar, but I just couldn't place you. With that in mind, what in God's name were you doing with Ryan?! You could have your pick of any guy!' he seemed genuinely dumbfounded.

Jessica readjusted herself in her seat to get comfy for her interrogation.

'We met at the radio station. He was nice, we were talking online for a bit, agreed to go on a date, then he left me naked in his hallway. It's simple really!'

Dominic smiled and whispered, 'I still can't believe you slept with that jerk.'

'Who I sleep with is most certainly none of your business, thank you!'

'It is when you make me go searching in his sex pit for your belongings!'

'Okay, enough about my ever dwindling sex life! I have a question, if you're some big shot lawyer with his own company, why on earth are you sharing an apartment with him?'

'I told you, the rent was a bargain and it's only temporary. I'm actually moving out in the next few weeks.'

'A bargain…? But, you must be loaded…!'

'And how do you think I've stayed loaded… not wasting money on rent when it's not needed…' he smirked, making Jessica laugh.

His smart watch vibrated, breaking the flow of conversation.

'Ah, I'm afraid I've got to head off to my next appointment. Listen, don't worry about mailing the clothes, either pop by my office again sometime or I'll come your way? It feels like it's my turn!'

'Thank you again for paying. And, I don't mind coming to you. It's my fault we have to meet again anyway!'

'I'm actually kind of glad you forgot them; a good excuse to see you again,' he smiled, formally kissing her goodbye on the cheek.

When she got back, Jessica contemplated just packing the clothes up and sending them on their way in the mail, but she actually wanted to see him again too. There was something a bit mysterious about him that she couldn't quite put her finger on, the way he could go from being deadly serious and formal, to making jokes, then back to being formal. Her phone chimed and she already sensed it was Dominic.

Hey, I had a nice time today. If you're so insistent on bringing the clothes to me, why don't you pop by my office tomorrow while it's still fresh in your mind? x

The kiss at the end certainly didn't go unnoticed and this one letter made Jessica beam, despite it probably just being a typo. Either way, she was going to risk it with her reply.

Hey, me too. Good idea, I'll put the bag in front of the door so I trip over it when I leave! X

:) About 10:30? Meetings all afternoon! :(

Bummer for you! See you then. :) Xx

Jessica felt like a giddy teenager, counting the number of kisses on the messages. The fact he'd sent two to make up for the lack of one on the previous message was the result of the big grin plastered on Jessica's face. Something was happening here! As she was re-reading the messages, her phone started ringing with an incoming call. Her dad.

'Hey dad, how are you?'

'Hello sweetheart. I'm glad I've caught you. I always lose track of what the time difference is. How are you?'

'I'm good, how are you? How's everyone back there?'

'Can't complain! I've got Henry here for a few days. He's had some time off work so thought he'd pop in and see his old man. Hold on, I'll put you on speaker.'

After a brief moment of fumbling and clear poking of buttons on his phone, he'd managed to get the loud speaker on.

'Hello? You still there, love?'

'Yep, still here. Hey Henry, how are you?'

'Hiya! Not bad thank you. Just got a new car. How are you getting on?' Henry shouted from afar.

'Standard; of course you did,' Jessica laughed; her brother was forever upgrading his car to the newest model.

'I'm fine,' she continued.

'Hello love, dad again. How's the new music going? I saw you on some chat show the other day – I watched it on the YouTube website.'

Jessica smiled at her dad's attempts at joining the technological era.

'Yep, seems to be going well. Sales are increasing each day. We spoke about doing a tour but didn't feel like it was necessary.'

'I see. Maybe a tour that brings you back to the UK?' he offered, hopefully.

'Aha, not sure if that's in the works I'm afraid,' Jessica admitted.

She heard her dad audibly sigh in response and she felt guilty once again that she'd not seen them in so long.

'Maybe I'll come out and visit you!' Henry shouted from the background, and she just laughed in response.

Her dad went on to update her about the outrage of the local pub closing down, his new hobby of tennis and the day trip he'd had with ex-colleagues to Bridlington. He finished by asking if she'd met anyone since they last spoke and as there was no way she was going to tell her father about the Ryan debacle, she debated mentioning Dominic. Then she remembered, nothing had actually happened there, other than her holding his clothes hostage after he rescued her from the aforementioned situation.

'Nope, nothing on that front!' she cheerily said.

Barely a minute after they hung up, Jessica had a message from Henry.

I wasn't joking about coming to visit you! X

Are we talking just you, or you and dad? X

Just me! C'mon! I'm dying to see where you live and hang out with the rich and famous! ;) x

Well, you're going to be bitterly disappointed with the significant lack of rich and famous folk to hang out with...but okay... why not? (Regrets this instantly!) xx

Yayyyy!!!! I'll look at flights and let you know!

Fire over any dates that don't suit you. X

Jessica wasn't overly sure what she'd just agreed to, but she had to admit that it would be nice to see her brother. Maybe he'd forget and it wouldn't come to fruition. No, this was her brother she was talking about. Not a chance he'd forget. She looked at her calendar and decided on a week for Henry to come over. She often wondered how he managed to take so much time off work. He was always travelling and surely there was a limit to how much annual leave one person had per year.

FIFTEEN

Jessica had some last minute work on in the morning, so Henry made his own way from the airport. When she pulled up at about 3pm, she saw him sat by the front door, playing on his phone. She suddenly realised that she'd told him the number for the gate so he could let himself in, but she'd completely forgotten to tell him the pin code for the door.

Oops. She texted him the code but didn't hear back. As she clambered out the car, Henry was sarcastically slowly clapping as if to well *'well done, moron.'*

'I'm so sorry! I completely forgot about how you'd actually get in! Have you been waiting long?'

'Fortunately not!' Henry laughed.

'I did text you!' she protested but he waved his black phone at her.

'Phone died,' he shrugged.

Jessica swiftly unlocked the door and gestured him inside. He dumped his bags down and threw his arms round her tightly. Jessica sunk into the embrace, being reminded of everything to do with home and the close bond she had with her brothers. She found herself starting to well up and swiftly wiped her face to hide any potential tears.

'Right! Get that kettle on, I fancy a brew!'

'Umm, I don't think I've got any tea bags, I tend to drink coffee these days.'

'Ugh, you've become so American!' Henry groaned.

'Electrical kettles aren't really a thing here and I'm not forcing down a cup of lukewarm milky water with a tea bag floating round in it!'

'Fair point…I'll have a coffee then…' Henry pulled a face.

Jessica pointed Henry towards his room as she made the coffee.

'Bloody hell!' she heard from the other room.

He'd obviously seen the stunning view of the sea from the guest bedroom window. They got comfy on the couch with their coffees and spent half an hour catching up on general life updates. Henry then delicately told Jessica that their dad did seem a little bit hurt not to be invited along to visit with him.

'What's really going on with that?' Henry quizzed her.

'Ugh,' she sighed.

'Okay, fine. Look, I'm just embarrassed about the last few years. I feel like an idiot, and I don't want him to judge me anymore than he already is. I love my job and there's parts of it that I wouldn't change for the world, but living out here, sometimes it's hard. I miss home. I miss my family. I miss my friends. I often wonder what my life would've looked like if I never left.'

'Easy. You'd be married to Jake and have two kids, living somewhere down South just like you always wanted. Christ knows what you'd be doing for work, but you'd still be earning the big bucks, I'm sure.'

Jessica didn't reply, but the mention of Jake's name and the potential life she could've had made her feel a sting in her chest.

'Oh, that reminds me,' he said, 'Matt's gonna propose to Lucy.'

'What?' she gasped. 'Oh my gosh! When? How do you know?'

'Not sure when, he just says he's been looking for rings and he told me, duh.'

'Wow, and she has no idea?'

'Don't think so. So don't say anything!' he warned her. She made a lips sealed gesture, pretending to zip her mouth closed. As she leant forward to place her coffee cup on the table, her eyes caught sight of a brown paper bag near the front door.

'Oh, for fuck sake!' she groaned, throwing her head back dramatically.

Henry looked up, startled, and confused, following her eyes to the bag.

'Erm...you good?' he asked, still looking confused.

'Yeah, I just forgot about something I needed to do this morning,' she sighed, getting out her phone. 'Just give me two mins.'

I've just realised.... I'm so, so, so, SO sorry! I'll drop them off first thing tomorrow, I promise!!!

Almost instantly came a reply.

Yeah, yeah. I've heard that before. I'm not too far from your place now actually. I'll just swing by. Saves you a trip.

I've actually got company at the moment. I promise I will drop them at your office tomorrow. I swear!

No reply. She hoped he wasn't too peeved with her; she felt like such an idiot. Henry didn't say anything but gestured comically for some kind of explanation.

'Okay, well it's a long story, but I met this guy, and we hooked up. Then he basically scarpered while I was in the shower, leaving me locked out of his room with all my belongings in. One of his flatmates lent me some clothes to get back home; I'm just trying to return them, but I keep forgetting.'

Henry pulled a face.

'Okay firstly, eww, you're my sister. Secondly, what kind of prick ghosts you like that? Thirdly, just chuck the clothes and erase the entire thing from your memory! Then help me erase it from mine...'

Before Henry could finish his sentence, there was a buzz at the gate. Jessica pressed the microphone to find out who it was.

'Hey, Jessica? It's Dominic.'

Her mouth fell open and she garbled something about opening the gate as Henry was poking her in the arm, asking who Dominic was, with a big grin on his face. Jessica swiftly batted her hand towards any further interrogation and examined herself in the mirror. She still had some remnants of make up on from her job earlier, but her hair was looking a tad worse for wear. She patted it down as best she could, raking her fingers through it like a comb. A knock came from the front door and Jessica grabbed the bag of clothes nearby, hearing Henry gasp with realisation.

'I get to meet my sister's hero?!' he jokingly said, clapping his hands in excitement.

'Shut up and stay there!' she turned round and threatened him with a point of her finger.

She opened the door to find Dominic stood there looking like a stereotypical American jock, yet weirdly he was able to pull it off. He took off his Ray Bans and met her eye. The late afternoon sun helped to carve out his cheekbones and jawline, making Jessica wish she'd put an actual comb through her hair.

'You may be talented, but your memory is shocking...' he laughed.

'I'm so sorry, it really is!' Jessica laughed. 'Didn't you get my last message? I've got company,' she added.

Henry took this as perfect timing to swing the door wider open and introduce himself. Dominic obviously wasn't expecting this and took a slight step back. Jessica subtly kicked her brother in the shin.

'Oh, sorry, I'll leave you to it. I just came for those things. Then I'll let you get on. Sorry to intrude.'

It was the first time Jessica had seen Dominic appear flustered; he usually came across incredibly composed and collected. Jessica handed him the brown paper bag and asked Henry to go make her another coffee. Dominic shoved the bag under his armpit and shoved his hands into his jeans pockets and thought of what to say. He thought they'd had a nice time on their date. *Maybe she didn't see it as a date. Had it been a date at all?* He found himself questioning his own thoughts. He felt a wave of protectiveness again.

'I suppose you do right; inviting them to yours means you won't get locked out of any bathrooms!' Dominic awkwardly chuckled.

'Excuse me?' Jessica replied, slightly taken aback by his personal dig.

'Sorry, I didn't mean offence. Just, yeah...Never mind...Sorry,' he ruffled his hair at the back of his head.

'He's my brother,' Jessica said plainly, realising what was happening.

Dominic's stance instantly relaxed and Jessica noticed his jaw unclench as he apologised for his misunderstanding.

'Oh crap, I'm so sorry! I just thought...' he stopped mid-sentence.

'I would invite you in,' Jessica continued to explain. 'But with him here, he will bombard you with inappropriate questions. Think of it as me saving you this time!'

Dominic smiled and stepped forward again, holding eye contact with her, regaining his suave and collected persona.

'That's fine. I was wondering though, how would you feel about going for dinner sometime?'

'But I've given you the clothes back,' Jessica said, puzzled.

'Yeah, I was thinking without the clothes...' he said. A loud laugh and wolf whistle came from the kitchen where Henry was, making them both blush.

'I didn't mean...' Dominic smiled, holding her gaze.

'I know what you meant. Sure, I'd like that,' she replied with the same smile. For a brief moment, she thought he was going to lean in for a kiss, but he stepped back and put his sunglasses back on, telling her that he'd text her some dates and restaurant options so she could choose. She waved him off and closed the door, feeling butterflies in her stomach and beaming like a

Cheshire cat. Back in the kitchen, she was met by Henry grinning and crossing his legs on the stool. Before he could even open his mouth, Jessica darted him a look, 'Shut up.'

SIXTEEN

Jessica was getting ready for her date with Dominic and had been debating for the last hour on what to wear. She knew he'd rock up in a smart suit, so she was onto trying on her fifth outfit. Looking herself up and down in the mirror, she assessed the black dress that was slightly too tight on her hips. She decided it was slightly too funeral-y and instead opted for a looser skirted dress that nipped in at her waist, along with some heeled sandals. It looked smart, but not obviously try hard. Perfect for the warm summer evenings that LA had to offer. She arrived at the restaurant and after fighting past a few paparazzi folk, she scanned the room to see Dominic perched on a stool at the bar, sipping what looked like whiskey. As expected, he was donned in a smart, slim fitting navy suit with a white shirt, open collared and no tie like before. He just oozed confidence, Jessica thought as she once again took a moment to admire his strong jawline once again. What was it about a man's jawline that made girls swoon?

Just as she was heading over to him in full on model walk mode, another lady materialised next to him and delicately placed her hand on his shoulder. Jessica abruptly stopped in her tracks and saw the scantily clad woman whisper something in his ear and romantically stroke his hair. He gently pushed her arm away from his head and said something back to her, leaving her to shrug and strut off with her clutch bag. Jessica cautiously approached him and gave him a slightly questionable look.

'Hey…Who was that?'

'I think she was an escort… she asked if I required any services…' Jessica's eye widened, not expecting that answer, then started to laugh.

'Dare I assume that you declined…?'

'I most definitely declined; explaining I had a better offer!' Dominic laughed.

'God, LA is weird sometimes…'

'Where have you brought me?' she laughed.

You picked from the list!' he joked.

'Good evening to you both!' the Maître D' said as he gestured for them to follow him to their table.

'May I get you a drink Madam?' he asked.

'Could I please get a gin and tonic?'

'Most certainly. I shall return shortly with your menus, but please do peruse the specials on that board over there by the window in the meantime. I highly recommend the duck ă l'orange.'

This unlocked a memory for Jessica; back at university when Jake had promised her a romantic night in with a homemade meal of the same course. Unfortunately, he didn't follow a recipe and didn't realise that the duck was supposed to be cooked with the orange. He flung some duck breasts in the oven, toughening them up in the microwave because 'they didn't look done' and then poured them both a glass of orange juice to swill it down with.

'I thought it was like eating duck, but with orange juice as opposed to wine or something!' he'd protested.

Ah, the mind of a nineteen year old boy who had never lived away from home before.

'You look lovely by the way,' Dominic said, breaking Jessica's thought. 'Thank you. As do you,' Jessica smiled.

'Been up to much? Is your brother still staying with you?' he asked, taking a swig of his drink.

'He flew back last night. It's been really nice seeing him actually; I have to admit I was a bit hesitant to have him stay. I've not had family come visit me since I've been here.'

'Why not?'

'Meh...the whole LA vibe wouldn't really be their thing. I'm not entirely sure it's mine!' she chuckled.

'Yeah, I know what you mean,' he raised his glass in acknowledgement.

They had both decided against the special, and instead they both ordered chicken dishes. *Easy first date food. Was this a date?* Jessica thought about what Dominic has actually said when he asked her to dinner. She took the implication that it would be a date, but now she wasn't so sure. *Was she dressed up too much for a casual friendly dinner? Argh, stop thinking!* Dominic broke her train of thought again, this time asking more about her family and where she was from. She explained that she was from a sleepy little place in Yorkshire, England and went on to explain to this naïve American that the UK was bigger than just London.

'I'm a lawyer... give my brain some credit,' he joked.

'Sorry, it's just quite common for people to say, *'Oh, England! I'd love to visit there! Big Ben! Buckingham Palace! Have you ever met the Queen?'* and it gets quite annoying!'

Dominic smiled in response, his charming grin making Jessica feel all tingly. Thinking back to when she first met him, she asked him if he'd managed to move into his new house yet.

'Ah yes! Last week in fact!' He suddenly lit up, seemingly more animated. 'I'm really pleased with it; the kitchen is insane, and the main bedroom is really stunning. You'll have to come check it out sometime!'

Jessica raised her eyebrows in response, and he suddenly realised what he'd said.

'Argh, sorry! Didn't mean it like that, honest! That wasn't some poor attempt at flirting, I promise!' he went red as he began awkwardly laughing.

Jessica simply smiled and shook her head.

'I'm sure your bedroom is just lovely,' she said before taking a sip of her drink and winking. Dominic wondered what it was about this girl that made his brain stop working properly. She had some weird effect on him that he couldn't figure out how to stop. Very obviously and quickly trying to change the subject, he started telling her about the architecture of it all and how long it all took from designing to building. He got out his phone to show her some photos, swiping away through the reel as Jessica nodded approvingly at the house. *Wait, what.* Jessica nearly spluttered her drink as Dominic quickly turned the phone back.

'Oops, sorry about that,' he chuckled awkwardly.

Jessica shook her head to tell him it was fine but she trying incredibly hard not to blush. As he'd been swiping through his camera reel, a photo popped up of him stood on the beach with a surf board and another man. She only got a brief glimpse of it before he snatched it away, but she managed to get an eyeful of his tanned, muscular body. *Phew*, she debated fanning herself with the menu, feeling rather hot under the collar.

'Sorry, just a photo from the other weekend. Me and my pal, Blake, like to head out surfing when we can. You'll have to excuse the posey photo!' he laughed as he put his phone back in his pocket.

Jessica thought about how much time Daniel would spend with his friends, surfing. Then again, maybe he was actually spending time with Riley rather than that. She focused her attention back on Dominic.

'You surf? That's cool. I have to admit, I can barely float, let alone surf!'

Dominic cut a piece of chicken and paused with it halfway to his mouth.

'Didn't you date a swimmer?' he laughed, still looking down at his plate.

Jessica widened her eyes at him.

'Oh, so we've done some research before the date, have we?' she winked.

'Date?' he asked very matter of fact.

Shit. Feeling herself blush, she swallowed and tried to think of something to say. As she opened her mouth to speak, he winked back. She jabbed at some vegetables on her plate and desperately tried to think of something to change the subject. It was weird, sometimes she felt really confident in herself around Dominic, then he'd randomly just throw her off guard and catch her out. Part of her found it unsettling, part of her was intrigued. Little did she know, he was feeling exactly the same way about her. They sat for another hour, enjoying a bottle of white wine together and talking about everything from work to family, even a brief discussion about exes. Despite wondering how much he already knew from Googling, she told him about how she thought Daniel was the one, but then found out he'd cheated on her, so she called it quits. Dominic told Jessica about how he was with his ex for five years but was left heartbroken when she left to go volunteer in Ghana. He admitted that he had never been able to forgive her for leaving. Jessica thought, if he couldn't forgive his ex-girlfriend for leaving him to selflessly volunteer in Africa, she felt even more sympathy for Jake when she left to pursue a career in stardom.

'But!' Dominic gently hit the table with his hand, 'that's in the past and you move on to pastures new, don't you.'

Jessica smiled and nodded. With the bottle of wine empty and the bill paid by Dominic, who wouldn't take no for an answer, they made their way out into the evening. Dominic arranged a car for them, which arrived in no time and opened the door for her, before coming round to the other side to join her in the car. During the short ride, Dominic had slyly rested his hand on Jessica's knee and was gently stroking her leg with his thumb. Trying to play it cool and act nonchalant, Jessica just stared out the window the whole time, watching the people fly past. The reality was that her body was on fire; this gentle touch was sending shockwaves through her entire body. She wondered if he knew what he was doing to her.

Arriving at her place, Dominic jumped out the car and raced round to open her door for her. He said something to the driver who nodded in acknowledgement. Dominic gestured for

Jessica to lead the way and she wondered if he was making the assumption about where this date was going next. Through the gate and stopping at her door, Jessica turned to face him.

'Thank you for this evening; I've had a really lovely time.'

'Thank *you*,' he emphasised.

They smiled at each other and all that could be heard was the rustling of trees nearby, in the gentle warm breeze that was flying around. Dominic cleared his throat and edged slightly forward. He locked eyes with her, and Jessica watched as a gulp descended down his throat. He gently clasped her hand and pulled her towards him. If his hand on her knee was enough to spark electricity in her bloodstream, the moment when he gently planted his lips on hers was enough for her to power a generator. He slightly pulled away and Jessica grabbed him back towards her, this time kissing him back more passionately. This time, he pulled away with more purpose which took Jessica aback, wondering what she'd done wrong. He looked down and ruffled his hair with hand.

'Umm, I think we should call it a night here,' he squeezed her hand and let it fall back to her side.

'Oh, yes, of course,' Jessica laughed, determined now to get to the other side of the door and be alone with her embarrassment yet again.

He quickly realised how it looked and started babbling to explain.

'Argh, no! Wait, sorry. I just meant as in I don't think it's a good idea to take things any further on the first date. Not that that's what you were suggesting either. I just don't want you to think I'm just after that. I'd like to really get to know you. Plus, he's waiting for me to walk to you to the door and go back,' he gestured back towards the driver.

'Okay,' she nodded and smiled as she turned to open the door.

'Thank you again for a lovely evening,' she managed before making her way inside and smiling at him before closing the door.

The minute the door was closed, her face dropped the fake

smile and she felt deflated and rejected.

'Fuck!' she heard Dominic scowl outside, then the sound of the gates opening to let him out.

Sat in the back of the cab, he had to fight his urges not to ask the driver to turn back around. It took so much self-restraint for him to let her go. All he wanted to do was carry her upstairs and rip her clothes off. However, he didn't want that to be it; he wanted to get to know her, so he didn't want to fuck it up. He tried to suppress the thought that he may have just fucked it up anyway.

Jessica exhaled and rested her head on the door. It's not that she desperately wanted to have sex with him tonight, but she couldn't help feeling unwanted and slightly rejected. Over the last few years, she'd had to fight men off. She knew deep down it was because Dominic was obviously being a gentleman and genuine, but her confidence had certainly taken a battering by its good friend humiliation. She'd been sat up in bed reading for an hour when her phone pinged with a message. From the first few lines she could see on the notification, she knew it was Dominic with the whole 'it's not you, it's me' spiel.

Hey, I'm apologising in advance for the lengthy message and for chickening out and doing this by text rather than ringing you. I just wanted to say sorry for how things ended tonight. I truly had a fantastic time with you, and I just didn't want to rush things. I didn't want you to think I was only after one thing, like that scumbag Ryan. Sharing a living space with him for even just a short space of time, I've seen all sorts of girls he brought back with him. The first time I saw you, you were different from them. I was surprised that you'd fallen for the bullshit that he said to you. Sorry, that sounds like I'm blaming you for falling for his tricks. I'm not; he's a disgusting idiot but clever with his pick-up lines! Anyway, after speaking to you in the flat and our endless encounters whereby you kept forgetting my clothes, I was utterly enchanted by you. I apologise for sounding like some guy out of a rom com movie, but I really like you and I don't want to rush anything/ruin anything. Now I'm worrying that will scare you off... argh! With my job, I'm so used to being organised and meticulous, but you make my brain go all funny! Hope to hear from you soon. x

    Well, that wasn't what she was expecting. Jessica smiled at his formal sign off, as if sending a business email. She went back and forth, typing out a reply then deleting it and starting over. In the end, she stayed simple and hit send.

No apologies necessary. I'm sorry if I seemed too forward/keen. I'd very much like to get to know you further. P.S. I love a rom com movie! :)

She watched the message change to 'read' and put her phone back on the nightstand and continued with her book. She had a busy week ahead with assorted meetings, meaning she didn't have much spare time for a social life. Dominic worked a 9-5 Monday to Friday job anyway, so he was equally as tied up throughout the week, with meetings too. They'd arranged to meet on Saturday down at the beach; Jessica had reluctantly agreed to let him take her surfing. A decision she was already regretting as she kept having images in her head of her having to be rescued by the lifeguards.
    When people thought of Hollywood, they initially thought of the glitz and glamour, not sat in four hour meetings about contract clauses and what each word specifically could be interpreted as. Then again, the money she was earning from such contracts meant Jessica couldn't really justify any complaining, she knew that. Also, she had learned that she really should read these contracts meticulously after the debacle with Michael when she left treatment.
    Saturday morning rolled around relatively quickly, despite Jessica dreading each new day of meetings for the last five days. She knew full well she was going to end up looking like a drowned rat by the end of the day on the beach, so she ran a brush through her hair but left it at that. She didn't want

Dominic to see her make up free just yet, but she also didn't want him seeing her with mascara running down her face. She applied a tinted sunscreen, a small amount of concealer to cover her eye bags, curled her lashes and applied a tinted lip balm. She was embracing the beach babe look, or the unwashed/unkempt look, whichever way you wanted to look at it. Dominic was picking her up with his boards and they were heading to Santa Monica beach. As they got nearer, Jessica began to feel incredibly nervous, the butterflies in her stomach were practically doing extreme sports at this point. She carefully managed her breath, trying not to show her nerves; she knew she was in good hands.

'You okay?' Dominic side eyed her.

'Yep. Just promise me that you'll rescue me if I start to drown!' Jessica laughed.

'I promise,' he smiled, remaining focused on the road ahead.

They arrived at about 9:30am and Dominic pulled one of the boards off the roof of his car with ease, handing it to Jessica.

'Just lay it down gently there,' he said, handing it over to her.

She didn't realise the weight of it and stumbled slightly. Fortunately, he was busy undoing the other board so didn't notice while she composed herself. Placing the other board down, he looked around.

'Okay, you can use the car to get changed into the wetsuit. You can go first.'

'What?' Jessica said, thinking she'd misheard him.

'Your wetsuit. It's in the back.'

'My wetsuit...okay...didn't think of that. I'm supposed to get into a wetsuit in the back of a car...erm, right... challenge accepted...!' Jessica said, hopping into the backseat and closing the door behind her.

Dominic stood with his back close against the front of the car so no-one could see in. Fortunately, the other windows were tinted so that was safe. Jessica huffed and puffed, trying to discreetly get into the skin tight wetsuit, pulling it up each leg with earnest effort. It made it more difficult that she was starting to get a sweat on from this workout. She peeked round to make sure no-one was in sight before slipping her top off, so she was down to her bikini top; yanking the wetsuit over her top half.

'Ouch!' She yelped as she accidentally uppercut herself in the chin.

Dominic turned round and shouted, 'You okay?'

'Turn back around!' Jessica screeched as she tried to cover up.

'Sorry!' he put his hands up and turned back. Jessica sat panting before sighing.

'Actually…can you help…?' she called out to him, admitting defeat.

He came round to the back door, looked round and clambered in.

'How can I be of assistance?' he said cheerily with a hint of sarcasm.

'Just…help!' Jessica snapped. He laughed and told her to lift her arms up slightly. He effortlessly yanked the suit up and over her shoulders, tightening the neckline slightly and gently brushing the back of her neck with his fingers.

'There we are.'

'Thank you. God, I'm knackered!' Jessica collapsed back into the seat.

'Right, my turn, out you get!'

Jessica obliged and went to stand guard at the front of the car as he had done for her. In what seemed like thirty seconds, she heard the car door slam shut and turned to see Dominic donning his wetsuit.

'How did you do that so quickly?!' Jessica demanded.

'Years of practice I guess,' he laughed in response.

'Come on, let's get out there. Grab your board.'

She followed his lead and hauled the board under her arm, trotting in the direction of the sand. Despite the wetsuit bearing a tremendous similarity to shapewear that Jessica owned, it felt tight around her stomach, making her feel self-conscious. They sat on the shoreline while Dominic explained the do's and don'ts. He showed on her the sand how to climb the board, how to kneel, then jump up. Jessica chuckled internally, knowing full well how this was going to go down. She was glad she'd opted for no mascara. They paddled out to the water, clutching their boards and as they were in deep enough water, Dominic expertly hopped over his board, so he was straddling it. Jessica ended up in the same position, it just took an extra three minutes to get there.

'Okay, now there's some good waves coming in, so you've just got to go with it. If you lie down and start paddling with your arms, riding the waves as they roll in. Then, when it feels right, onto the knees like I showed you, and stand up!'

He made it sound so easy, not at all like the technical logistical manoeuvre that Jessica saw it to be. She lay forward and began to glide her arms through the water, either side of the board. She felt perfectly content at this stage so decided to follow Dominic's instructions and get to her knees. *Okay, all good so far, now just for the...*

'Argh!' she came crashing down with a splash.

'Almost!' he laughed as he looked back at her. You'll get it, just keep doing that.'

After lots of swearing, laughing, and falling, Jessica sat upright and let the waves take control. She bobbed up and down on the board, feeling more in control as she watched Dominic stood on his board, gliding across the incoming waves. She could see the outline of his muscles under the suit, and yes, she couldn't help but notice the large package in the downstairs region too. Trying not to ogle too obviously, she occasionally glanced around the beach in the distance, seeing couples and families enjoying the morning sun. He paddled up beside her and used some bungee cord contraption to tie the boards together, so they floated together.

'How was that?' he asked, sweeping his hand through his wet hair.

'That was...interesting,' she said with a smile.

'I thought you did very well for a beginner,' he said kindly, if not a little patronising.

Jessica kicked some water in his direction, making him smile. They both sat in silence, looking at the views surrounding them.

'I might not be taken by the surfing, but the views sure are nice from out here,' Jessica gazed towards the pier.

'Mhmm, sure are.'

She could feel his gaze on her while she pretended not to notice.

'Hey,' he got her attention and pushed a piece of bedraggled wet hair behind her ear.

He scooted forward on his board, so he was more in line with her, then placed his hand under her chin and lifted it slightly so she was looking right into his eyes. As they were bobbing up and down, she knew full well what was about to happen and braced herself for the electricity. *Surely this amount of electricity couldn't be safe in the water!* He leant in and gently met her lips, causing her to taste the salt water on his skin. They pulled back in sync and looked at each other before smiling and laughing, before a big wave came and took them both out by surprise. They both yelled as they were swept clean from the boards.

'Oh my god, please don't make me laugh, I can't float when I'm laughing!' Jessica shouted through giggles.

Dominic grabbed her to help steady her while she got her breath back.

'Come on, let's get you back on terra firma,' Dominic hauled the boards (and Jessica) back towards to shore.

'So, bad news. You're not getting in my car with that on,' Dominic pointed at Jessica's sopping wet suit.

'What was the point of getting changed inside the car for modesty but now I've got to peel this off in broad daylight?!'

'Because I didn't know to start with if you were wearing a bikini or anything underneath. Now I know you are, you can just take your wetsuit off here. You're decent enough.'

'Decent enough?' Jessica repeated back to him.

'Look, we'll do it together,' he offered in moral support, and he began unzipping his own suit, peeling it from his toned shoulders. As she began to disrobe too, she kept a side eye glance in his direction. Partly to see where he was looking, partly to check out his body. *Damn, there were those abs from the photo.*

'Enjoying the view?' he said without looking up. Oops, he'd caught her.

'Erm...umm...haha!' was all she could manage in response as she fought yet again with the garment on her body. She found her way free and slipped it down her legs to her ankles, yanking it off. She exhaled at the freedom from the tight, second skin, stretching her limbs with the new found freedom. This time, she noticed him ogling her and she felt herself blushing yet again in his company.

'What?' she asked, instinctively covering her stomach podge with her hands.

'Just enjoying the view,' he smirked.

Inviting her back to his new place to show it off, as promised it was fantastic. She loved her place, but she couldn't help but feel a pang of jealousy as he gave her the grand tour of his house. Then again, it was incredibly modern and stylish, which looked very swish, but Jessica personally felt it lacked a homely feel. Ever since she moved to LA, she never felt her house as being 'homely' like her dad's. She couldn't quite put her finger on it, but there was something about the modern, but comfy furniture back in England that just felt cosy. He showed her the back yard, which housed a reasonable sized outdoor pool, with lounger chairs scattered round the outside. Jessica looked at all the borders of the garden and thought again about her dad's house; those borders would be filled with flowers of all types and colours. Dominic's garden just felt very sterile and boring.

'What you do you think?' Dominic asked, both proud and excitedly.

'Yeah, it's stunning!' Jessica lied.

'I got a landscape gardener in,' he added to which Jessica's eyes widened a bit too much.

'What?' he asked, noticing her look.

'No, nothing...well...it just looks a bit...plain,' Jessica said without making eye contact.

Dominic looked around and slowly nodded his head.

'I suppose you're right. I should ask for a refund!' he joked.

'Sorry,' Jessica laughed, 'I didn't mean offence!'

'None taken at all! I know nothing about gardening so if you have any pointers, please be my guest,' he smiled.

Jessica could feel her phone vibrating away in her pocket and chose to ignore it, until it became a constant barrage of vibration that made her hip start to feel numb. She opened her phone and saw messages from assorted friends and members of her team.

Wow! Where have you been hiding him?! xx

Ooh, hello! Do tell me more! Damn girl!

He's fine!

Where did you find him? Also, let's do lunch sometime soon! Dying for a catch up! Xxxx

You've certainly upgraded! I didn't know that you surfed?! ;) xx

She cleared the string of messages on her notifications and opened her Instagram to see she'd been tagged in copious amounts of photos, all within the last hour. She was often tagged in things by fans, but it was rare they all came in one go, unless there was some news story out. *Oh God.* She gently gasped and rammed her phone back into her pocket. Dominic had been watching her and had a look of both concern and intrigue on his face.

'What's wrong?' he asked.

'Nothing!' Jessica said brightly with a forced smile.

'Okay...' he didn't seem convinced by her response.

'So yeah,' he continued, 'that's the house. Pretty pleased with it!'

Jessica smiled, 'It really is lovely. Listen, I'm sorry but I better go. I need a shower; I've got a Zoom call later this evening. Thank you for a lovely day though.'

Jessica swore she saw Dominic's face drop to a look of slight disappointment, but he nodded and thanked her for a lovely day too. He escorted her back inside and towards the door, where they parted with a hug and a brief peck. Dominic watched the Uber drive off and as he ambled back inside, closing the door, the house suddenly felt empty. He wandered back out into the garden and sat on the edge of the pool, rolling his jeans up and putting his feet in the warm sun-heated water. He found himself thinking about his kiss with Jessica as they bobbed up and down, afloat in the sea. He thought about her soft lips, gently kissing him back. He wanted her.

SEVENTEEN

The next morning, Jessica was woken by her phone pulsing away on the bedside table. She rubbed her eyes and stretched her body with a big yawn as she rolled over to reach for the phone. Dominic. She smiled as she swiped to answer the call.

'Hi,' she sleepily offered.

'So…why is my face plastered in magazines around America?'

Jessica rubbed the sleep out of her eyes and sat up in bed, the smile abruptly disappearing from her face. She debated in her head whether to act vacant and question what he was talking about. Instead, she decided against lying.

'Oh, erm…yeah, I saw that yesterday. Sorry, there must have been some paps at the beach.'

'My friends have been sending me screenshots of stuff on social media too. There's some terrifying stuff on Twitter. People referring to me as '*Daddy*' and obscenities that they'd like me to do to them!'

Jessica tried to stifle a laugh. The poor guy seemed so shocked, and she wasn't sure just how upset he was.

'Are you laughing?' he asked bluntly.

'No!' She protested a little too much. There was a brief pause and Dominic said, 'There's zoomed in photos of my crotch in magazines, referring to my apparently pleasingly sized package...'

Jessica put a hand to her mouth and held her breath to stop from laughing. 'My Mom will be so proud...'

Dominic said and Jessica exploded into laugher.

'I'm so sorry!' she pleaded, through gasps.

'Par for the course when dating someone like you I suppose' he said, chuckling.

'That's what you saw in the garden yesterday wasn't it?' he quizzed.

'Yeah, sorry. I didn't know how to tell you. I know you don't have social media, so I didn't think you'd find out to be honest. A bit too naïve on my part there. Seriously, are you okay? I know it must seem a bit weird. I completely get it if it's not for you. I'll understand if, you know...'

As she said this, practically offering Dominic a get out clause, she felt anxiety in her tummy just thinking what his answer would be. She was really enjoying his company and didn't want it to end. There was a pause and a sigh from him, as she held her breath awaiting the inevitable response.

'Okay, so it's not quite like any dating experience I've had before...but I really like you...So I just suggest we crack on and ignore it?'

Jessica blinked and took a small intake of breath which caught in her throat.

'I mean, are you sure? Most people run a mile. Or you get people like one of my exes who loved the limelight and actively went searching for it,' Jessica said a little too sharp.

'I can assure you that there will be no limelight searching from me. Also, I prefer surfing to swimming.'

Jessica blushed and felt embarrassed, knowing that Dominic knew she was referring to Daniel.

'So, are we okay?' Jessica bit her lip.

'We're okay. In fact, what are you doing next Friday? Fancy going out to that new Thai restaurant?'

Jessica was about to answer, until she realised Dominic hadn't finished.

'Or I could cook? I make a mean lasagne. If you don't mind copious amounts of carbs and fat of course,' he said.

'How do you maintain a body like yours by eating full fat lasagne?' Jessica remarked casually.

He just chuckled in response and they both agreed that she would meet him at his office on Friday evening, as she was in the area, and they'd head back to his place together for a meal. Jessica didn't want to assume anything, but it's safe to say she would most definitely be shaving her legs the night before. You know, just on the off chance.

She had a quiet week ahead, so she'd arranged to catch up with her group of girlfriends at a cocktail bar. Fortunately, most of her friends were either in the industry in some form or they worked flexibly so they were able to meet up mid-week. That was the only downside with Dominic, he worked a 9-5 job. Then again, he was his own boss so he could move things around if he wanted to. When she arrived at the bar, a few of the girls were there already.

'Hello!' Jessica said jovially.

Each of the girls turned and greeted her with big smiles and individual hugs. Just as they were finding a table, the other girls rocked up and exchanged similar greetings. Once seated and with their first set of cocktails in front of them, the updates began.

'So, I dumped Jamie,' Alison said, met with gasps from the other girls. After this topic was discussed at length, all agreeing that Alison could do so much better than Jamie, it was straight onto the next topic of conversation.

'Me and Lyle have booked to go to Paris for our anniversary next month!' Ellie squealed.

All said how jealous they were as they'd love to go to Paris. Jessica had said that she went for a weekend at university with her friends (Jake) and loved it. Then to the next topic. Christie proudly held up her hand, showing the girls an enormous diamond ring on her finger.

'That's my news!' she giggled as everyone gasped and grabbed her hand to get a good look at the beautiful ring. Christie had always been adamant that as a staunch feminist, she would never get married and be chained to a man for all eternity. How times had changed! Now it was Jessica's turn.

'So, the album did well. There was talk of doing a tour but that was quickly thrown out. My brother came over to stay for a bit, that was nice.'

Everyone nodded along, listening intently. When Jessica stopped and took a sip of her Cosmopolitan, they all looked at each other and Alison piped up.

'You're really not going to tell us?'

'Tell you what?' Jessica asked, knowing full well what they were waiting for an update on as she continued sipping her drink.

'Who is he? How did you meet? Come on! Tell us! Or is it over before it began?' Alison said, frowning.

Jessica smiled coyly as she placed her glass down on the table, fiddling with the stem.

'Okay fine,' she held her hands up in defeat. 'He's called Dominic and he's a lawyer.'

They all furrowed their brows.

'How the hell did you meet a lawyer?' Alison questioned, looking bamboozled.

'Long story that doesn't actually involve his job but,' Jessica felt herself grinning, 'he's really nice!' A collective 'ooh!' came from the girls, making Jessica laugh.

'From the photos online, I just assumed he was a model or something,' Christie said as she took a swig of her Manhattan.

'Has he seen the photos?' Alison asked Jessica.

'Erm yeah...we just laughed about it and fortunately he seemed to take it quite well!'

'When do we get to meet him then?' Ellie asked.

Jessica didn't need to reply – she just raised her eyebrows and rolled her eyes. They spent the next few hours downing more cocktails and putting the world to rights. A young waiter expertly picked up handfuls of empty glasses from the table.

'Are you ladies sure I can't get you anything to soak up your cocktails?'

'Ooh! Nachos!' Alison clapped her hands together and the waiter smiled sweetly and nodded.

'Ooh, he's a bit of alright isn't he.'

'Alison!' Christie exclaimed.

'He's young enough to be your son!' They all laughed as Alison batted her hand away.

Ten minutes later, a large sharing plate of nachos materialised in front of them, smothered in melted cheese and sauce. The girls dived in, stuffing their mouths like they'd been starved. Jessica looked up and nearly choked on the three nachos she'd shoved in her gob.

'Well, well, fancy seeing you here,' the familiar voice of Dominic said. *God, he looked good,* Jessica thought as she eyed him up and down in his dark navy suit. All the girls glanced round to look at him too, each with nacho dust covering their hands.

'Damn...' Alison said, half joking, half flirtatiously.

Christie thumped her in the arm and Jessica giggled, desperately trying to swallow the dry tortilla chips that were now lodged in her throat.

'Hi,' she managed. Finally swallowing and taking a big deep breath, she introduced Dominic to the group.

'Guys, this is Dominic, the guy I was telling you about,' Jessica smiled at him, wiping her mouth to make sure she didn't have any nacho remnants hanging around.

'Oh, don't worry, she didn't tell us anything! We've had to practically pry your name out her mouth!' Ellie laughed.

Jessica mouthed 'shh' at her and winked.

'Well, it's nice to meet...'

'Dom!' a female voice interrupted him, causing him to turn back towards the other end of the bar.

A long legged, tanned woman with straight jet black hair was gesturing at him and beckoning him over. She was stunning and her toned legs made Jessica fiddle with her dress and stretch it further over her thighs, covering them up. *How did people get so toned? She regularly went to the gym and ate well. Nachos weren't part of her usual diet, that's for sure. Why weren't her thighs like that?* Jessica found herself reflecting.

'Ah, I best go…' Dominic said apologetically, nodding at the woman. 'It was nice to meet you all,' he added before heading back.

Jessica noted that he didn't say goodbye to her, but she brushed it off.

'Who is that?' Alison nodded towards the woman.

'I don't know, someone from work. It is the middle of the afternoon remember,' Jessica shrugged nonchalantly.

Although, she couldn't help feeling a little unnerved by the woman.

Over the next hour, Jessica was able to keep an eye on the Dominic situation thanks to a very handily placed mirror. Whatever the conversation they were having, it looked tense, with Dominic repeatedly collapsing back in his chair and rubbing his brow.

'Right! We all done?' Christie slapped her credit card onto the table and made a check sign to the young waiter who nodded and made his way over.

The rest of the women skirted out of the booth they were sat in.

'Eurgh,' Alison groaned as she stumbled to her feet. 'No more daytime drinking please ladies. Next time, let's do coffee and cake!' Jessica glanced over in Dominic's direction then into the mirror on the wall. She fluffed up her beachy waves and straightened her dress to hide her protruding food baby. They had to walk past Dominic and his guest to leave, and she was feeling increasingly self-conscious, assessing the woman he was sat with. Alison strutted out first and tapped him on the shoulder as she passed him.

'Nice to meet you, Dominic!' she called back, to which he raised his hand in acknowledgement, smiling.

He turned his head to watch the parade of women walk past him, each smiling at him and receiving a polite smile in return. Next it was Jessica's turn. She certainly didn't strut; she shuffled her way towards the door and smiled at him, mouthing 'bye.' He opened his mouth to speak, but he stopped abruptly as the woman at the table placed her hand on his and smiled at Jessica. Dominic tried moving his hand, but she persisted and maintained her sickly sweet smile. Jessica noticed that there was a hint of viciousness to her smile.

Arriving back home, Jessica felt deflated about what she'd seen at the bar. She found herself wondering why Dominic was there and who the woman was that he was with. It seemed more than a lunchtime business meeting. She decided that the woman must be someone he worked with, so Jessica brought up the company website on her phone. She scrolled through the many numbers of employees photos and job titles. Nothing. She let out a sigh and flopped onto the couch, closing her eyes. The afternoon alcohol in her blood stream had made her suddenly very sleepy and within minutes, she drifted off into a slumber.

She spent the rest of the week tidying the house and enjoying the sunshine, hiking up some of the Californian hills, stopping for the occasional selfie with fans who recognised her. In the evenings, she spent her time playing around on the keyboard trying to come up with new music. She'd not heard from Dominic all week and when Friday came round, she debated texting him to check their date was still actually on. Fortunately, a message from him popped up.

Hey! Hoping to finish at about 6pm if you want to head over for then?

She relaxed and hit reply.

Sure. See you then.

She arranged a cab to pick her up at about 5pm to give her

enough time in the Friday afternoon rush. She had to raise the topic of the woman in the bar, but she wasn't yet sure how to do this without coming across needy and clingy. They weren't officially in a relationship so technically he could see as many girls as he wanted. Sure, it was a dick move but they were just dating. In her eyes, she thought they were officially dating but not dating other people. She should have kept her options open. Arriving at his office, she approached the desk and was greeted by the same receptionist as last time, with a wide eyed, quizzical look.

'Hi, I'm here to see to Dominic Paxton. He's expecting me,' Jessica added the last part to avoid having to be asked by Kelsie. She'd learnt from the last time.

'Okay, he's just in a meeting now but you can go up and wait. There are some chairs outside his office, next to the water cooler. He shouldn't be much longer,' she said.

Jessica thanked her and tried to remember the way to his office. Reaching the corporate style couch and chairs she recalled from the last visit, she knew she was in the right place. She plonked her bag down by her feet and waited, got out her phone and did the obligatory scroll through social media platforms. This is what modern age folk did when waiting for something. Less than five minutes later, the door to Dominic's office opened and out walked the same woman from the bar. This time she was wearing a slinky emerald bodycon and dark green high heels. Her gorgeous long black hair was pulled back into a high ponytail, further enhancing her sharp cheekbones. She did a double take of Jessica.

'Wow,' she said sarcastically, rolling her eyes.

'Dominic, darling, I'll see you later. Have a nice evening,' she gestured towards Jessica before planting a kiss on his cheek and strutting off down the corridor.

Dominic stepped back and held the door open for Jessica, but he too did a double take as she walked past him.

'Umm, Jessica…' he stepped forward and rubbed her cheek with his thumb.

'Wh…Oh god…what?' Jessica stuttered, as she pushed his hand away and searched for a compact mirror in her bag. Holding it up to her face, she gasped as she saw unblended contour, sat on her face in two thick stripes either side.

'Oh my god!' she began desperately rubbing at her face, trying to blend it in. No wonder Kelsie and that woman were giving her funny looks. Come to think of it, so did the cab driver. She now remembered getting distracted by a phone call from her agent when she was getting ready. She was mortified and put her face in her hands. Dominic smiled at her and pulled her close.

'What must you think of me?' she laughed, feeling herself achieving a warm rosy glow without the need for blusher.

'I think you were clearly so excited to see me that you lost your mind!' he joked.

'Shut up,' she slapped his arm.

'I'm so sorry – I probably embarrassed you in front of…' Jessica gestured towards the door and when he realised, she meant the woman just in here, Dominic finished her sentence for her.

'Lena.'

'Lena,' Jessica repeated. Then there was silence.

'Umm… sorry but I must ask, who is she?' Jessica instantly regretted asking this question so boldly and bluntly but decided it was better than spending the rest of the evening worrying. Dominic smiled, understanding what she was asking.

'She's from a rival firm, Beester & Langton. She's trying to poach me to partner with her. Them,' he quickly corrected himself, noting the potential ambiguity.

'Oh right, sorry,' she laughed awkwardly.

'No don't worry, I'd rather you ask than be worrying about anything. 'She can be a little, let's say forward,' he emphasised the last word.

'So, I saw…does she always kiss her colleagues?'

'God knows but that's partly why I don't want to be her colleague!' he said.

'It's a great deal…' he continued, 'but I'm so proud of what I've built up here, I can't just walk.'

'Well, you've got to just do what's right for you,' Jessica shrugged.

'Speaking of what's right for me...let's go,' he kissed her gently on the lips. He grabbed his jacket and threw it over his shoulder.

'After you,' he held the door open as Jessica brushed past him.

'Just give me two secs,' he popped his head into the office next door.

'Sandra, I'm off. Have those invoices gone out today? Great. Okay, don't stay too late, please. Go enjoy your weekend!' Jessica smiled at his interaction with his PA, the fifty something year old lady with mushroom coloured hair and thin maroon coloured glasses.

'Thanks Mr Paxton, you too!' Sandra called back.

'Sandra... for the billionth time...'

'Sorry! Dominic!' Sandra sung back at him.

Dominic muttered to Jessica, 'Sandra's used to working as a PA/Receptionist in very corporate, stuffy offices where it's all 'Mr' this and 'Ms' that. I can't stand that. First names for everyone here; no-one is better than anyone else.'

'The one with the highest income in the building says...' Jessica mocked cheekily. Dominic looked uncomfortable and Jessica quickly dropped her smile. 'I just meant...' she began.

'No, it's fine,' he assured her.

'I just really do believe that you get what you give when it comes to the workplace. I've had bosses who treated me like shit on their shoe and it's awful. It just makes you not want to put the effort in to help them. I swore I'd never be like that as a boss. It makes my skin crawl when you see middle aged men talking down, often to women, just because they earn more money or they have more *'power'*,' he used air quotes.

Jessica placed her hand on his back and rested her head against his arm as they stood in the descending lift. She only lifted her head when the doors opened into the bright foyer.

'Bye Kelsie, have a good weekend,' Dominic slapped his hand on the reception desk where Kelsie was clearly starting to wind down for the day, doing an online crossword. She jumped at the noise of his desk hit and smiled innocently.

'Oh! Erm! You too Dominic! Thank you! Sorry!' she garbled as she closed the window down on the screen, just waiting until he was out of sight to reopen it again, Jessica thought.

'Right, I brought the car today so just down here,' he pointed towards the underground car park.

Adjusting herself in the leather seat, Jessica watched as Dominic hung his suit jacket up in the back and hopped into the driver's side. She openly acknowledged she knew nothing about cars, but she knew this was an expensive one.

'What happened to the other car?' Jessica thought about the standard, scruffy saloon car he drove when he took her surfing.

'That one is for pleasure, this one is for business.'

'Crikey, so what am I? Business or pleasure?' Jessica laughed and Dominic joined in.

'Depends!' As they headed down the street, Dominic fiddled with the air vents, so they were both getting a cool blast of air in their faces. He unbuttoned his shirt sleeves and keeping one hand on the wheel, rolled them up with his free hand. Jessica noted his tanned forearms and the veins that stood proud. Jessica pondered what it was about certain men's hands that could be a turn on. It was bizarre really; *'hey here's some hands that will make you want to have passionate sex with me.'* It wasn't long before her thoughts were interrupted.

'I don't think I've ever actually asked, do you drive?'

'I can drive manual back in the UK. What do you lot call it? Stick? But I can't drive an automatic. The thought of just two pedals scares me...' Jessica admitted.

'To be honest, I'm impressed by anyone who can drive stick, all those gears and the *extra* pedal scares *me*!'

'Also, I passed my test first time. Only one in my family to do so. Major bragging rights!' Jessica proudly announced.

'You don't really speak much about your family. What are they like? Obviously, I've met your brother,' he commented as he joined the freeway, eyes remaining glued to the road. She instantly and shamefully regretted bringing them up.

'Well, there's my dad and my four brothers. I'm adopted...' she said, suddenly feeling shy.

'Oh really? Wow. I never knew that. I hate to ask as I feel there may be a story, but seen as you didn't mention...'

'She died,' Jessica said bluntly. Dominic adjusted his hands on the steering wheel and opened his mouth to speak before Jessica got in first.

'Cancer. When I was eight. I'd only known her for a year. My real parents were killed in a car accident a few years before.'

'Jesus...' Dominic looked away from the road and at Jessica. He placed his right hand on her knee.

'I won't say 'it's fine' because it's obviously not, but I don't really remember my real parents to be honest with you. I only really know them from photos. Despite only being a year older, I've got way more memories of my adoptive mum. My dad and my brothers took me in as their own and raised me.'

Dominic puffed out his cheek and exhaled. 'Wow. I'm sorry,' he squeezed her leg again. 'Do you see much of your other brothers and your dad since you moved out here?'

Jessica shifted in her seat.

'Not as much. How about you? Any siblings?' she tried to take the attention off herself.

'Just me! Only, lonely child!'

'Ah, a spoiled little brat then?' she jested.

'Sorry to disappoint you, but I'm afraid not! Pretty average upbringing in a very humble home,' he protested.

'So, I have a confession. I cheated...' Dominic said flatly, changing the subject suddenly as he opened the car door for her.

'What?' Jessica's eyes widened. She assumed this was where he was going to tell her the real story about Lena.

'I made the lasagne last night to heat up tonight,' he sheepishly admitted as he let her inside his home.

'Oh!' Jessica exhaled, relieved.

'Bit of a cop out, I know, but I realised I felt nervous about cooking in front of you. Don't ask me why!' he laughed, dumping his briefcase on the side.

'No problem with me, but I am starving so get the oven on!' she instructed, and he obliged.

'Can I get you a drink?' his hand hovered over some wine glasses in a cupboard as Jessica nodded enthusiastically.

The oven came up to temperature and Dominic placed the dish inside, setting a timer. Jessica admitted that it looked delicious, and she couldn't wait to try it.

'Shall we?' he signalled to the couch in the living room. He exhaled loudly as he collapsed into the seat next to Jessica, ruffling his neatly quaffed work hair into a more casual look. For men, that was the equivalent of a woman taking her bra off at the end of the day.

'Urgh, what a week!' he moaned. 'What have you been up to this week?' he asked, taking a big swig of red wine, before placing the glass on the coffee table in front of them. Jessica told him about meeting up with the girls and what a coincidence it was to bump into him there. She told him she'd also spent half the days trekking up the Californian hills.

'Pfft, easy life!' he joked, knowing full well her schedule was usually hectic. She drank from her wine and could see out of the corner of her eye that his eyes were fixed onto her. She could see his fingers began fidgeting slightly and he shuffled in the seat, so he was sat closer to her. Clearing his throat, he waited for her eyes to meet his and then leant forward to kiss her, his hand cupping her face. He took the wine glass from her hand and placed it onto the table next to his, then pulled her closer to him. She swung her legs round to get comfortable, but he lifted her left leg over his, so she was straddling him. He pushed his hands through her hair and kissed her eagerly.

'Forgive me, I forgot to say earlier, but you look absolutely beautiful...' he stroked her cheek.

'Even with the unblended make up?'

'Yep! Few can pull that look off!' he kissed her as he was smiling.

'Oh, and when I saw you in that bar the other day. Holy fuck, that dress. I was getting jealous of every other man eyeing you up in there!' he murmured as he began kissing her neck. Jessica didn't mention that she had quite different feelings of jealousy towards the woman wearing the other skintight dress. She sunk into him and as things got more heated, he led her towards his bedroom. Red faced and panting, they collapsed beside each other.

'Wow. Wow. Wow.'

'Right back at you,' Jessica said, patting his bare, muscular chest with a slight giggle. He took her hand from where it was resting on his chest, lifting it to his mouth, kissing it.

'Right, do you want to hop in the shower, so it gives me time to make a quick getaway?' he openly joked about the scenario Jessica found herself in with his previous flatmate.

'Prick!' she mimicked offence and then stopped to sniff the air, sitting upright, and looking round for clues.

'Ah shit!' Dominic's expression changed and he jumped up, stopping only to put his boxers on. He appeared again a few minutes later, to a semi dressed Jessica.

'So, lasagne's off the menu...' he cleared his throat. 'But I've ordered some pizza in. Still Italian, I suppose,' he offered, pulling a face. He walked across the room to Jessica, who was now sat on the edge of the bed, and she pulled him closer by wrapping her legs round his.

'So, the pizza will be about half an hour, if you fancy a quick shower,' he said in between kissing her.

'Very funny. You already made that joke,' she replied.

'I meant a shower together, but nope, that's fine!' he too mocked offence and began walking off before Jessica jumped up and grabbed his arm.

'Erm, I didn't say no!' she objected. He smirked and picked her up, her legs wrapping round his waist. He placed her to her feet once in the bathroom and turned the shower on, checking the water temperature.

'After you,' he said in the same way he did as they were leaving his office earlier. She slipped off the top and knickers she'd put back on and stepped into the shower, closely followed by Dominic. It wasn't quite as sensual as planned; one of them was getting jabbed in the back by the shower caddy, while the other was stood out of the water fall, shivering. They both had a quick rinse and got out to get dressed, ready for the pizza's arrival. There was still a significant smell of burnt lasagne in the air, despite Dominic's attempt to rid it by opening windows and lighting candles. The buzzer for the door went, signalling the pizza had arrived.

'You get that, and I'll find us a rubbish film to watch,' Dominic said, kissing her as he walked past her and into the lounge. He'd changed into some jogging bottoms and a T-shirt and Jessica questioned how he still managed to look so good. She opened the door, ready with some cash Dominic had given her for the delivery guy. Flinging the door open, her jaw dropped instantaneously.

'Hello again, I need to speak to Dominic please,' Lena said, already pushing her way past Jessica. Unsure what to do, Jessica closed the door and watched as Lena dumped her bag on the counter and pointed towards the lounge.

'He in there, is he?' she said confidently. Jessica nodded slowly but heard Dominic's voice approaching.

'Right, there's a new comedy on Netflix with Adam Sandler, it's...' he stopped as he saw Lena stood in his hallway. He looked at Jessica, then back at Lena.

'Le, what are you doing here?' It slightly stung Jessica to hear him use a shortened name for her, as if affectionately.

'I come by with more of your post because I've got nothing better to do on a Friday night apparently! Please change your address!' she demanded as she thrust several letters in his direction.

'Thanks,' he muttered as he cautiously took them from her.

'So, twice in one day!' she turned brightly to Jessica who said nothing. 'Ooh I used to love wearing that one! So comfy isn't it!' Lena remarked about the baggy hoody that Dominic had leant Jessica to wear after their shower.

'S... sorry?' Jessica stuttered.

'The hoody!' she confirmed, with a sickly sweet smile. 'Although it must have shrunk in the wash because it always looked baggier on me,' she said, this time with a vicious smirk.

'Right, thanks for stopping by Lena but we...' Dominic was interrupted by the buzzer again. This must be the pizza.

'Aren't you going to get that?' Lena said as she expectantly widened her eyes at Jessica. Like an obedient lapdog, she followed her orders and took the pizzas from the delivery man at the door. As she was handing over the money, she heard Dominic and Lena whispering and muttering. It sounded like arguing under their breath. Lena turned to look at Jessica holding two pizza boxes.

'Holy shit, that hoody will be even tighter if you eat all that!' she cackled.

'Lena!' Dominic snapped in a way Jessica didn't imagine he could. 'Please...' he rubbed his brow.

'Okay, okay, I'm going. Calm down. Enjoy your pizza darling!' she waved her hand and gave Jessica a set of hard eyes as she sauntered towards the door. As the door closed, Jessica looked up to see Dominic still rubbing his brow. She stayed perfectly still.

'Right...' he began. 'Firstly, I can only apologise for the things she said to you. Please ignore her cruel remarks. You are gorgeous, beautiful, sexy, intelligent, funny, kind...'

'Oh, just stop it,' Jessica snapped this time.

'Okay, I just...please, Lena has an incredibly vile side to her, and she has a way of making people believe what she says.'

'Is this the part where you tell me she's still just a business connection?'

'Oh, that part's still true. But I wasn't completely honest,'

'In a shocking twist...' Jessica said sarcastically.

'Please,' he held his hands out to her, but she refused to take them, so he accepted defeat and pulled out one of the chairs from the island. 'Basically, yes, we used to be in a relationship and yes, it was a committed relationship. We were engaged.'

Jessica's mouth fell open and she ripped off the hoody and threw it to the ground.

'Jessica, please, just hear me out!' Dominic begged and she stood with her arms folded, allowing him to speak. 'We were engaged, because believe it or not, she was a nice person when I first met her. We met at a conference when I was still learning the ropes in the industry, and we hit it off. She managed to get me a job working for her dad at his law firm. It really kickstarted my career, having a law firm like that on my resume. Anyway, eventually I managed to get another job on my own merit at another firm. We began drifting apart as I was working more. *'Daddy'* had paid for her to start up her own law firm, so her career was keeping her busy too. Eventually, we realised the relationship had run its course and we broke up. It was totally mutual and amicable. Then about a year ago, I started dating this girl called Eloise. I'd not heard from Lena since we broke up, then suddenly she appears back in the picture. She found out I'd started my own law firm too and she told me that she was struggling with some employees, so she wanted some advice on how to deal with them. Turns out it was all a rouse and next thing, she's all over me in my office.'

Jessica winced at the thought of someone else touching Dominic the way she had, not even an hour ago.

'I pushed her away, explaining that I was with someone else, and she got all defensive. She'd rock up at my office and turn up at places I was at with Eloise. To this day, I still don't know how she knew where I was. She'd use the same line about 'changing my address' and despite me thinking I'd changed all my details with banks, etc., she'd still show up with random post, even just junk mail that came addressed to me. One night, Eloise told me that she was fed up and couldn't deal with it all anymore, so she dumped me, blaming Lena. Once Lena found out that I was single again, she backed off. Now I'm with you, she's back again. It's like she doesn't want me, but she doesn't want anyone else to have me either.'

Jessica had listened patiently, but she still had so many questions.

'So why would you meet up with her for a drink and have a

meeting with her at your office?' she asked.

'Because I'm an idiot?' Dominic half smiled.

'Nope, proper answers. Why?' Jessica demanded.

'Okay, I lied about the thing at the bar; that wasn't a business meeting. That was because she told me her dad had died and despite him being partly responsible for producing the spawn of Satan, he was a good man. I was gutted for her.'

Even Jessica couldn't argue with that one, but she remarked that Lena had seemed in awfully good spirits at the bar to say that her dad had just died. Dominic shrugged.

'I doubted her at first, I have to admit, but I went to the funeral so...' *Fair enough*, Jessica thought.

'And the meeting at your office?' she pushed.

'That was genuinely because she told me that her dad had left her money in his Will to expand her firm. She wanted to hire three partners and approached me. It was a good offer that I'm sorry to say I did consider, hence me meeting with her. It became clear in the meeting that she was her usual self. She was constantly asking about you, commenting on things she'd read online, your past...' Jessica laughed and interrupted him.

'Let me guess, did you know she was in rehab? Did you know she's crazy? I've heard it all before!' 'Yep, that's exactly what she was saying,' he nodded.

'And that's when I knew I wanted absolutely nothing more to do with her.'

'And yet she still shows up unannounced at your house!' Jessica snapped, throwing her arms up in despair.

'Then I'll fucking move!' Dominic shouted, jumping up from his stool and knocking it over.

'What?!' Jessica gasped, slightly taken aback by his outburst. 'What are you talking about? You've just moved in!'

'I don't give a fuck! I'll sell up and move and have 24/7 security on the doors, or I'll get a fucking restraining order if I need to!' he yelled. Jessica just looked at him and frowned. He sighed and walked towards where she was stood, wrapping his arms round her waist. At this point, she felt her throat get tight and her eyes began to sting.

'I'll do whatever it takes. I'm not letting her come between us. I was a fucking idiot, and I shouldn't have been so naïve and stupid to answer her calls. As I said, somehow, she has a way of finding out what I'm doing and where I am anyway, but that's another issue. The only person I talk to about my plans is Sandra!' Something in Jessica started. *Was Sandra in contact with Lena? Could she be the link?*

'Jessica, I really, really don't want to lose you. I...well...I...' he paused and looked into her eyes. 'I'm really fucking hungry! Can we just eat that pizza before it goes cold, please?' he laughed and rested his chin on Jessica's head as he pulled her close. Despite being hurt and angry, she couldn't resist and collapsed into his embrace, half smiling. She felt safe with him, she trusted him, despite him skirting around the truth about Lena. She knew he meant well, and he'd just been taken advantage of and manipulated. He sighed and swayed slightly as he kept hold of her.

'And I think I love you...' he whispered. Jessica retreated slightly and looked at him, wiping her eyes with the back of her hand.

'You think?' she said, sniffing. He smiled and met her eyes.

'I love you,' he said clearly.

'I think I love you too...' Jessica shifted on her feet.

'You think?' he mocked her gently in return, making her smile. He pulled her even tighter, before leaning his face down to meet hers, running his fingers through her hair again as he kissed her firmly on the lips.

Later that night, they were lying in bed together, Jessica nestled into his shoulder, arm resting once again on his toned chest.

'So, all that stuff in my past...it really doesn't bother you?' Jessica asked.

'Not at all. Don't hate me for this, but if I knew all that before meeting you, I may have been a bit more apprehensive. I know that's an awful thing for me to say…sorry. But I got to know you and only found out about that after Googling.'

'You don't need to apologise, I'd be the same. I'm slightly horrified that you Googled me though. God knows what comes up when you search my name!' she laughed.

'Well, lots of photos of you with your ex to be honest, which just made me jealous, but there was nothing bad, even on the Daily Mail website!'

'Oh God,' Jessica laughed again, cringing.

'To say you've been through all that shit and overcome it, I think that's certainly something to shout about. Without sounding completely patronising, you should be super proud of yourself. I can only imagine the scrutiny you have to put up when you're in the public eye like you are.'

'I'm kind of used to it by now, sadly,' Jessica sighed. He curled his arm round her and squeezed her close, kissing her forehead as he did so.

EIGHTEEN

Monday came around quick after an eventful weekend and that morning, Dominic texted Jessica to say he was going to broach the topic of Lena with Sandra. Jessica had mentioned it in conversation that she was the one feeding information, but Dominic had brushed it off as ridiculous, despite agreeing that she was the only one he really opened up to and knew his diary inside out. She was his PA after all. At 9am on the dot, Dominic ambled towards his office, nodding, and greeting people he met along the way. He really liked Sandra and didn't want to upset her or accuse her of anything untoward, but the more he thought about it, the more he was beginning to doubt her. He was just going to ask her outright and go from there. He took the stairs instead of the lift, to try and burn off some of the anxiety he was feeling about broaching the topic. As he reached the office next to his, he stuck his head round the door to see Sandra sat there in her thin rimmed glasses, typing away at the computer.

'Good morning, Mr Pa...Dominic!' she beamed as she noticed him peering round.

'Good morning, Sandra, I wondered if you had five minutes for a quick chat?'

'Of course! Shall I come through to your office now?' she asked.

'Here is fine,' Dominic entered the room and shut the door

behind him.

'Sandra, I wanted to ask you something and I want you to be completely honest with me. It's going to sound crazy, and you'll have to forgive me, but I just need to know to put my mind at rest,' he said.

'Oh my, it sounds serious. I sent out those invoices like you asked!' Sandra became panicky, wondering what she'd done wrong.

'Thank you, it's not about the invoices though. I wondered if… have you…do you know a woman called Lena Beester?' From the glazed look of panic that took over Sandra's face, he knew instantly that it was true.

'I…I think I know the name, yes. She came in for a meeting the other day, didn't she?' Sandra stuttered.

'She did, she's been in a lot over the years actually…' Dominic nodded, wondering how to play this.

'Sandra, have you been giving her information as to my whereabouts when I was with Eloise and now Jessica?' he asked calmly. There was a moment of silence and Sandra hung her head, nodding.

'I'm so sorry Mr Paxton…' she whispered.

'Sandra…why?' he asked gently, genuinely confused, and hurt.

'She paid me for information on you, I'm so sorry! I really am! Honestly, I've never done anything like this in my life. It's just, it came at a time when I really needed the money. Martin had just divorced me, he kept the house, and I was really struggling. It was as if she knew that I was desperate for the cash,' Sandra said, sobbing.

'Oh Sandra,' Dominic sighed. 'Why didn't you tell me you were struggling? I could've helped, but instead you go behind my back and help Lena cause carnage in my personal life.' Sandra sobbed louder.

'Sandra, I'd have given you a raise, a bonus, a loan, anything you needed. You've been like my right arm since you started here. You know I'm going to have to let you go, don't you?' he said, and she nodded, sobbing.

'Look, we'll make a deal. You never speak to that manipulative, vengeful woman again and I'll give you a great reference and I'll make sure you get full pay for the next few months, until you can find something else. I won't say you were let go, I'll happily agree to go with the story that you left for progression or something. I'm gutted Sandra, I really am, but you've broken my trust...'

'I'm such an idiot, I know that now. I'll regret it for the rest of my life; you're the best boss I've ever had. Thank you for being so kind, even now,' Sandra sniffed. Dominic left the room and closed the door behind him once again; he could hear Sandra still sobbing and didn't want anyone else in the office to hear her. He felt like he'd just fired a family member; he felt dreadful but knew it had to be the way.

Later that morning, Sandra had packed up her desk and left. Dominic felt mentally exhausted and found his concentration drifting increasingly as the day went on. He texted Jessica to tell her she was right and explained that Lena had taken advantage of Sandra's financial and personal situation.

Fuuuuuck. So, you just let her go? X

Yup. I had to – I knew I wouldn't be able to trust her anymore. I'm genuinely gutted, it felt like I was sacking my grandmother! :(x

Rightly or wrongly, I feel sorry for her. Lena really is poisonous isn't she! x

She sure is! As I say, I didn't have a choice though. Can I come round tonight? In serious need of hug and Chinese food! X

Of course! Hug and Chinese food will be waiting for you. Love you. Xx

Love you too. Well done for figuring it all out, Sherlock. Xx

Dominic had to fight all his urges not to call Lena and give her a mouthful of profanities; as she was the real villain here. He'd found himself profusely apologising to Sandra and gave her a hug before she left the building. He assured her that he would keep to his promise of a good reference and full pay. He thought of her going back to her empty home and just felt more anger towards Lena. Unable to concentrate any more on the cases he was researching, he packed up his bag and made for Jessica's place.

NINETEEN

Over the next nine months, things were going from strength to strength with Jessica and Dominic's relationship. He'd had stern words with Lena, and she'd finally left him alone, finding herself a new boyfriend who was a Calvin Klein model. Jessica was simply happy she was out of the picture, as was Dominic. He had moved into Jessica's house, renting out his own place on Airbnb for a hefty sum, providing him with additional income that he didn't need. They'd had their first holiday together in Costa Rica, which was fantastic until the rag mags printed unflattering photos of Jessica's cellulite as she was sunbathing in her bikini. She'd met his parents several months ago and she'd finally agreed to let him meet her dad (over Facetime of course). She wasn't letting her brothers loose on him though; not just yet anyway. She'd properly introduced him to her friends at Christie's wedding too. He just slotted into her life perfectly and she into his; everything was just so easy. Granted, they were still very much in the honeymoon stage of the relationship, but even so, Jessica felt genuinely and utterly happy. She'd had a message from Lucy on behalf of her and Matt, saying that Matt had finally popped the question and they were getting married, so to save the date. Instead of the usual 'plus one' on the invite, Lucy and Matt had invited Dominic too. Jessica had been gushing about him on their chats and facetimes as he would amble round in the background, leaning in to say hello to them. They knew Jessica was absolutely besotted with him so if she was coming to their wedding, so was he. She'd even found herself writing some love songs about him – not the mushy type. They were still in her usual rock pop style but, a happy change from the songs she'd written about her struggles with addiction and depression. It was a pleasant change of pace, she thought. The songs that had been released proved successful with her fans too. The streaming figures were high, they were often played on the radio stations in both the US and UK, and she'd even booked some interviews and performances on some chat shows. Dominic had even attended a few with her, to show his support. The only thing that shook her slightly was when she performing her latest single, 'Eyes For You' on the Late Night show, it wasn't Dominic that kept springing to mind when she sang the words. She kept thinking back to her university days and the person she was then, thinking about how her life could've turned out if she hadn't moved to the States. It had taken her by surprise, and she felt guilty for even having these thoughts when she was so happy with Dominic. She brushed them off as just reminiscent. Backstage, after the performance, Dominic enveloped her in his arms.

'Incredible as always,' he said as he planted a kiss on her forehead. 'Also, you look fucking fantastic,' he muttered into her ear. 'Can't wait to get you home...' he winked, and she pretended to be appalled before laughing.

As promised, when they got home later that evening, they were barely in the house before they started ripping each other's clothes off. Lying together afterwards, Dominic was unusually quiet.

'Jessica, there's something I have to tell you...'
Oh God, what was happening? Jessica's mind raced to every possibility. *Had he been cheating? Had he met someone else? Was Lena back in the picture?*

'I've been offered a takeover at another firm for a rather handsome sum,' he began, adjusting his position.

'Wow, that's incredible!' Jessica gasped excitedly then stopped. 'Please tell me it's not at Lena's firm...' she said firmly and quickly.

'No, no, don't worry. But, it's in New Zealand...' he said bluntly. Jessica snorted with laughter.

'Ha. Ha.'

Except, Dominic wasn't laughing. He wasn't joking.

'Wh...' Jessica began but couldn't finish; unsure what to say.

'I know. It's insane and, really shit timing, but it's an incredible offer. Like, incredible. Life changing incredible. I couldn't turn it down.' Jessica's ears clocked onto the past tense he was using.

'You mean, you've already accepted it?' she asked.

'Mhmm,' he nodded.

'Were you even going to discuss it with me?' she suddenly felt a burn of anger in her chest.

'I thought you could come with me, it would be a new adventure for us both,' he said eagerly.

'What are you talking about? This should have been a discussion. You can't just accept a job on the other side of the world and expect me to be okay about it!' Jessica's blood was boiling; she was so angry with him, but she couldn't deny that most of the anger was stemming from the fact that she was hurt he hadn't mentioned it to her prior to this. He tried explaining how fantastic the job was and what it could mean for them (or him), but she couldn't listen any longer.

'I need to get out of here!' she said, jumping out of bed and throwing some clothes on.

'Jess, come back to bed and let's talk about this!'

'Talk about it? Dominic don't even...' Jessica couldn't finish her sentence. She was going to end up saying something she didn't mean. She stormed downstairs and then stopped halfway. Realistically, where was she going? It was almost midnight and she sure as hell wasn't going to drive out anywhere. Instead, she turned the outside lights on, lighting up her vast back yard. She curled up on the big comfy armchair and hugged her knees to her chest, trying to calm her breathing. She could see Dominic in the reflection of the glass.

'Rightly or wrongly, I just assumed you'd want to come with me. It's not to say it's forever, but this is something I really need to do.'

'Then you can do it by yourself,' Jessica snapped.

'Sorry?' Dominic was taken aback by her attitude.

'If it means that much to you, go by yourself. I'm not leaving. I have commitments here. If that means it's over between us, then fine, so be it.' Dominic's mouth fell open then quickly closed tightly shut as he clenched his jaw.

'You want to break up?' his voice trembled as his hands were fidgeting in and out of fists.

'Yep! I can't go with you, we won't last doing long distance so that's it. You do you and be selfish. I'll be equally as selfish and stay here.' she responded without looking at him. 'Selfish? You want to talk selfish? Jesus, Jessica what is going on?' Jessica knew she was being petty, and it was killing her to even think of her life without him, but she was going into defensive mode, trying to justify her anger and upset. All she wanted to do was hug him and never let him go. He scowled and marched back upstairs, slamming the bedroom door behind him. It suddenly dawned on Jessica that what Dominic was doing marked a significant resemblance to what she had done to Jake all those years ago. Was this karma? Was she being given a taste of her own medicine? Thinking about Jake, she typed in his name on Instagram and found his profile, going straight to his tagged photos. Sure enough, there were recent photos of him with his wife and children, out and about. His wife had a ginormous grin or some, then a ridiculous duck pout on others. Jake didn't look overly thrilled at having to pose for a photo. Jessica conceded that there was a substantial proportion of boyfriends and husbands who were forced repeatedly to pose for photos with their respective partners, and none looked particularly overjoyed about having to do so. She kept scrolling and the only photos where Jake had a genuine smile on his face were ones with his kids. It was obvious to anyone that he doted on them. Jessica couldn't help thinking how cute they looked, little mini versions of Jake. She heard the bedroom door open upstairs and quickly closed the app on her phone, pretending to gaze out the window. There was a clattering down the stairs and Jessica turned instinctively to see what the racket was. She was met with a fully dressed Dominic, dragging his suitcase down each step. She thought she was going to throw up as she stumbled to her feet. He cleared his throat.

'No point hanging around is there?' he said, his voice clearly shaky. His eyes looked bloodshot like when you're trying to fight off inevitable tears from falling.

'Dom, I didn't really mean it...please...' Jessica whispered, clutching his arm with her shaking hand.

'Nope, you were right. It wouldn't work and there's no point dragging it out for weeks or months, only to end up with the same result.' His voice sounded firm and assured but there was still a wobble in there. Tears began falling from Jessica's eyes and she didn't even try to stop them or wipe them away. They fell at speed down her cheeks and gathered on her jawline, before running down her neck and being absorbed by her T-shirt. Dominic found this hard to witness and tried to steel himself by clenching his jaw and inhaling deeply. All he wanted to do was hold her and tell her everything was going to be okay. But he couldn't, because it wasn't going to be okay. He was leaving and they were over.

'I really do wish you all the best, Jessica. Any guy would be lucky to have you and I'm already so jealous of the guy who ends up with you. I mean that. I...I love you so much. Goodbye.'

Jessica heaved and sobbed at the last part, watching him leave and begging him to stay. As the door closed, she collapsed back onto the armchair and left out sobs, dry heaves, wails, and moans. When Dominic got into his car, he punched the steering wheel and found himself sobbing. He'd never considered himself a crier, but he'd just lost the love of his life, and at what cost? For his career.

TWENTY

Six months later

The last six months had been a blur to Jessica. She'd spent the first two months refusing to see anyone, missing meetings, constantly crying, ignoring people's calls and worst of all, she'd been fighting urges to dabble with drugs again. This was the hardest part; she tried to remember everything she'd learnt during her stay at the rehab centre, but everything was becoming a haze. Dominic had called her the night before he flew out to New Zealand, and they'd chatted for nearly two hours. They found themselves reminiscing about happy times they'd shared and what they'd imagined their future to hold. This only made them both feel worse. They both agreed that they missed each other terribly, but they knew it was right to end things now. They also agreed that it would be best if they didn't talk as much, to allow them both the time and space to try to move on and get over each other. This was, of course, easier said than done. Jessica wasn't even sure she was missing Dominic anymore; it felt more than that. She'd been through breakups before and sure, they could be brutal, but as the weeks went by, she'd not thought about him. She wasn't even bothered about trying to social media stalk him. She just felt empty, numb, and fed up with life in general. She'd finally agreed to meet with her manager one afternoon but refused to leave the house – he had to come to her. When she opened the door for him, he visibly winced at the sight of her. It was fair to say, she looked like shit. There was no telling when the last time she washed her hair was, the dark circles under her eyes were getting blacker with each day. She had the persona of a shell that had been left behind by its inhabitant. They sat down on the couch, and he clapped his hands on his knees.

'Right, Jess, my love, no easy way to say this so I'll just come out with it. We think you need help. You're not doing well and that's completely fine and normal, but we can't sit and watch you self-destruct. We've made some calls, and we can get you into the same place you went to before if you'd like? Or we can arrange somewhere new? Whatever you'd prefer.' Jessica listened and despite struggling to fully understand the offerings, she appreciated that unlike her previous manager, Bill actually cared about her welfare. From the minute he took her on, he treated her like one of his daughters. She felt guilty that she'd let him down.

'I'm not doing drugs,' Jessica said. 'Don't get me wrong, I've definitely thought about it, but I haven't.'

'And that's great,' Bill nodded, seeming genuinely proud of her honesty, 'it really is, but we want to make sure we stop this in its tracks before you do end up going down that road. Is that fair to say?' Jessica nodded in agreement.

'Okay, so what do you think?'

'Same place, I guess' Jessica mumbled.

'Okay, I'm just going to make a call,' he got up, putting a reassuring hand on her shoulder. A few minutes later, he reappeared but this time he didn't sit, he knelt next to her and took her hands in his, clasping them tightly.

'I can take you over now if you'd like?' he said in a caring, fatherly manner.

'Okay,' Jessica whispered without hesitation. Less than an hour later, Jessica was being bundled into Bill's car with some essentials and they drove the familiar route to the centre. Jessica was in complete agreement that this was where she needed to be right now, but she felt a violent concoction of anger, guilt, frustration, and panic. Silent tears were falling from her sore eyes as she watched the buildings and trees fly by.

'I'm so proud of you,' Bill offered, making Jessica's eye scrunch up and causing more tears to tumble.

'I'm sorry,' she uttered in reply. She was having déjà vu; she'd been down this road before, quite literally.

'Hey now, don't you dare apologise. You're just going through a shit time, and you need some additional support. You've got nothing to be sorry for, you hear me? You'll fix yourself up like you did before and you'll be back to yourself in no time. There's no shame in asking for help, you know that better than anyone,' he pointed at her. She had a sudden urge to call her dad and tell him that she loved him.

'Bill, please will you call my dad and let him know? I don't want him to read it somewhere and worry.'

'Of course, I will. We'll take care of everything. You just focus on getting yourself better, okay? Is there anyone else you want me to call?' Jessica sat with the thought for a moment.

'Can you just let Dominic know, just so he doesn't see it anywhere too?'

'Of course, I will,' Bill smiled gently. When they arrived, Jessica was greeted in the same way as before by the same people as before. She'd hugged goodbye to Bill and thanked him. As he drove off, she could just see him wiping his eyes with a tissue. The tour of the centre was the same and she even recognised some of the other members of staff. Each one greeted her with a smile and a welcoming nod. Jessica had forgotten just how calming the atmosphere was here; she instantly felt her shoulders relax. It was explained to her that unlike 'first time guests,' it wouldn't be mandatory to attend certain sessions, instead she would be able to choose her own timetable, to an extent anyway. There would be more individual sessions to identify why she'd ended up back here. She was assured it was completely normal for people to return and very rarely were problems solved following the first stay. She was told that this time, whilst it may seem harder and more of a challenge, she would feel more determined and stronger to get through it. She was also well established on her medication so apparently this would help her to access the therapies from a better mindset from the get-go.

Just like last time, the first night was incredibly difficult; coming to the realisation of where she was and why she was here. However, it was true, she did feel a sudden determination to crack this and move on with her life. She unexpectedly found herself craving Dominic's embrace and longed for him, despite not feeling that way for months. She lay awake, thinking about what the rag mags would have to say, if anything at all. She thought of her dad, thinking *'here we go again'* when Bill contacted him to let him know. Her dad hadn't met Bill in person, but he knew that Bill looked out for his daughter as if Jessica was his own. Jessica thought about her brothers discussing with each other on the group chat how they'd been down this road before. She found herself putting words in their mouths – *'That sister of ours, what a mess!'* *'She's such an embarrassment to the family name;'* *'Mum and dad should never have adopted her.'* She knew full well they wouldn't be uttering words even remotely like that; they were equally as protective of her as her dad, if not more so.

Back in the UK, Jessica's dad saw the caller ID as his phone sprung into life. His heart in his mouth, he answered the call without delay.

'Bill? What's wrong? Is she okay?'

'It's fine, she's fine. She's gone back into the treatment centre but it's not like before. I promise you. She just needed a little 'boost' if you like, but we're not back at square one.'

'Is she back on drugs?'

'Nope. I mean, so she says but I believe her.'

'Okay, okay, that's good. So, what's happened?'

'Well, her and Dominic broke up a few months ago and...'

'What?' Jessica's dad interrupted.

'Ah, okay, sorry, I assumed she'd told you. Apologies. Yes, they called it quits out the blue to be honest. I think the basic gist was that he had to move to New Zealand for work and she didn't want to go with him. I believe it was a mutual decision. After that, she just became a bit of a recluse and it fed into other things. She didn't want to book any performances in, and she just kept talking about you all back home and her university days. She kept talking about how this was when she last felt genuinely happy. I've been keeping a close eye on her since the breakup, but we decided as a team that I'd convince her to get some help again. Fortunately, she didn't need much convincing; she was wise enough to realise it was what she needed. That's something she should be proud of,' Bill explained down the phone. Bill heard a long exhale of breath and found himself doing the same.

'Thank you, Bill, sincerely. I know how highly she thinks of you as a manager and a friend, thank you for looking after my little girl.' Finding himself welling up, Bill sniffed and took a moment to compose himself as he listened to Jessica's dad.

'We'll get her back again, don't you worry,' he managed. As they hung up, her dad started drafting out a message to the family group chat to let the boys know before they read anything online.

Just had a call from Jess' manager, Bill, all okay but she's back in treatment. She's fine and not using again but struggling again with some stuff. Her and Dominic broke up apparently?! News to me!! Wanted to let you all know and will let you know if/when I found out anything else. Dad xx

Unbeknownst to Jessica, all her brothers read the message, marking her dad's phone with two blue ticks to show this. Each of them typed out individual messages to her and hit send, knowing the messages would be waiting for her when she switched her phone on. Dominic had also received a message from Bill, explaining that situation and saying that Jessica just wanted him to know that it wasn't his fault she was back there. Despite this, Dominic found himself feeling guilty about moving away. He still loved her, and he genuinely believed that a part of him always would hold her close to his heart. He thanked Bill for letting him know and asked him to keep him updated. Scrolling through Twitter, Jake saw his ex-girlfriend's name trending on the home page. He clicked on it, assuming she'd released a new single or album, then found himself feeling dizzy and queasy. His eyes flew over the tweets from TMZ and random accounts posting a mixture of support and horrific abuse. Reports were pretty vague, but he got the gist that Jess was back in rehab and once again, all he wanted to do was see her. He messaged Tom.

Seen the news about Jess?

Ah shit. :/ I'll drop her a message for when she comes out. Bless her.

Gutted for her. Pass on my best wishes.

TWENTY ONE

Six months later

Jessica's four weeks at the centre ended and she truly felt like a different person as she walked out. She felt that half of this was purely down to the fact that she'd been catching up on weeks of lost sleep and eating a nutritious, balanced diet. She'd forgotten how tasty the food was at the centre; even suggesting they should branch out into delivery. She spent the next couple of months keeping her workload to a minimum but doing just enough to keep her busy and top up her pension. She'd spent copious amounts of time in the studio, writing and recording music that she'd written. Some of the tracks she wasn't even sure she wanted to release; it was simply a cathartic exercise for her. She didn't want to get too complacent, but everything was falling back into place and her team had been incredible. She would be forever grateful to Bill for everything he had done for her. Unfortunately, she had something to tell him...

It was unusual for Jessica to call a meeting with her team; she was usually the one being told where to go and at what time. She smiled and welcomed them all as they materialised, thanking them for coming in.

'It's all very cloak and dagger!' Bill said jokingly but with a degree of concern clearly in his face.

'Sorry,' Jessica laughed, 'there's something I've decided, that I need to tell you all. I've been debating when to tell you, but I kept chickening out and putting it off.' You could hear a pin drop in the room, each of them wondering what she was going to say.

'I'm moving back to the UK,' she said quickly, cutting through the silence. No-one said anything, they all just looked at each other and then back to her.

'Obviously, I'll fulfil any contracts and it's not like I'm going next week or anything, but I've made my decision and I've been really terrified of telling you all. You've all been incredible to me, and I wouldn't be where I am today without each one of you. It just feels like it's time for me to go home. I want to keep making music, but I can't keep up with this lifestyle and to be quite honest, I don't want to keep up with this lifestyle.' She paused for breath, but Bill raised his hand while his face remained still. It was impossible to tell whether he was angry or not and Jessica's breathing rate was rapidly increasing, waiting for him to speak.

'If I may?' Jessica nodded to let him speak.

'Firstly, why do you look like you're about to barf? Secondly, selfishly, I'm obviously gutted but I'm happy for you for reaching that decision on your own,' Bill said before abruptly stopping and bowing his head. Everyone was staring at him as he sniffed and cleared his throat, his head still bowed towards the table. Jessica rested a hand on his arm, and he lifted his head, nodding and smiling at her. He lay his hand on top of hers and winked at her. As he did so, a droplet formed in his tear duct. Bill was a large man in both height and width. He looked like he should be a security guard rather than a manager and didn't look like the type of man that would shed tears. Then again, Jessica thought, what does that man look like these days? She recalled seeing him wipe tears away as he drove off from the treatment centre that day.

'Urgh, what are you doing to me!' he laughed, wiping his eyes with the back of his hand, and clearing his throat again. Everyone else was still looking gobsmacked to see him in this way.

'Listen, if you've taught us anything, then it's to do what's right for you and do what makes you happy!'

'Here, here!' the others cheered, and Jessica felt her shoulders suddenly relax. She'd had sleepless nights, wondering how to break the news to Bill and the team. She discussed it with her girlfriends, explaining that the team had given her so much, she didn't want to let them down. Christie had assured her that every decision they made to do with her career, they had her best interests in mind. She reminded Jessica of her previous team who would actively sabotage her if it meant making more money.

'So, you're not quitting music?' Bill clapped his hands together.

'Well, no. You know how much I love writing,' Bill interrupted her.

'Well, why are we saying goodbye then? Why do we have to part ways?' he opened his previously clasped together hands, as if opening the question to the table. Jessica frowned.

'What do you mean? I'm moving back to the UK.'

'You never heard of the internet and airplanes?'

'Huh? But...you mean...really?' Jessica stuttered. Bill winked at her just like her dad used to do and everyone at the table clapped and cheered again.

'So that's settled then! You move back home, and we create a new contract for you. Ella, could you get working on that, please?' Bill gestured to his assistant, who nodded enthusiastically in response, grinning at Jessica. Back home, later, Jessica felt a concoction of relief, exhaustion, melancholy, and glee all in one weird cocktail in her mind.

As she delicately removed her make-up from the day, she felt sorrow about leaving her life here, but bliss at the thought of going back to her home comforts. Forget her family, she already knew the first thing she was going to do back in the UK was go to Tesco, buy some sliced bread and a jar of marmite. Marmite on toast for breakfast every day! She was mentally creating a food shopping list as she wiped mascara from her lashes. Getting in bed, she was scrolling through her social media when she felt a sudden urge to do a bit of cyber stalking. She typed in the name 'Dominic Paxton' and there he was. Clicking on his Instagram, she felt a sudden thud as her stomach dropped through the mattress she lay on. Firstly, she clicked on the photo of him with a gorgeous brunette, embracing each other with a stunning sunset behind them. The caption read, *'Reunited with my forever.'* Clicking the next picture of the black and white polaroid type photo, she read the caption underneath. *'Love wins,'* with a man, woman, and baby emoji. With the way her stomach dropped after seeing photos of Dominic and his (no longer) ex, she was waiting to feel sad. She touched her eyes but there were no tears. She felt weirdly okay about seeing her beloved ex with another woman, announcing they were expecting a baby together. She felt unexpectedly happy for him and not in the least bit spiteful, angry, or even jealous that he had reunited with his first love. Wow, that last bout of therapy really had done her wonders, she thought as she closed the app. She opened her messages and hit send on one to Henry.

Guess who is coming home...xxx

Football?x

Moron. You're dearest sister, of course!! Xxx

Awww, don't talk about yourself like that! My dearest sister isn't a moron! X

She sent back a punching fist emoji to her brother in response before the three dots showed Henry was typing.

Can't wait! Dad will be over the moon! Have you told him yet? Have you told the others? Why are you coming home? Are you okay? Has something happened? When are you leaving? Xx

Feeling slightly bamboozled but understanding of all the quick fire questions, she slowly answered them one by one, before saying goodnight and leaving it to him to tell their dad, so she didn't have to go through the same question and answer probe.

TWENTY TWO

Jessica had been back in England for about three months now and she was finally starting to get settled back into British life. It had rained consistently since her plane touched down at Heathrow, which wasn't much of a welcome, but it certainly felt like home. Despite her dad hinting not so subtly about a house for sale in the next village from him, Jessica found a stunning, recently renovated, five bedroom house in between Bournemouth and Poole. When they were younger, they'd go on family holidays down there and the area always held a special place in her heart. At university, her and Jake even spoke about how they'd save up to move down there. She never imagined she'd be able to afford a £2.7m house in the BH13 postcode though. It was quite different from the semi-detached holiday cottage lets they'd stayed in as kids. The house had been put up for sale by a Bournemouth football player after he signed with another club. The house was modern, but it had large wooden beams which remained, as a nod to its history. The garden was abundant with enormous trees of all varieties, towering high above thick, green bordering hedges. All the rain in recent weeks had given the garden a gorgeous bottle green glow. She'd put bird feeders out so she could sit and watch from behind the bi-folding doors. Granted, it was pigeons, seagulls and starlings that landed, nothing exotic but Jessica could sit there for hours watching them.

Usually, if an unrecognised number was calling, like everyone, Jessica would watch it ring, then Google the number to see who it was. This afternoon though, it was a mobile number which intrigued her enough to answer the call.

'Hello?' she sang cautiously.

'Hi, Jessica? It's Luke, Luke Jones.'

'Oh wow! Hey! How are you?' Jessica replied, in slight shock at hearing her old friend's voice. Luke was part of the 'SHU crew' - the group of friends at Sheffield Hallam University. He was the drummer in Jake's band.

'I hope you don't mind, but Tom gave me your number. I'm going to be cheeky here and ask you something. Please feel free to say no; I won't be offended but my thinking is that if I don't ask, I'll always wonder!' Jessica felt a feeling in her stomach that emulated that of little winged creatures flying around in there. God, he wasn't going to ask her out, was he? He was a close friend but nothing more. Plus, that would be so awkward, dating one of her and Jake's mutual friends.

'Go on...' she hesitated.

'I've recently opened a recording studio, and I'd love to have you on the books. Also, I may have written a song which I think would be perfect for you. What do you think? You up for meeting?' Luke garbled with apprehension clear in his voice. Jessica wasn't entirely sure what he was going to ask, but it certainly wasn't that. She felt relief that it wasn't a request for a date.

'Oh, ermm...' she faltered, 'I mean, I'd have to check with my management. You'd have to send over the song too, so we could get a feel for it,' she continued.

'Yeah, yeah, of course. I can get that sent over after this call. I hope it's not too presumptuous of me to ring. As I said, the worst you can say is no; I'd completely understand,' he said, still garbling. Jessica smiled as she began speaking.

'Listen, I would 100% love to work with you. You're incredibly talented, you're a good friend and I think it would be fabulous. I just have to check with my management, but it's got my vote.'

'Oh wow, cool. Thanks Jessica, really. That means a lot. You just let me know yeah? I'll get that track sent over now.'

She could tell from the tone of his voice that he was smiling too. If it was anyone else, Jessica would've politely turned them down, but she'd been witness to Luke's creation of his studio via his Instagram page that she followed. Based over in Leeds, he'd spent several months doing up an old studio, making it his own, working with upcoming, local artists on reduced rates to help get them started in the industry. She knew he dabbled with song writing but she was taken aback as she read the insightful, poetic lyrics he'd sent over. She hit play on the downloaded track and heard his hoarse voice singing along. He wasn't gifted with a good singing voice, that was clear, but quite often, when you had songs sent over, they'd often be sung by an out of tune voice. It was only really so you could get a feel for the song and the melody, but then turn it into your own version. There were quite often deals going on too, like bargaining; if you took their song, they'd pass your songs to others they had contact with. Jessica knew that simply by accepting to record in Luke's studio, he'd be happy to give her the song. Despite the lack of tune and pitch to poor Luke's voice, Jessica was really taken by the song. She knew in that moment that she wanted it; it had a really similar sound to her own catalogue of songs. It was a kind of heartbreak type song, but not the whining sort, a really soft type that she related to instantly and she knew others would too. She was sold, she just had to convince her management. She quickly texted Luke to say she loved the song, and she was on board but would speak to her management. Later that week, she'd arranged a Zoom call with her team and played the track for them. None of them seemed phased by the monotonous singing voice, with this being the norm, but Jessica could see a few nodding of heads and brains working away amongst her team. When the song came to a delicate piano end, Jessica looked around at her colleagues, raising her eyebrows.

'So...?' she asked. They all nodded and agreed the song was a good match. Not one person had any thoughts otherwise, which was a slight surprise. Jessica was half expecting a bit of a fight on her hands, but alas not. As the team went on to discuss logistics about recording and assigning tasks to each other, Jessica discreetly texted Luke with a bunch of thumbs up emojis and smiling faces. She got a text back a few minutes later with excited clapping hands emojis and hearts.

'So does that sound okay then, Jessica?' *Oops*, she hadn't been listening.

'Ah sorry, the connection went a bit weird, could you repeat that please?' *Ha. Perks of internet meetings in the modern age.*

'I was just saying, I'll arrange to fly over and check the place out, meet your guy, Luke, and we'll get a schedule set up,' her manager, Bill repeated.

'Oh cool, yeah that sounds great. I'll send you over his details,' Jessica grinned.

Less than a month later, Bill was expertly looking around the small studio in Leeds, asking Luke lots of technical questions, to which he expertly replied. Jessica just watched on, keeping everything crossed that Bill would approve. It was pretty much a 99% done deal but she knew that Bill was a stickler for details and would be assessing every minute aspect. This was why he was so successful as a manager; he could've sent over his PA to check out the place, but he like to get his hands dirty, so to speak. As Jessica sat, swivelling on a chair like a child waiting for their parent to stop talking to a friend, she saw the pair shake hands as Bill looked over to her and nodded his head.

'Eeee!' Jessica jumped up, hugging the both of them in turn.

TWENTY THREE

'Right, so we've got tracks 1,2,5,6 and 8 done and dusted. Beautiful rendition of 'Stolen Thoughts' by the way,' Luke said. This was the song he had written for her, and she'd loved recording it, accompanied by just a piano. It was a beautifully delicate track that allowed her to really test her vocal range to bring power to the song and make it her own. The songs that were left to record were some of the more personal ones she had written; they covered the topic of her bouts in rehab and the standard cliché heartbreak songs. She wasn't sure if it was because she was working with Luke, but as she was writing and recording the songs about lost loves, she expected to picture Dominic's face, but she didn't. Instead, she kept picturing Jake's face. She put it down to the fact that it was because she was working with Luke, their mutual friend, so it was simply reminding her of old times. As she was recording her track 'Leaving' she found herself welling up and having to take a short break. It really hit her how different her life could have been if she hadn't left for the States at such an early age. She managed to finish the rest of the recording by throwing all her emotions into the vocals, making it sound real and raw, which it felt like too. She was releasing a single from the new album in a few days and her team had been fielding many requests from radio stations and chat shows who were trying to secure a live performance. Jessica reluctantly agreed to do Good Morning America and The

Ellen Show. Kill two birds with one stone as they say. She also agreed to be a guest on the Radio 1 Breakfast show and Graham Norton's show, both of which she would perform on too. There was no need to even bring up the topic of a tour in any sense, as her team knew better than this by now. Country wide tours had proven to be a no-go area of stress that did nothing for Jessica's mental and physical health. Performing one off shows were more her forte. Thus, she agreed to be one of the main headliners at Leeds and Reading festival. Her team almost politely declined until she managed to jump in and explain how much it would be a dream come true. This took her team back somewhat, but she explained that her dad used to take the family to Leeds festival every year when they were younger. She used to love it, especially on those years where the heavens opened on Yorkshire and the site became a mud bath. She could still recall the rancid smell of stale beer in the tents and the porta-loos that always had queues of complaining festival-goers, even in the green campsite which was more for families. Once everything was booked and attendance was confirmed at the festival, Jessica rang her brother, Henry.

'Guess what!' she squealed.

'No idea!' he replied.

'I'm headlining Leeds fest!' she squealed again.

'I'm sorry, what?' Henry stuttered.

'You heard!'

'Holy shit! Have you told dad?'

'Not yet. I'm gonna tell him before the line-up is officially released,' Jessica said.

'Holy shit,' Henry repeated.

'I'm so proud of you! I assume this means VIP tickets for us all, yes?' Jessica laughed in response.

'Also, did I tell you who I'm currently in the recording studio with?'

'Adele?' Henry said.

'Not quite...' Jessica laughed, before telling him that Luke was handling the recording of her new album.

'Luke? Wow! No way! That's awesome. I didn't even know that's what he was doing these days.'

'Yep, got his own studio here in Leeds…' Jessica paused, waiting.

'Leeds? You mean you're there now?' he questioned.

'Mhm!' she responded cheerily.

'You are back in Yorkshire, and you didn't tell us. Right, Sunday lunch at dad's this weekend. Deal?'

'Deal,' Jessica smiled as she agreed. She hadn't told her family about her homecoming as she wanted to really focus on her album and not get distracted by anything. Just hours later, she already regretted telling Henry she'd go to their dad's on Sunday. They were working flat out to get this album done due to clashing schedules; meaning she would have to work over the weekend in the studio. She'd message Henry that evening to send her apologies.

'Right, so you want to try that last one again?' Luke said as he set everything up. Jessica complied and blasted out another vocal range to her song. It was a hard one to perform as it really tested her abilities; so, it was tiring trying to get it right. There were two key changes in the chorus alone. Fortunately, after another take, they were both happy with the result. Pausing for a cup of tea, Luke looked at Jessica with his head on a tilt, clearly wanting to ask her something but not knowing how to start.

'What?' she smiled, bemused.

'Sorry,' he laughed, 'just wondering who some of these songs are about…' he paused to sip his tea.

'By the look on your face, you don't really need to ask that,' Jessica said with a look of derision, causing him to pretend to be shocked.

'When was the last time you spoke to him?' he asked, sipping his tea again as he waited for her to answer.

'Umm, not properly for like ten years. We had a brief chat on Facebook several few years ago, where I wished him a Happy Birthday and we had a few stilted messages back and forth. Then, when news broke that I was in rehab the first time, he messaged me to wish me well.' Luke swirled the tea round in his cup and stared down at it.

'I don't think he ever got over you leaving,' he said.

'He's married with two kids. I think he's doing fine,' Jessica snorted.

'You think he loves her the same way? Not a chance,' Luke shook his head.

'Oh, give over, it's not some Hollywood movie!' Jessica laughed, but clutched her cup tightly at this revelation, whether it was true or not. Luke held his hands up in defeat.

'Fine, don't believe me, but despite the common misconception, guys do sometimes talk to each other!'

'Right, come on, let's crack on,' Jessica said, jumping up and heading back into the booth. Later that evening, she texted Henry to let him know she wouldn't be able to attend the Sunday lunch at their family home, expecting backlash. She was pleasantly surprised when he was understanding and simply made her promise, she'd attend one soon. With a date in the diary for the album release and the new single out in the world, Jessica was feeling a mixture of relief, excitement, and apprehension. After finishing the album, Jessica had headed back to base in Bournemouth before jetting off to the States for the chat show appearances. She'd got a few more appearances on assorted platforms to do in the UK, before she could settle and bask in her new album. Not wanting to sound too cliché, her writing and recording of the latest album felt as cathartic as ever. She'd been taking the time to look back at parts of her life that were really difficult and voicing those times on a page. Once the album was out for the world to hear, she felt instantly relaxed. Sales were doing well, all promo was done and dusted, meaning she could relax and take some time out. She found herself spending the evenings looking round on Airbnb for a getaway somewhere. She'd been scrolling through assorted properties along the South Coast of France when a message pinged up.

Hey, just wanted to say that the new album is great. You should be really proud. Luke's not stopped talking about it. Jake x

Jessica stared at the message for a while, frozen in shock. It was from Jake. It was a very nonchalant, platonic message but all she wanted to do was call him and tell him how much she missed him. Of course, she didn't do such a dramatic thing. Instead, she sent a simple reply.

Thank you! :)

She put her phone down, taking a deep breath, debating whether to get herself a drink. It wasn't really a debate she realised as she reached for bottle of gin. After flopping back down on the sofa with a pink gin and tonic, her phone buzzed again.

How are you? X

It seemed a conversation was beginning between the pair. Jake sat in bed, waiting for a reply. He could see that she'd read the message and willed for her to press send on something. Ever since Luke had shared in the group chat that he was recording with Jess, he'd been going back and forth on whether to contact her. He'd managed to hold off until he had a genuine reason – the album release. Luke would share pictures of the two of them in the studio and all Jake could do was reply with thumbs up in the chat. In reality, he had to stop himself getting in the car and driving up to Yorkshire. He instinctively locked the screen on his phone as his wife climbed into bed next to him.

Good thanks. You? X Kids keeping me busy haha. How did you end up working with Luke then? X

I'll bet! I've seen photos on Instagram by the way, ridiculously cute! Yeah, he rang me with an offer I couldn't refuse. Really pleased with how it all turned out and he was great to work with! Xxx

Oops. Jessica was so used to texting her girlfriends and ending the messages with masses of x's that she was on auto pilot.

He was chuffed to bits you agreed to work with him. :) So, are you living back in Yorkshire permanently? xxx

Ooh. Okay, she thought. The three x's in reply meant they hadn't gone unnoticed by him either.

Nah just here for recording. I'm living in Bournemouth now. Can you believe it?!

Just like you always wanted! :) I'm in Eastleigh, so not too far away.

Jake had to stop to rewrite his message after initially typing, *'Just what we always wanted.'* Realising that Jake lived relatively nearby, she decided there wasn't much else to say to him; nothing that was appropriate to send to a married father of two anyway. So, she didn't reply. She knew she'd see him in a few weeks anyway for Lucy and Matt's wedding, so she didn't want to use up too much of the stilted conversation topics before then. She needed to leave some of her mental conversational cue cards in her brain's reserve. After waiting twenty minutes for a reply, Jake accepted defeat and laid his phone to rest on the bedside table.

'What happened to our no phones in the bedroom rule?' his wife said.

'Sorry, just checking in on a friend,' he replied with a sigh.

TWENTY FOUR

Taking a deep breath, Jessica stepped one foot into the room. Everyone was standing around, deep in conversation with one another. She was just beginning to survey the room for signs of someone she knew when Matt came bounding over.

'Jess!' he exclaimed as he flung his arms round her without hesitation. She instantly relaxed in this unknown environment.

'Hey Matt. How are you?' she said as she returned his embrace.

'I am marrying the love of my life! I'm fantastic. How are you keeping kiddo? Long-time no see. Still can't quite believe you're actually here! I'm so pleased you could make it.'

'I wouldn't miss it for the world,' Jessica said, giving his arm a squeeze.

Despite it being clear he'd had a swig of something as Dutch courage for the day ahead, there was no doubt that he worshipped the ground that Lucy walked on. He always had done. They broke up briefly in second year of university for about a month, then realised they couldn't keep apart from each other. It was clear to everyone that they were soul mates. Everyone had said the same about Jessica and Jake too, but of course Lucy didn't run off to America, so they were always going to work out. It wasn't long before Matt's brother, who was best man, ushered him away to get into position ahead of Lucy's arrival. Everyone was beginning to take their seats in the beautiful grand hall. Clearly no expense was spared on the wedding. Then again, Lucy's family were certainly not short of money and with their only child getting married, they'd clearly thrown everything they own into it. Everyone seemed to be sitting in cliques and groups, so Jessica hung around near the back until the majority of folk were seated, before taking her place on a spare chair. The sounds of gentle piano, flutes and violins piped up from the back of the room. Wow, really no expense was spared for this, Jessica thought to herself. As everyone took to their feet, Lucy entered the room, followed by the enormous train of her ivory, lace dress. Her arm was looped into her dad's arm, and he looked proud as punch, beaming broadly as everyone turned to look at his daughter. The photographer was stood halfway down the aisle, clicking away in Lucy's direction. She looked stunning and to acknowledge this, a unanimous murmur of awe spread through the hall like a Mexican Wave as she walked by everyone. All eyes were on her. Jessica was dying to see Matt's reaction. Gazing towards the front to try and get a view of Matt, her body went cold, and she had to catch her breath. Of course, he was going to be here. She had known that, but it was nevertheless still a shock. Jessica ducked down as best as she could, trying to avoid the vision line of Jake.

The elderly man next to her took her arm and helped her upright. He whispered, 'She looks beautiful doesn't she. I almost went a bit light headed myself. You'll be okay in a minute. Just hold my arm for a bit.' Jessica smiled sweetly, not wanting to tell him that she was actually trying to hide from an ex-boyfriend. She tried to free her arm from his, but he just gripped it tighter.

Great.

Lucy and her dad were still only halfway up the aisle, but she was just passing the row of seats that Jake was sat on, so his head was turned just enough towards the front now, that Jessica could relax. She smiled again at the old man stood next to her before gesturing to him that she was fine, and he could let go of her arm. Fortunately, this time he did allow her freedom, as everyone took their seats. Lucy reached the front of the aisle, flashing an enormous grin as she stood face to face with Matt.

After they'd exchanged vows and rings, they undertook the obligatory kiss to seal the deal, which was met with an eruption of cheers and applause. They headed back down the aisle, arm in arm, as they smiled and waved at everyone, they met eyes with. Jessica had to admit, she felt a pang of jealousy at how in love they clearly were. Row by row, like a school assembly, everyone filtered out of the ball, some headed straight to the bar, others made a dash for the loos and the rest were herded into yet another grand hall. Thinking of the vast expense, Jessica couldn't help thinking that she wished Lucy's parents had adopted her. There was a ginormous board with a seating plan in the corner, with people swamping round it to see where they were sat. Jessica waited until the crowd dissipated somewhat, before having a look.

'Shit,' she murmured under her breath. Table 4 was labelled as *'SHU Crew!'* and there was her name, in between Tom and Ben. She wasn't surprised, it was the only thing that linked them all together, so of course they'd be sat together. Jessica had completely forgotten to let Lucy and Matt know that her and Dominic had broken up though. It never came up in conversation, even when they messaged her supportively after her second bout in treatment. To top it off, as part of the *'SHU Crew,'* Jake was seated directly opposite her.

After an hour or so of mingling, or in Jessica's case, avoiding, everyone was directed by the events manager to take their seats for the wedding breakfast. Not wanting to draw too much attention to herself, Jessica found the table and plonked herself down first, placing her clutch on what would've been Dominic's chair. She could see Tom and the others still fighting to see the seating plan. Tom managed to squeeze through and then called back to the others.

'Table four! SHU Crew!' As they were walking up, Jessica panicked and didn't know where to look so she just kept her eyes down, gulping down the urge to vomit from her increasingly dry mouth. Where was the wine when you needed it?

'Oh my god! Straight from the high life of LA, look who's here!' Tom's mocking voice pierced her panic.

'Who is it?' she heard a girl say. Jessica looked up at the wrong time, locking eyes with Jake. He froze and she could see him gulp something back, like she had just been fighting to do. He looked away briefly as he took his seat opposite her, then glanced back up at her. He couldn't believe she was sat here, less than a metre away from him. Her blonde hair was half up, half down with wavy curls falling near her face. She was wearing a stunning lilac dress which had straps that accentuated her neckline and chest, to the point where Jake found his eyes wandering South a little. He knew she'd been invited to the wedding but didn't even consider that she'd actually be able to make it. He'd been thinking about her nonstop since their brief exchange that night. He hadn't mentally prepared himself that he might actually see her today, let alone be sat opposite her. His thoughts were interrupted by an old man who had rested his hand on Jessica's shoulder.

'Are you okay now sweetheart?' the man asked Jessica, causing her to jump and turn. Before she could answer, the man addressed the rest of the table, 'This one had a funny do earlier!'

'Are you okay?' Jake asked a little too eagerly, concern on his face. His familiar voice hit Jessica in the chest. She hadn't heard that voice for ten years and she forgot how much she missed hearing it.

'I'm fine, really. It was nothing!' she said brightly, thanking the old man and shrugging off his hand from her bare shoulder. As he pottered off to his own table, Jessica adjusted in her seat and just as Jake parted his lips to speak, he was interrupted before he could begin.

'Oh my god! Hi! I still can't believe you went to university with this lot. Whenever you're on telly, I say to people *'She went to University with my husband!'* Harriet excitedly garbled as she rushed round the table towards Jessica. Harriet was Jake's wife.

Jessica only knew her name through her social media stalking, which she regularly did these days whilst sat on the loo. When else do you get a quiet moment to yourself? She didn't know if it was Harriet's excitable character or the fact she'd got her arm round Jake, that made Jessica instantly dislike her. She decided on the former this time, but knowing it was the latter in reality. Jessica sheepishly nodded along, not knowing just how much she actually knew.

'Yeah, we used to hang out all the time. We were a proper little gang.'

From the side eyes from Tom and smirks between Luke and Ben, she realised very quickly that Harriet had no idea about their past. It was probably better to remain that way and play along for the night. She suddenly realised everyone was staring at her as if waiting for a response.

Oops, what did I miss this time? Jessica thought.

'Sorry, I was away with the fairies there! What did you say?' she recovered.

Harriet's high pitched voice piped up again, 'I was just asking why you never really stayed in touch?'

Umm, because I broke your now husband's heart by essentially running away with the circus, Jessica thought, before reconsidering her response.

'Ah well, you know how it is, life just gets in the way, and you lose contact,' she settled on the vaguer answer, much to Jake's clear delight from the way his shoulders relaxed. Everyone took to their seats at the table ready for the meal and sure enough, on this round table, Jessica and Jake were forced to look directly at each other.

'Well, that was fun!' Tom whispered mockingly in her ear. All she could do in response was mumble a profanity back in his ear.

'Why is there a spare seat?' Harriet squawked before picking up the place card next to Jessica. 'Dominic,' she said with confusion. 'Who's Dominic? Never heard you mention that name before,' she looked at the rest of the table. Jessica had to pipe up.

'My boyfriend,' she said, noting that Jake rubbed the back of his neck, like he always did when he was uncomfortable. 'Ex-boyfriend, I mean,' Jessica clarified.

'Aww. He broke up with you before a wedding? That's awful!' Harriet exclaimed assumingly. Jessica didn't want her feeling sorry for her in the slightest so decided to correct Harriet, whether true or not.

'I actually broke up with him,' Jessica said before nodding to the waitress that yes, she would very much like some wine please. Everyone ate the food put in front of them in relative silence, bar the odd stilted conversation about what everyone had been up to since University, and Harriet moaning about the lack of vegan aspects to the wedding. Most interestingly to Jessica, apparently Jake was a vegan now; a far cry from his university days where KFC, tuna pasta and cheese toasties were weekly staples in his diet. The speeches were made in between the main course and dessert. Even Jessica found herself welling up at how Matt gushed over Lucy in his speech. His brother's best man speech was vastly different from the usual; there were no embarrassing stories about the groom or dirty tales to tell. He simply said how much he looked up to his eldest brother, reminiscing on life events they'd shared together, travelling they'd undertaken together and how Lucy just integrated into the family perfectly. Jessica thought about what her brother's would say at each other's weddings during the speeches. It would certainly be more akin to the usual idea of speeches – crude and verging on inappropriate! When things were being cleared away ahead of the evening do, Jessica circulated the room twice and then suddenly spotted familiar figures back near the bar. She set off in their direction excitedly. 'Hi you!' she said as she flung her arms around her older brother.

'Ah! There you are!' he responded, embracing Jessica back before her younger brother did the same. In a weirdly small world, they knew Matt from school, so they'd been invited to the evening do. Jessica instantly felt more comfortable now her brothers were here. Every time she saw them, she was reminded how long it had been since they last saw each other. 'So, have you been to see dad yet?' Henry asked her.

'Not yet! I'm stopping by on Tuesday for that family meal, but I'll probably drop in tomorrow to see him,' she replied, almost defensively. Their dad knew everyone would be in the area for the wedding, so he'd arranged a family get together. They did it once several years ago, with their dad announcing it a success and confirming it would be a yearly calendar item. Needless to say, they hadn't done it for three years. It wasn't long before Tom popped again. He had a particular habit for creeping around and appearing out of nowhere. Some may say like a phantom, Jessica said more like one of those fruit flies that just won't go away. However, Tom was Tom, and she wouldn't change him for the world, no matter how annoying he was. Her brother's band did quite a few shows with Tom and crew, plus with Jessica and Jake being together, they got to see quite a lot of each other.

'Hey man, how are you keeping? You've been travelling, haven't you?' Henry said, shaking hands with Tom.

'Yeah, I headed over to the States for a while, then made my way back to Vietnam and I've been working over there for the last nine months.' Tom's job as a data analyst kept him busy and he'd since started his own business a few years back, which presented him with countless opportunities to travel the world. Jessica was very much the odd one out in the group; everyone had *'normal'* jobs. Then there was her. Some people thought it was glamorous and exciting, which it definitely was some of the time, but she had to admit that it could be a little embarrassing at times, when people who didn't know her would ask, *'So what do you do for work?'* A question she loathed. She thought she really should be grateful for her success and yes, even the money that comes with it. She still always tried to evade the question though. After catching up with Henry and Billy for a while, it wasn't long before Tom had dragged Jessica back to the circle that included the two cackling twin witches. *Urgh, what an annoying cow*, she thought. She then made a mental note to slow down with the wine before she said any of this stuff out loud. Out of nowhere, a chorus burst forth and everyone turned towards the stage at the front of the hall. A rendition of The Lion King's 'Circle of Life' was being sung by a gospel choir. After being initially jealous at how fantastic the lead could sing, Jessica watched in awe and even pushed her way forward to get a better view. Matt had proposed to Lucy during the show's interval when they went to see it in London, hence this inclusion in the wedding. Jessica could think of nothing worse; being proposed to surrounded by groups of gawping strangers.

Her and Jake had had a weekend city break in London back at Uni. They managed to get one of those deals where you book a train, hotel, and a show for a discounted price. They spent the entire day Saturday exploring the sites, riding around on the tube, before spending the evening at the Lyceum Theatre, watching The Lion King themselves. This was after they'd got the tube to Covent Garden and trekked up the ridiculous number of steps back up to civilisation anyway.

As she stared on in absolute delight at the choir, she suddenly felt a familiar presence to her left. She looked up to see Jake had joined her to watch. He remained looking straight ahead, so Jessica followed suit. She could see Matt hugging Lucy from behind, swaying side to side with her. Jessica and Jake both continued to hold their gaze straight ahead as Jake delicately brushed his pinkie finger against hers. An electric current shot through Jessica's left arm, despite her thinking it was an accident as he was just stood too close to her. As the chorus continued and everyone was still stood agape at the enthusiastic choir on the stage, Jake stepped back slightly and interlaced his fingers with hers, holding her hand tightly in his. Again, neither of them spoke and their eyes didn't move from centre forward. Jessica gulped, realising that he'd stepped back to block any views from behind, hiding the fact that their hands were holding. He was married, of course, she reminded herself. The music ended and they unlocked their hands to applaud with everyone else. Without making eye contact or saying a word, Jake walked back towards the bar and ordered himself a shot of tequila. He didn't waste any time and threw it straight down his throat. Jessica watched as she saw the familiar reaction of the alcohol burning the throat; that universal face that everyone pulled after doing a shot. Composing himself, he walked back to join his wife and sister-in-law, putting his arm round Harriet. Jessica kept expecting him to turn around and confirm that did actually just happen and it wasn't her imagination. He remained with his back to her though, so she ordered herself a tequila shot and then another glass of wine which she nursed at the bar, playing with the stem with her fingers. The fingers that Jake had just played with.

The party continued into the night and as her feet were beginning to ache from being propped up at the bar, she decided to explore the grounds outside. She smiled as she walked past Tom and Henry, who were deep in conversation about something, looking highly suspicious.

'So, how's she doing?' Tom asked.

'I mean, she seems okay. I've not seen much of her since she's been back though. You probably know about as much as me,' Henry replied.

'Hmm…Luke was saying that when they were in the studio together, they were having quite long chats about stuff. He was trying to convince her that Jake still had feelings for her, but she was just brushing it off.'

'It's been ten years, they've grown into adults. How can they still have feelings for each other? I don't get it. They don't know each other anymore. Maybe it's like a fantasy thing?' Henry shrugged.

'I beg your pardon?' Tom laughed, a quizzical look on his face.

'No, hear me out. Like, because they ended so abruptly and they've never had closure, maybe it's like they almost need a night together to say goodbye?' Henry reasoned.

'Are you really trying to pimp your sister out to a married man?' Tom laughed again. Henry fake gagged and screwed up his face. 'You might be right, but I'm not so sure…' Tom said.

Outside, each tree glistened with fairy lights, sparkling away as the night sky loomed from above. Jessica could hear the gravel crunching under her heels as she ambled round, following the hedgerow. The further away she got, the fainter the sound of music and laughter became. She sat on an old wobbly bench, wondering if it may collapse, closing her eyes and inhaling the chilly night air.

'Christ Almighty!' she yelled as she opened her eyes to see Jake stood in front of her. 'You frightened the life out of me! Why didn't you make a noise?' Jessica gasped, catching her breath. Jake just did that half laugh he always did and mumbled an apology before sitting himself down next to her.

'What are you doing out here?' he asked.

'What are *you* doing out here?' Jessica retorted, a little more brashly than she meant to. 'I just wanted some air,' she added to soften her reply.

'*I* just wanted some air,' he mocked in return. They both then sat in silence for what seemed like ages. For the first few years after they broke up, Jessica always had this inexplicable belief that she would bump into Jake at some point, somewhere. Needless to say, as time went on that belief subsided. She knew he'd be at the wedding, but she thought ten years would be enough for her feelings to lessen. 'Jess, about what happened in there...' he stuttered.

'I won't say anything, don't worry. It was a spur of the moment thing, whatever. It's fine. Just forget it ever happened,' she reassured him. Another long silence. He took her hand in his and made eye contact with her. *God, his hazel eyes were beautiful,* she thought. *Why couldn't he have aged horribly? This was torture!*

'I don't want to forget it...' he whispered, as he made circles on the top of her hand with his middle finger. He then let go of Jessica's hand and delicately but deliberately stroked her cheek with his fingers, looking deep into her blue eyes. She felt the voltage strike again, this time throughout her whole body. He lifted her chin with his thumb and finger, then leant in. The electricity was absolutely ebbing through Jessica's veins as she waited for his lips to touch hers. But they never made it to their destination.

'What the hell is going on here?' A familiar screech pierced the silence of the night. *Uh-oh, it was the twin.* 'Jake, what the hell are you doing? Is this for real?' Her voice seemed to reach new heights of screeching. She had just seen her sister's husband try to kiss another woman, so you can't blame her, Jessica thought. Jake had already cast Jessica aside by this point.

'I...' he began.

'Save it for Harriet!' she yelled as she stormed off with Jake following quickly in tow, not looking back. By this point, Jessica decided she was most definitely ready for home. She texted her brothers to say she was leaving and trooped off towards the taxis that were waiting nearby, all lined up to take guests back to their hotels.

'There she is!' the familiar screech penetrated the night again. Jessica turned around, assuming the screech was referring to her as she was the only one in sight.

Fuck. It was the evil twins with a sheepish looking Jake. Tom had appeared from nowhere too as usual. He really should have made his career in magic. Jessica debated slipping off her heels and making a run for it towards the taxis but decided against it for assorted reasons. The primary reason being that she couldn't be bothered to run after a hefty wedding breakfast.

'Who do you think you are?' Harriet was marching towards her with a purpose and anger in her eyes. Like her sister, you can't blame her for her reaction, Jessica supposed.

'Hang on,' Jessica said, suddenly realising that she didn't initiate anything. She was innocent in this situation. She suddenly felt armed to stand her ground and fight her corner. It was clear that no-one else was going to.

'It wasn't her fault, Harriet!' Jake shouted after her. Okay, so maybe one person would fight her corner.

'Who do you think you are?' Harriet repeated, by now face to face with Jessica. She could see that the tears rolling down Harriet's cheeks were filled with anger. Jessica debated whether to say anything further to protest her innocence, but thought she'd let Harriet say her piece first. 'You think you can just go around stealing other people's husbands just because you're rich and famous?'

No.

'You think men will just throw themselves at your feet?'

Nope.

'You think that just because you and Jake were friends all those years ago that he'd magically be besotted with you?'

No.

'Maybe you were more than friends.' *Uh-oh. She was figuring it out.* 'Maybe you were both actually together. Even if you were, do you really think he would still have feelings for you after all this time?'

Maybe.

Jake shuffled his feet awkwardly, the sound of the gravel crunching awakening Harriet from her rant. She turned to look at him, then back to Jessica.

'You were together, weren't you?' she asked, knowing the answer.

'Yes,' Jessica said the words out loud, 'but it was over a decade ago. I've not seen him since then.' Suddenly a piercing volt of electricity was shooting through her again. Only this time it was from the fierce slap Harriet just greeted Jessica's left cheek with. *Ouch.* Jake suddenly sprang into action, whilst the other twin clapped and laughed mockingly.

'What the fuck are you doing? She's done nothing wrong, and you can't just go around slapping people!' Jake pulled her away from Jessica. 'Are you okay?' he asked, stupidly holding Jessica's face adoringly.

'Fine,' Jessica muttered, shrugging him off but trying desperately to hold back the tears forming in her eyes. She was still in somewhat shock, her cheek throbbing, and her eyes stinging. She had to hand it to Harriet, she had a bloody good right hook.

'You need to apologise to her right now!' Jake spat.

'Are you for real? I am not apologising to her!' Harriet argued.

'Jake, whatever, it's fine. She's just upset, just leave it,' Jessica managed to find her voice.

'In Jake's defence, he's been besotted with her for that decade, and I don't think you can fight feelings,' Tom helpfully piped up. Simultaneously, everyone turned around and stared at him. Jessica caught his eye, widened her own eyes, and raised an eyebrow at him, giving him a look of bemusement. He started to look sheepish and sauntered off. Harriet turned back to Jessica.

'Stay away from my husband. I don't want you dragging him into your drug habits and him ending up a nut-job crack head like you,' she said plainly. *And there we have it*, Jessica thought as she took the words on board. Jake stared at his wife, gobsmacked and jaw quite literally on the floor. Jessica took a deep inhale and found her voice again.

'One...' she began counting on her fingers, '...fuck you. Two, you have no idea what you're even talking about. Three, fuck you. Four, do you really think that's the worst I've been called? Five, FUCK YOU!' Jessica shouted before barging past and clambering into a taxi, deliberately elbowing Harriet in the right arm. Jessica remained stone faced as the taxi pulled away, fully aware everyone was still staring at her. As it pulled out onto the main road, she crumbled into her seat and felt silent tears falling down her flushed cheeks. The driver glanced in his rear view mirror but didn't say anything, instead choosing to turn the radio up. Jessica mentally thanked him for this.

TWENTY FIVE

'Hi dad!' Jessica lunged towards her father's open arms the next morning as he opened the door. There was something about a parent's hug. You instantly felt safe, wanted, accepted, loved, and protected. After the dramatics of last night, she truly needed it. She'd had a message from Jake apologising for both his and Harriet's behaviour. She'd had a few missed calls from him too.

'Sweetheart. It's been too bloody long!' her dad chuckled. He led her through the family kitchen and pulled out one of the bar stools for her. He was such a gentleman. Jessica's eyes wandered around the kitchen as her dad made a pot of tea. They landed on her favourite photo of the two of them. It was taken at Boscombe beach when she was 10 years old. They were pictured in the sea, in an action shot of splashing each other with water. Both had carefree grins plastered across their faces. She smiled as she reminisced about simpler times and then felt a burning in her throat and behind her eyes. She began to sob so heavily that her dad turned swiftly around in shock.

'Oh sweetheart! What's wrong? What's happened?'

'Everything is just shit!' she said, matter of fact. 'Have you relapsed?' he cautiously asked. This was always the first question Jessica was greeted with when she told people things weren't going well. You can't really blame them for jumping to that conclusion, Jessica thought.

'No, no. It's not that. I was at the wedding last night and Jake was there.'

'Ah.' Her father knew exactly what this meant.

'He's married, but he was saying all these things to me, and his wife found out. She went ape shit and...' at this point her work phone began to vibrate loudly against the sound of the marble effect worktop. It was her publicist. She never had good news. Jessica debated ignoring it, but her dad slid the phone towards her.

'Answer it. It might be important,' he said.

She sighed and swiped up to accept the call.

'Hey sweetie, just a heads up. Some British chick is claiming you've been having an affair with her husband. She's sent the story to all the rags and gossip mags.' Jessica felt numb but resigned. 'There are photos too. I'll send them you now.'

Within seconds, Jessica was greeted with staged photos of Harriet looking directly into the camera with a sad look on her face. Her sister stood behind her with her arms round her, showing support. Jessica was sure it looked like she was smirking at the camera, looking directly at her.

'Jesus! She didn't waste any time. It was only last night! Just let it run. I don't even care anymore.'

'So, it's true?' she pressed.

'No! Of course, it's not true!' Jessica barked in response, rubbing her brow. Her dad took this as a cue to step away, deciding to intensely focus on the washing up and pretending not to listen to the conversation.

'Sorry Jess. I can block it. It's just some silly bitch trying to get her five minutes of fame. She's probably only being paid about £100 for it. You know the type, I reckon the photos are done DIY too. They're too grainy for a pro.' Jessica couldn't help wondering if Jake knew about this. Part of her wanted to let it run so he could see for himself. Weighing up her options, she made her decision though.

'Okay. Block it, please,' Jessica said, somewhat defeated. They hung up and she picked up her personal phone, typing out a message to Jake.

Fairly sure you aren't aware of this...your wife and her sister have sold a story to the press. Jess.

Almost instantly, she got a reply back.

I know.

This took her aback and she made the decision not to reply; she wasn't sure how to take his response. *Was he cross? Was he okay that his wife had done this? Why hadn't he warned her?* She switched her phone off and looked at her dad. He didn't need to ask any questions, he just came round the counter, kissed her head, and held her in his arms. It wasn't long before he was cracking dad jokes and making her laugh.

'Things will sort out; I just know it,' he said. They spent the next hour chatting about everything from the weather, her dad's neighbours, what each brother had been getting up to and even the current music scene.

'I better get on; I've got a meeting at 3pm. I'll see you on Tuesday though,' Jessica said, referring to the family meal her dad had organised.

'A meeting on a Sunday?' her dad raised his eyebrow, curiously.

'I'm afraid so! As I say, I'll see you on Tuesday though,' she reasoned.

'I'm looking forward to it,' her dad said with a smile. He walked her to her car and did the usual parent thing, where they walk to the end of the drive and wave you off into the distance before you watch their lonely figure disappear out of view and feel a pang of sadness. It doesn't matter how much older you get, it always seems to hit the same nerve. Tuesday came round quicker than expected and she was actually looking forward to it. It was her birthday too and she'd not spent a birthday with family for years. Her family loved an excuse to dress up, but with it being a day time meal, Jessica decided to go casual and threw on a pair of skinny jeans and a loose fitting, comfy jumper. She decided on wavy hair that was half up, half down and minimal make-up. When she pulled up to the house at about 1:30pm, she had to slam the brakes on before she swung into the drive. *Why were there so many cars?* Her other brothers must have come back too, she thought. She expected it to just be her, Henry, Billy, and their dad. She had two other brothers, Ollie and Chris who were younger than her. She saw less of them than the other two, partly because they were still in different stages of their lives. Chris was living it up in London with his friends and Ollie was currently renovating a house in Warwick with his partner, Lisa, so this kept them busy. *Maybe they'd come up too?* She'd just assumed that not all would've been able to get time off work mid-week, so numbers at the meal would be limited.

Excitedly, she pulled up alongside a flashy Jaguar, which was definitely Henry's car. He was such a show off with his cars. Henry had always been very much the guy who drives past you with music blaring out and his tinted windows rolled down. The type that you'd just laugh at and assume he's compensating for something. Jessica would always knock on the door whenever she came home. Despite it being her family home, she'd not lived there for so long that it felt rude to just walk in unannounced. Her dad came to the door just as he did the other day and she had to say, he was looking very smart in his shirt and chinos.

'Hello again sweetheart. You look nice. Come on in,' he beckoned, before adding, 'there's no need for you to knock! How many times do I need to say?'

Jessica could hear voices in the kitchen and there seemed to be a lot more than she had expected. She reasoned that if her brother's had brought their respective partners along, that must be it.

'Here's the birthday girl!' her dad announced as they walked into the kitchen.

'Wahey!' Everyone cheered and clapped.

'The big 3-0!' a voice shouted. Jessica looked around the room and then back at her dad, before realising her mouth was hanging open. She abruptly closed it.

'What's all this?'

'Well sweetheart, we've not spent a birthday with you in ages and seen as it's a big one, we thought we'd have a little get together.'

'A *little* get together?' Jessica air-quoted, 'I thought it was just a cooked lunch!' Her dad laughed and handed her a glass of prosecco before pulling it back.

'Wait, is alcohol, okay? When you say you're sober I lose track what you're sober of.'

Classic dad, Jessica thought. 'Just cocaine! Drink is fine in moderation!' Jessica cheerfully replied before snatching the glass, taking a swig, and raising it in a cheers motion, winking at him. He chuckled, sharing Jessica's dark sense of humour. Whilst it wasn't something they thought of lightly, humour was most certainly their way of dealing with stuff. They'd been through so much pain and hurt together, they always got through everything with jokes and laughter. A lady who Jessica didn't recognise watched their exchange and looked appalled. Her dad explained later that she was some relation of her mum's, whom he didn't particularly like but felt he always had to invite to family events as she was the only left on her mum's side. Her dad's loyalty and love for her mum, even after she'd been gone for so long really did have to be admired. Drinks were flowing and despite expecting a nice, quiet family meal, Jessica had to admit that she was enjoying herself. Albeit feeling slightly under dressed as Chris' girlfriend, Lindsay, sauntered past in heeled boots and a cocktail dress. She looked fantastic though, Jessica noted, enviously.

'Happy Birthday you haggard old witch.'

'Tom!' Jessica turned around in shock. 'Why do you just appear out of nowhere? And what are you doing here?'

'Your brothers invited me!' he replied defensively. 'What are you wearing...?' He looked Jessica up and down, clearly judging her baggy jumper.

'I was told it was a family meal!' she argued, poking him in the ribs with her finger. There was suddenly a collective noise of appreciation from everyone in the room and confused, Jessica glanced round to see what was going on. Her eyes locked on to the couple near the doorway. *Why is my little brother holding a baby?* She thought as she stared at him.

'Ollie? What? Is that? Huh?' Jessica managed to stutter.

'Ava, this is your Auntie Jessica,' Ollie said with a beaming smile.

'I'm so confused!' Jessica spluttered, clapping her hands to her mouth as she tried to come to terms with the situation in front of her.

'Well, when two people love each other very much, they...' Ollie began.

'Shut up you clown!' Jessica laughed, taking Ava from him. 'Oh, my goodness, you are just the most beautiful!' she cooed. Angrily, she turned back to Ollie. 'Why didn't you tell me!' she demanded, making him laugh.

'We knew dad was organising this and we thought it would be a fun surprise. Sorry!' Ollie explained.

'Were you just hiding in there, waiting?' Jessica said, furrowing her brow.

'No, you fool, we were upstairs. She'd just woken up from a nap, so we were feeding her,' he chuckled.

'Tell me all about her!' Jessica gushed, besotted with this gorgeous, tiny baby in her arms.

'Well, her name is Ava Bethany Jessica Cooke. She was born in September weighing 8lbs 9oz.' Ollie's fiancée, Lisa said, putting emphasis on the middle names and smiling dotingly.

'I'm sorry, what?'

'You heard,' Ollie said in response to his sister. Bethany was their mum's name, so it was of course only right to honour her in this way, but Jessica too?

'Why...?' she asked, genuinely confused.

'Because, believe it or not sis, I think Ava is going to be so incredibly lucky to have you as not just an auntie, but a role model too. Also, Lisa has liked the name since she was a little girl, so it was partly that too,' he added laughing, to which Lisa rolled her eyes at him.

'Me, a role model? Christ. God help the girl if she looks up to me!' Jessica laughed. Jessica couldn't stop fussing over Ava. The gurgling little baby was making her so broody, and she spent the next half hour refusing to put her down. Ollie and Lisa seemed a little too happy that someone had taken her off their hands for a while. They seemed to be enjoying conversing with adults rather than cooing over their child. It was getting a bit loud in the kitchen and Ava was stirring, so Jessica took her into the garden for some fresh air to try and calm her. After a few bounces and sways, she was soon settled again and drifting off in her arms.

'You're a natural. It suits you,' a recognisable male voice said, causing Jessica to turn round with a start.

'Jake...What are you doing here?' she asked.

'Happy Birthday,' he simply replied, not answering Jessica's question. 'You weren't answering my calls and Tom said you'd be here.'

'Oh, okay,' she replied quietly, not apologising for ignoring his messages and calls.

'I instructed my solicitor to send divorce papers to Harriet,' Jake said, no emotion on his face.

'What?!' Jessica had to really focus not to drop Ava.

'Mhm,' Jake nodded, still emotionless. They both stood in silence for a while, Jessica's eyes flicking between Ava and the grass below. She couldn't quite bring herself to look at Jake.

'At least you don't have to pretend to be vegan anymore,' Jessica said with a side eye and a smirk, breaking the still, solemn mood.

'Only you would figure that out! 'How did you know?' Jake laughed.

'Are you joking? I saw you not so subtly scoffing sausage rolls and quiche at the wedding buffet!' Jessica chuckled. 'Did she *really* think you were vegan?'

'Believe me, if she knew she would've cut my balls off!'

'I think that would go against vegan rules...' Jessica pointed out. 'Also, you know my dad was a solicitor, he could've done you mates rates on the divorce...' she said, instantly regretting her supposed joke. Fortunately, Jake laughed as he shook his head in amusement. 'In all seriousness, I'm sorry, that's got to be rough,' she said.

'It's okay. We've not been good for a long time anyway. We've been living apart for the last six months,' Jake said, while playing with Ava's tiny hand.

'So, at the wedding...?' she hinted for an explanation, feeling a bit bamboozled by this revelation.

'Separated. Just putting on a show...' he raised his eyebrows before adding, 'her idea.'

'But if you were separated, why did she get so mad when she saw us together?' Jessica asked, bouncing Ava as she began to fuss again.

'I guess she always thought we might resolve our issues. That was never going to happen, with or without you in the picture,' he admitted. 'Jess, I...' he began again but they were interrupted. Her dad appeared at the doorway.

'There's my beautiful granddaughter! I'm going to steal her for a cuddle if you don't mind.' He took her and winked at Jake knowingly. Jake smiled back. That was weird, she thought. Maybe her dad didn't recognise him; it had been over 10 years since we were together. He probably just thought it was one of her brother's friends, she pondered. Just as she was thinking about the odd exchange, Jake placed his beer bottle on the table and got down on one knee.

'Jake? What the hell are you doing?' Jessica asked, suddenly feeling panicky.

'Jess, since you've been back, I cannot stop thinking about you. Even when you were away, I couldn't stop thinking about you. You always did have this weird effect on me even as a teenager. I don't know how you do it, but just one look at you and I absolutely melt inside. I'm in awe of how you've been through so much and come out the other side every time. You know I don't believe in that nonsense, but if this isn't fate then I don't know what is.' *Was he proposing? Was this really happening?*

Jessica tugged his shirt at the shoulder, 'Jake, get up. People are looking!'

He just smiled and continued, 'So, I'm still technically married…but I'm asking you to make me the happiest man in the world and go out with me?' She could hear various people were sniggering, watching from the bi-fold doors.

'Jake, get up!' she hissed again, feeling her cheeks flushing a shade of crimson.

'I won't get up until you give me an answer,' he smirked, knowing just how much this was torturing her with embarrassment.

'Go on love, he asked my permission and everything!' her dad shouted from across the garden. Jessica looked at Jake with her most vicious glare, trying to resist smiling.

'Okay, fine!' she murmured, reluctantly. He nodded then grinned and jumped up, grabbing his beer bottle. He then began waltzing back towards the house and leaving everyone, including Jessica, confused.

Noticing everyone's stares and very much enjoying their confusion, he shouted back, 'I'm a gentleman! I don't kiss until after the first date!' Still somewhat bemused and embarrassed about the whole debacle, Jessica ambled back over towards her family.

'That was the cheesiest thing I've ever seen…' Henry said. He had a point, Jessica agreed in her head.

'Did he really ask your permission for *that*?' Ollie asked their dad.

'That was the sweetest thing I've ever seen!' Lucy exclaimed, with Lindsay nodding enthusiastically in agreement. The men just rolled their eyes while the ladies gushed over the romantic gesture. Jessica looked around, flabbergasted, inclined to agree more with her brother's responses.

'So, he's just left now, has he?' she laughed, still bemused. Her dad smiled and pulled her in for a hug.

'He's a good one that one. Don't you let him go this time,' he muttered in her ear.

TWENTY SIX

When the day came around, Jessica actually felt more nervous about the date than she did going on stage or being on live television. It had taken various video calls to Lucy (and Tom) to decide on what to wear; trying to find the right balance of looking good but also not trying too hard. The final decision was a teal coloured, floaty A-line dress that really nipped her in at the waist, paired with a wedge heeled sandal. Assessing herself in the full length mirror, she suddenly felt a wave of self-consciousness. When her and Jake were last together, she was a lot slimmer. Granted, she was a teenager so hadn't exactly developed by that point, but even so. She shook her head to get those intrusive thoughts out her mind and applied a slick of nude lipstick to finish her make-up. She'd not long poured herself a small glass of white wine to calm her nerves, when the gate buzzer rang.

'Umm, hi, Jess? It's me, Jake?' She saw him awkwardly inspect the camera on the gate from inside his car.

'Hi! I'll open the gates now!' she replied through the phone, a little too excitedly. She heard the clanking of machinery from the gate at the end of the drive, the little camera showed Jake driving in and the gates closing behind him.

'Jeez, you've gone up in the world...' Jake's first words to her were as she greeted him at the door, locking up. She laughed, almost slightly embarrassed by the charade of the gate and the buzzer. Thank God he never saw her house in Los Angeles, she thought. Still, in this day and age, Jessica felt safe behind those gates. It gave her the privacy and peace of mind that she very much needed these days. Jake paused and took a step back to look her up and down before fixing his eyes onto hers, his face suddenly serious.

'You look incredible.'

'You don't look so bad yourself...' Jessica admired back, before letting herself into the passenger side of his car. In reality, she wanted to tell him how absolutely incredible he looked too. She was taken aback by him at the wedding, but he looked even better. Something which she hadn't thought possible.

'Fuck, I should've opened the car door for you! Sorry!' he said, seeming genuinely annoyed with himself for this plain faux pas.

'Not quite the gentleman you proclaim to be!' Jessica mocked, before reassuring him that it was fine, and she most definitely could manage to open and close a door without aid from the opposite sex.

'Sorry, I'm just a bit nervous and this place is insane!' he gestured to the gate as they pulled out and continued to ogle at the big houses as he drove. Jessica had gotten used to living in large complexes or gated communities when she moved to LA, and it just became the norm for her. She recalled Dominic's reaction to the grandness of her home. The whole gate access did feel a little bit over the top and pretentious now back in England.

'Remember how we always used to say we'd move down here?' Jake reminisced as he turned to check his blind spot before changing lanes on the dual carriageway. Jessica smiled and murmured an acknowledgement as she remained looking out the window. It wasn't long before she clocked where Jake was taking her. It had been a surprise, but knowing the roads well from family holidays, she knew he was headed for the acclaimed seafood restaurant on the front at Mudeford, boasting idyllic views out to sea. She had initially worried that he might be taking her to the Captain's Club in Christchurch, thinking that she would like it because of the 5* rating. She was even happier to figure out where they were headed.

When Jake had joined the Cooke family holidays, Jessica's dad would book them a table at the Noisy Lobster and drop them off for a little date night. Looking back, how tragic to be dropped off for a date, aged 18, by your parent. Nevertheless, the pair felt like grownups, being waited on by a professional looking waiter or waitress, topping up their wine glasses. Neither really liked wine at that age, but it made them feel grown up, sat sipping it as it burned their throats and caused them to pull a face.

'I hope this is okay...' he said nervously as he pulled into the car park near Avon Beach. Despite it being a weekday evening, families and couples were still strewn on the beach, some even braving the sea.

'I've got so many memories from down here,' Jessica said as they sat in the car looking out to sea.

'Same. I remember the first time I came here, with your family that summer. Remember? Your dad would drive us past the big houses at Sandbanks to point out where Harry Redknapp lived. They'll be people driving past your house now, saying *'Look kids, that's where Jessica Cooke lives!'*" Jessica made a noise to show she was cringing and shook her head.

Upon finishing their food, they both sat sipping the rest of a bottle of white, looking out to sea. It seemed Jake had become a bit of a connoisseur of wine, selecting a specific type from the wine menu, testing it, and approving it. It was a far cry from the 18 year old boy who pulled a face as the over-priced alcohol hit his taste buds. Jessica was simply happy it numbed her nerves and inhibitions so she could hold a conversation with the handsome man sat opposite her.

'So, you thoroughly enjoyed your vegan fish, did you?' Jessica nodded as a waiter cleared the empty plates for them.

'Oh! Miss, I'm so sorry, but the fish wasn't vegan!' the young waiter said. He couldn't have been more than University age, Jessica thought.

Jake smiled and shook his head as Jessica garbled, trying to explain it was a joke.

'Oh, I'm so sorry Miss. You had me worried for a second there. We have a gluten free menu, but not a vegan menu. Would you like to see the gluten free dessert menu?' he asked.

'Coeliac and vegan aren't quite the same thing...' Jessica began.

'I'm so sorry Miss. We don't do vegan food here,' he apologised, still clutching the empty plates.

Jessica widened her eyes at Jake, in a request for help.

'I think we're both a bit full for dessert. The food was absolutely beautiful. Can we just get the bill please?' Jake smiled at the young waiter.

'Bless him,' Jessica said, pulling an apologetic face. 'Let's give him a decent tip!' she giggled.

'But, to answer your question, never...again...' he groaned, rolling his eyes as he exhaled.

'Eating fish or being vegan?'

'Being vegan! Most miserable time of my life!' he laughed.

The young waiter returned with the check and Jake insisted on paying for everything, batting Jessica's hand away as she tried to grab it. She managed to get him to agree to let her leave a tip for the waiter; that would be her contribution to the meal.

'Let's go for a walk on the beach!' Jessica said eagerly as Jake helped her put her jacket on outside the restaurant. He glanced down at her shoes and met her eye with a mix of intrigue and humour.

'Obviously not with these on...' she rolled her eyes and began taking the wedges off.

'But your dress...' he pointed at the near floor length number.

'Hmmm...give me your belt,' Jessica demanded after a few seconds thought.

'Pardon?' he asked, and she repeated her request. He looked around, sighed, and handed her the belt from his waist, seemingly confused. She gathered up her dress and with a bit of folding up and tucking in, she was now fashioning a much shorter, knee length dress.

'Come on!' she beckoned, jumping over the low wall onto the sand. They walked with the sea on their right up until Highcliffe Beach before they realised how dark it was getting. The sound of the waves gently and rhythmically crashing was truly sublime. It was like one of those meditation apps you could play as you try to drift off to sleep.

'Wanna head back?' Jake asked and Jessica nodded in agreement as they both played out an overly dramatic U-turn to walk back the way they came.

'Argh! That's bloody freezing!' Jessica yelped as the arctic water lapped over her ankles, now she was walking with the sea on her left. Much to Jake's amusement, as she was hopping around and screaming, another wave came crashing in unbeknown to her, causing her to scream even louder.

'Come here!' Jake yelled as he tried to control his laughter.

'Jesus Christ!' Jessica laughed, trying to hide the fact that her feet felt like they'd been slapped by blocks of ice.

'Right, change of plan. Sit down,' he said, taking off his jacket and laying it on the sand for her to sit on.

'You don't need to do that...' she said, poking his jacket with her icy toe which was definitely a blue-ish white colour.

'I didn't think you'd want to ruin your dress,' he pointed out.

'Ah, sod that,' she plonked herself down on the sand next to his delicately placed jacket.

'Okay then,' he picked it up and sat beside her on the sand, before lifting her frozen feet onto the jacket and creating a warming blanket wrap for them. 'There we are,' he said proudly, admiring his handy work.

'I look like a deformed mermaid...' Jessica said, trying to lift her feet, only causing her to fall backwards into the cool sand. Her abs clearly weren't as strong as she thought they were. She laughed then sighed, rubbing her face trying to understand the absurdity that was happening. Jake went quiet and lay down beside her. Everything suddenly felt incredibly quiet and dark. She could see the stars starting to peek through the black blanket up above. She could still hear the sea lapping away, fortunately nowhere near her feet. The cool air smelt salty, with the distinctive faint smell of seaweed nearby.

'Jess, there's something I need to tell you...' Jake began. 'Do you remember that night at university when...' he stopped.

'When what?' Jessica pushed.

'When I thought you'd cheated on me?' he finished.

Jessica felt her body stiffen up; she'd not thought about that night in years. They'd reconciled the following day, but she still found it hard to get over and forget. She nodded.

'I haven't been completely honest with you,' he admitted as he lay still next to her on the sand. She didn't say anything, just waited for him to admit whatever he was going to admit.

Oh God, did he sleep with her? she thought, feeling an ache in her chest. Even after all these years, it hurt. She mentally prepared herself to hear the words out loud.

'It was Harriet,' he said.

Jessica froze, only able to blink. She managed to utter a word resembling 'what?' and inhaled the cold, salty air into her lungs. She wasn't quite sure how to feel.

'Was it still just a kiss?' she asked, and he sat up abruptly. She joined him but remained looking towards the black horizon in front.

'Yes. 100%' he said assuredly. Jessica's brain couldn't quite comprehend what she'd just heard. She wasn't angry or upset, she just felt weird. 'I... I'm not really sure what to say,' she confessed. 'Did you keep in touch with her afterwards or did you meet again years later?' she asked.

'I had to see her at university again, but neither of us really mentioned what happened. A few months after we graduated, she added me on Facebook. She messaged me asking what I was up to, and we just got talking really.'

Jessica nodded in response. 'Does she know who I am?'

'What do you mean?'

'Did she know I was your girlfriend at the time?'

'No. I mean, I don't think so. She's never mentioned it. Even after the wedding when she'd figured out that we had been a couple, I don't think she clocked it.'

'Can we leave it that way please? I don't want her thinking she won,' Jessica said, drawing circles in the sand with her thumb.

'Won?' he queried.

'Won *you*,' Jessica said, lying back down in the sand. Jake mimicked her action and lay back down too.

'She didn't win anything; she just got the remnants of a broken man who had a broken heart and was yearning for someone else.'

'How very poetic,' Jessica said mockingly, after a pause.

The sand grains next to her hand began to move slightly and she felt Jake's fingers brush her own, almost asking a question if he could get closer. She responded by lightly echoing his movements. He took this as approval and interlaced his fingers with hers. They were mimicking their actions from the wedding, only this time Jake was single, kind of. A dog barking nearby made Jessica jump and sit up with a start, dropping Jake's hand as she did so. She suddenly remembered her feet were tied together and quickly untied them, handing back the sandy, crumpled jacket. Jake stood up and held his hand out to help her get up.

'Still scared of dogs?' he asked. She smiled at the thought of him remembering something from so many years ago.

'Very much so! I want to make sure I can run fast if needs be!' she admitted, wiggling her toes.

'Come on, let's head back,' Jake said, this time offering his hand out. He interlocked her fingers with his as they set off back towards the car.

'Wait,' Jessica said and unhooked her fingers, leaving Jake looking confused. She jumped round to his other side, taking his right hand in her left. Realising he was still looking puzzled, she explained. 'Didn't want to get caught by the sea again.'

'Great, so I'll get wet and cold instead. Thank you,' Jake said bluntly. She smiled innocently at him in response. He just smiled and shook his head. Even though it was her idea to go for a walk on the beach, she was certainly feeling it in her calves now.

'Right, nearly there. Pop your shoes on,' Jake said, freeing her hand from his.

'My shoes…' Jessica muttered, looking around.

'You didn't…' Jake chuckled.

'Oh, for fuck sake!' she sighed; exasperated as she realised, she'd not picked her shoes up after they'd been sat on the beach.

'Do you want me to go back for them?' Jake offered kindly but Jessica shook her head, explaining it was fine, they weren't expensive. She did pull a face looking at the painful looking rough tarmac of the car park. She also noticed the smashed glass bottle. 'Right, only one thing for it. Fireman or piggy-back?' he said with his gorgeous half smile.

'I'll flatten you! I weigh a bit more than I used to!' Jessica hesitated.

'Give over. Decide or I'll decide for you,' he threatened jokingly.

'Piggy-back,' she said after a moment, sulking. She manoeuvred herself onto the low sea wall and Jake crouched down in front of her, allowing her to grab his shoulders and mount his back. She'd not been given a piggy-back since she was, well… probably a teenager and Jake had given her one. She hopped on as he instructed her to and he trotted off across the gravelly car park, weaving around to try to scare her, instead making her laugh, with an added snort laugh too. If she was in anyone else's company, she'd have been mortified but Jake used to always take the mickey out of her when she did that. Even now, he laughed out loud in response, snorting back to mock her. They arrived back at the car just a short distance away and he gently helped her down to a standing position before turning to face her. He cleared his throat and this time, looked straight into her eyes. It was Jessica who looked away and refused to make eye contact, instead looking at her feet which she was shuffling around. His hand lifted her chin, so she was now looking at him, however his eyes were looking towards her lips as he began to lean in, gently pushing her back into the side of the car. She could feel the warmth of his lips getting closer to hers before a flash out the corner of her eye caught her attention. She swiftly pushed him away and scanned round the car park.

'Sorry!' Jake seemed panic-stricken, 'It felt like the right moment.'

'No, no, it's not that. I thought I saw something, that's all.' Just as Jake was glancing around with her, his gaze settled on something, and his face went to steel.

'That's Harriet's car…'

'What? Where?' Jessica scanned the cars parked up in each of the bays. He pointed to the car parked over two spaces, where two women were blatantly trying to duck down in the front seats. Jake began storming over angrily, but the car sped off. Jessica considered it quite impressive actually, as the driver was still ducking down as she drove away.

'What the fuck is she playing at?' Jake shouted.

'I think she was taking photos…' Jessica said, confused.

'Probably going to try and sell them again,' he sniggered. Jessica's face dropped with realisation, which he instantly noticed. 'Hey, it's okay. I was joking; she wouldn't try that again.' He reassured her somewhat and she nodded but felt numb. She knew how this story was going to go. They got in the car, and he dropped her off back at her place. She wanted to be alone so opened the gates with her phone and made a quick escape from the car, shouting goodbye and shutting the door behind her. Jake knew not to follow her, instead watching to make sure she got inside safely, before driving back out the large iron gates. Driving back to Eastleigh took him longer than expected due to assorted overnight roadworks. The air in the car suddenly felt stale and stuffy, so he wound the window down, inhaling the cool nighttime air. There was something about the air at night that just felt fresher. He debated turning round and driving back to Jessica's to check in on her, but he recognised the look on her face as she jumped out the car. It was the same look he'd experienced many times throughout their university years. It was a look of *'Give me some space and I'll be fine in a bit.'* He got back, threw the keys indignantly onto the sideboard and tapped out a quick message to her.

I had a really nice evening. Thank you. Xx

He wasn't expecting a reply, so it was no surprise when his phone stayed silent the rest of the night. He spent the evening thinking how he could desperately persuade Harriet not to mess this up for him.

TWENTY SEVEN

The headlines and stories in the tabloids and gossip magazines were exactly as predicted. Jessica did wonder how her publicist didn't get wind of them this time, so she decided to call her. 'New man for Jessica?' 'Jessica breaks up a marriage!' 'Straight out of rehab and into the bed of a married man!'

'I'm so sorry!' her publicist answered the phone straight away. 'No-one called me!' she continued with a groan.

'No prizes for guessing who...' Jessica said as she went on to explain the situation in the car park and the fact that the photos were clearly taken on a bad zoom with a harsh flash.

'What a petty bitch!' her publicist said. 'She apparently approached the usual suspects and spun some dramatic story. Sadly, I imagine she got more than £100 for this one!' She went on to explain that it was best to just ride it out and ignore what the rags and online trolls were saying. She was right but it was certainly easier said than done. Jessica toyed with putting something on social media, professing her innocence then decided against it, choosing to follow her publicist's advice instead. If it was anyone else but Harriet, she would just ignore it and laugh it off. There were always stories about her that simply weren't true; they'd print anything if it was a slow news day. With that in mind, she picked up her phone and called Jake, firstly apologising for ignoring his calls for the last few days and then she listened to him apologise for Harriet's behaviour. This was becoming a bit of a habit, she thought.

'She fessed up,' he said straight out. 'She said she just let everything get on top of her, and her sister was encouraging her to follow us to see what we got up to. They emailed the photos and story over to all those gossip sites and apparently within the hour, they were calling her for quotes. She said she ranted it all out, so they had everything they needed, then regretted it instantly. She said she feels terrible, and she just let her emotions get the better of her.' It was almost as if he could sense Jessica's frowning. 'Not that it's an excuse...' he added, then went on to say that she'd already requested the piece be pulled.

'Too late,' Jessica said, matter of fact.

'I'm so sorry, I wish there was something I could do,' he said, with an irate tone to his voice. Hearing his anger at Harriet and his concern for Jessica, something in her brain flipped and she asked him bluntly to come over. He obliged and within the hour, he was pulling up outside the house.

'I'm sorry...' he offered again on behalf on his soon to be ex-wife.

'I don't care,' Jessica said with a firm smile before flaunting back into the house, leaving the door open for him to follow her. After a slight minute of confusion and hesitation, he followed and shut the door behind him. She was waiting for him in the hallway and taking his hand, she led him to the sofa, gently pushing him down before straddling him. She leant back slightly so she could look him in the eye. She ran her fingers through his dark hair. Last time she did that his hair was jet black, now it had flecks of grey throughout it. Jake held his hands on her waist, looking deep into her eyes. Less than a week ago, he could only dream of experiencing a moment like this with Jessica. Now it was actually happening, he didn't quite know what to do or how to feel.

'Are we okay?' he said as he fought every urge not to kiss her, instead sitting back to look at her.

'Mhm!' she nodded.

'Sure?' he checked, still feeling confused as to her sudden mood change.

'I promise,' she assured him. 'You're not together anymore, you weren't together at the wedding either. We both know we've done nothing wrong. I'm not going to let her mess this up,' she said assuredly.

'My sentiments exactly,' he said as he gently ran his hands up her back, slightly lifting her top up. His fingers gently grazed her waist, giving her goosebumps. Breaking eye contact, she leant forward, and their lips met. Just as things were starting to get more intense, Jake felt a buzzing coming from his pocket. *Come on, not now*! he thought. He briefly broke free of the kiss, yanked the phone out of his pocket and without looking to see who was calling, threw it down onto the rug. Jessica had waited so long for this moment, she felt like a giddy teenager. He held the bottom of her shirt and asked permission with his eyes, before lifting it up and throwing it on the floor, near his discarded phone. Jake's brain couldn't quite understand what was happening; he had waited ten years for this moment. As gently guided her shirt above her head, his breath caught in his throat as he watched her hair fall back onto her bare shoulders. He'd seen so many photos and videos of her over the last ten years, but he couldn't quite fathom just how beautiful she was. When they were at Uni, she was always a typical, beautiful British Rose type girl. Now she was beautiful, but sexy too. He felt movement in his trousers as she tugged his shirt above his head, adding it to the pile. Helping her to remove her jeans was interesting. There were some definite logistical manoeuvres taking place, but after they managed to resolve it, Jake moved Jessica's thong to one side. Exhaling, she collapsed into him. Trying his best to keep hold of her, he managed to slide his jeans down just enough. Jessica had concluded that sex was actually usually one of the most un-romantic, messiest debacles that humans partake in. This was different; she felt like they were in a film. She felt Jake pick up pace and he made it noticeably clear that he was finished. He exhaled loudly and stroked her face, before lifting her up and throwing her back down onto the sofa.

'Your turn now…' he said smirking. They both collapsed down onto the sofa together, side by side. Neither of them knew what to say so they just looked at each other and burst out laughing.

'I love you,' he said with a smile.

'I love you too,' Jessica replied without missing a beat, holding his hand. Despite not seeing each other for nearly a decade, they both truly felt like they knew each other. Sure, they'd changed physically and to an extent, mentally but the reality was, they were both the same besotted teenagers they were back at university. They sat on the sofa, semi-naked, snuggling up to each other under a blanket for over an hour to keep warm. Jake rested his chin on her head and played with her hair, twirling it round his finger repeatedly. This is all Jessica had been thinking about for years; to be back in his arms. He'd made it clear he felt the same too and Jessica felt warm inside thinking about their future. She was snapped out of her thoughts by the sound of Jake's phone vibrating again. Jessica used her foot to kick it closer to him as he bent forward to pick it up, it was obviously important.

'Jesus Christ,' he said, running his hand through his hair. Jessica had spotted that he'd got a fair few missed calls from Harriet. Just as he was letting out a sigh, it began to vibrate again.

'Harriet, what the hell is going on?' he said sternly as he accepted the call and held the phone to his ear. Jessica saw colour drain from his face and as he sat there half clothed, he suddenly looked really vulnerable. Jessica could sense something wasn't right, so she slipped her clothes back on and stood waiting for him to finish the call.

'Wait, slow down. What's happened? How? Where are you?' he stuttered. 'Okay, fine, I'll be there as soon as I can,' he finished before hanging up and looking to meet Jessica's eyes. 'I need to go… it's Harry, he's had an accident,' he said with a sudden urgency as he looked round for his shirt.

'Oh my god. What happened? Is he okay?' Jessica spluttered in the same way he did, just thirty seconds ago, her hand clasped to her mouth.

'I... I don't know. She said they're at the house,' he said, nearly filling up. He threw his shirt on and tracked down his shoes, slipping them on in a hurry, before stopping and taking Jessica's face in his hands. 'I'm sorry. I'll call you when I know more. In fact, come with me,' he suggested. Jessica almost laughed but managed to hold it in due to the seriousness of the situation.

'I don't think that's a clever idea. It's not the time for fireworks with your ex-wife. Go be with your kids and just let me know what's happening.'

'Okay. I love you,' he said before kissing her and making a dash for the door. Jessica looked round the room as she heard his car pulling out the drive and the gate closing behind him. She slumped back onto the sofa and switched the TV on, snuggling back under the blanket. She must have fallen asleep as when she woke up, the TV had switched itself off via the energy saving mode and the dark of the night was looming in through the window. She stretched with a yawn then hauled herself up to get some food. She looked at the clock and decided on ordering in rather than cooking something, as it was past 9pm. Within twenty minutes she was sat back under the blanket, munching on enormous slices of pizza. She hadn't realised just how hungry she was until she noticed she'd got just one slice left. She checked her phone and debated texting Jake to check how things were. She decided against it because as much as she wanted to know, his priorities were understandably elsewhere at the moment. He needed to focus on his family. She was quite sure he wouldn't be coming back tonight but she remained hopeful, so stayed up watching TV until midnight. At which point, she was struggling to keep her eyes open, so she accepted defeat and headed up to bed after having a quick shower.

TWENTY EIGHT

When she woke the next morning, she grabbed her phone and expected to see a text from Jake, but nothing. She opened up their chat and noticed that he hadn't been online since he left last night. Her stomach turned, wondering what on earth had happened to Harry. She didn't want to call him just in case Harriet was there and picked up, but she couldn't not message him at this point.

Hey, just checking in on you. Is Harry okay? Xxx

She waited a few minutes to see if she got anything back but once again accepted defeat. Jessica was well aware that she had no rights to receive constant updates, but she did think that due to the way he left, Jake would have at least messaged her to let her know all was well (or not). Her phone suddenly burst into life, the screen showing that Jake was calling her.

'Jake, hi, is everything okay? I was getting worried when I didn't hear from you. Is Harry okay? What happened?' she gabbled.

'Jess?' a familiar voice spoke.

'Hello?' she answered, confused, looking at the caller ID on the phone. Definitely Jake's number.

'Jess, it's Tom.' 'Tom? What are you doing with Jake's phone? What's going on? Is Harry okay?'

There was a brief pause and Tom stuttered, 'Harry? He's fine. Listen to me, Jess. Jake's been in an accident.' Feeling an enormous knot form in the pit of her stomach, Jessica clutched the kitchen worktop. She felt dizzy.

'What do you mean?' she managed.

'Jess, it's quite bad. They've put him in a coma to reduce swelling on his brain.' Jessica gasped for air but only managed a squeak instead. She listened to Tom give directions to the hospital and grabbed her car keys, ignoring his cautions to reconsider driving for public transport due to her being upset. With Harriet still living near Eastleigh, Jake had obviously managed to get as far as the M27, or near enough as he was currently in Southampton General Hospital ICU. It was only about an hour or so drive from Jessica's house on a good run. She was fortunate for relatively clear roads as she illegally broke the speed limit in the fast lane on the M27. She pulled into a space, which she wasn't entirely sure was a legitimate parking space but abandoned the car nevertheless in a space on the road before the two storey visitor car park. Some of the spaces around hers were labelled as being reserved for nurses only. Fines, towing, clamped, she didn't care. She just needed to see Jake. Jessica weaved her way round assorted medical staff, walking wounded and general public, winding through the corridor towards the ICU department. Everything suddenly went silent, and Jessica noticed everyone had disappeared. It felt like she'd just stepped out of reality and into some alternate universe where the human race was non-existent. She found her way towards a glowing box which read 'Reception' above it. She couldn't help noticing how it all looked very new and swish. *Was it even open? Was she in the right place?* A lonely looking figure sat behind the desk and looked at her over his glasses. 'Can I help you?' he asked with a kind smile.

'Hi, I'm looking for Jake Taylor. He's been in an accident, and I was told he was here?' she replied with a wobble in her voice, trying extremely hard not to cry.

'Let me have a look,' he said whilst tapping at a computer. 'Ah yes, so just off to the left here then straight ahead and you'll see a room off to your right,' he pointed vaguely, before realising Jessica hadn't paid attention to a word he'd just said. 'I'll show you, come with me, love.' He appeared out from his large glowing box and guided her through the corridor. They made it to the large, open plan style room and he gently knocked on the door before opening the handle and ushering her inside. He had explained that the room would usually have other patients in, but they were pretty '*q word*' at the moment so he was in there alone. Jessica had heard of this superstition amongst medical staff before. Apparently, the minute you say the word 'quiet,' things ramp up and it becomes a mayhem shift for them. Jessica stood still for a while in hesitation, while he looked at her wondering why she wasn't going in.

'Don't worry, love. I know it can be scary when you don't know what you're walking into. I can get one of the nurses to come and have a chat with you first?' he kindly offered, still holding the door ajar. Tom materialised at the door and threw his arms round Jessica, leading the receptionist to smile.

'It's okay, I'll take it from here,' Tom offered. Jessica mouthed a 'thank you' to the receptionist and offered a weak smile, before collapsing into Tom. 'Okay, now listen to me,' he said sternly, holding her shoulders. 'There's lots of tubes and all sorts of machines and shit, but the nurses have said he can probably hear us, so we need to talk to him and let him know we're here,' he explained, his voice breaking slightly. She held Tom's hand as she walked into the room, expecting to see Harriet at his bedside, instead she saw Jake's younger brother.

'Oh my god, Jess!' Patrick jumped up and embraced her. They pulled apart and Jessica realised she hadn't actually noticed Jake yet. At the same time her eyes darted over to him and took in the sight, her body seemed to collapse from under her and strange noises came from her mouth. Tom managed to catch and steady her, before comforting her as best he could.

'Remember what I said, they said to talk to him, okay? Maybe you should sit with him and let him know you're here,' Tom offered, rocking her in a hug. Jessica nodded and awkwardly took Patrick's seat. She stared for a while at Jake's battered and bruised face. He looked dreadful. Every shade of purple and red was spread across one side of his face. All she could hear now was the rhythmic beeps of assorted machines that were attached to him. She lifted his hand, so it sat in hers, then lay her other hand on the top. His felt so lifeless and heavy.

'Jake...' she started and filled up. She took a breath and tried again. 'Jake, it's Jessica. I'm here,' she began sobbing, 'Please wake up! Please open your eyes!' she begged through loud heaves. Patrick and Tom looked at each other, filled with emotion themselves and nodded, before announcing they would go get some coffees for them all. Jessica leant down so she was resting her chin on Jake's arm. 'Please Jake, please wake up. I love you. I can't lose you now, I've only just got you back,' she wiped her eyes before the tears could fall onto his motionless arm. Once Jessica had grasped that even if he could hear her, it wasn't as easy as him just opening his eyes as if he was asleep, she sat silently with him, not letting go of his hand. Tom reappeared but without Patrick, handing her a black coffee in a putrid coloured, small plastic cup. The thought of trying to digest anything at the moment was enough to make her heave, so she politely thanked Tom and put the cup on the side table.

'His mum and dad have just arrived,' Tom told her. 'And Harriet too,' he added as if less important.

'Fuck, I should go,' Jessica panicked, wiping her tears as she jumped up. Tom placed his hands on her shoulders and pushed her back down into her chair.

'You're not going anywhere,' he instructed. She didn't have the energy to resist. The door flung open and the familiar, if not slightly older, faces of Mr and Mrs Taylor appeared, closely followed by Harriet.

'Oh, my baby!' Jake's mum cried out, rushing to the other side of the bed. Jessica didn't need to look up, she could feel Harriet's eyes burning on her. She saw Jake's dad mutter something to Patrick, who nodded in response, whilst Jessica became suddenly aware that Harriet's presence was now right behind her.

'Do you mind? I'd like to sit with my husband, please?' she firmly asked. Although, Jessica knew it wasn't really a question, more of a statement of intent. Jake's mum, Julie looked up and clocked Jessica's face before gasping.

'Oh my God, Jessica! Sweetheart, what are you doing here? Come here!' she beckoned Jessica round to the other side of the bed and embraced her, while Harriet planted herself firmly into the chair Jessica was obviously just keeping warm for her. Julie looked across at her husband, David and requested he go find another chair for Jessica.

'No, honestly, I'm fine. Please!' she begged David not to leave.

'Nonsense!' Julie protested and David knew better than to ignore an order from his wife of forty years. He came back in with another chair and planted it next to Julie, despite Jessica offering desperately for him to take a seat instead. Mainly, because she didn't want to be sat directly opposite Harriet. Shuffling in the chair, feeling increasingly uncomfortable in this situation, Jessica felt Julie's arm round her. As she did this, Jessica heard Harriet inhale deeply through her nose and just to match Harriet's pettiness, she rested her head lightly on Julie's shoulder. Jessica then suddenly felt guilty, knowing Harriet had a poorly husband (ex-husband) and a poorly baby too. It wasn't the time for pettiness. She dropped her arm from Julie and addressed Harriet directly.

'How's Harry?' she sensitively asked, with genuine sympathy and concern.

'He's fine,' she curtly responded, and Jessica nodded. Tom muttered something to Patrick who looked back quizzically at him.

'Hey, Jess would you mind helping me with some drinks for my folks?' Patrick asked. Grateful for an excuse to take a breather from this increasingly unpleasant situation, Jessica rather too keenly jumped at the chance. The pair ambled slowly down the corridor to the coffee machine and Patrick casually asked, 'Why do you keep asking how Harry is?'

'Oh, well, I just wanted to be sure he was okay. When Jake left, he seemed pretty concerned,' Jessica offered as response.

'Harry and Joseph have been staying with me and Izzy the past few days. He's fine.' he said before stopping. 'Jess?' he looked quizzical.

'But Harriet said...' she began. *She wouldn't lie,* Jessica thought. *Or would she? But why?* Patrick pulled a face and swiftly turned back in the direction of the room. 'What about the coffees?' Jessica shouted, throwing her arms up. Receiving no response, she abandoned the coffee machine and picked up to match his pace, almost at a jog now.

'Harriet?' he pushed through the door, 'Why did you tell Jake there was something wrong with Harry? He's been at ours since Saturday,' Patrick demanded. 'You dropped him off,' he continued, face like stone. Jessica knew instantly that she'd lied, just by the horrified look on her face and the fact she was speechless, her mouth just gaping open and closed, like a fish at feeding time. Everyone looked at each other with confusion and Jessica felt a sudden burst of energy and anger.

'He was driving from mine to get to yours! He'll have been speeding along and crashed because he was trying to get to you!' Jessica shouted. Harriet obviously got the same burst of energy and anger that Jessica did.

'If he was at home to begin with, I wouldn't have had to call him back! But oh no, you come flouncing back and think you can just steal him back because of who you are!' she spat back.

'What the hell are you talking about? He's waiting for you to sign off on divorce papers! That happened long before I came back on the scene! Did you really use your kids to try and lure him back? You actually pretended your kid had had an accident? What the fuck is wrong with you?' Jessica shouted even louder. She felt her throat burning and her eyes stinging. It felt like a fire was slowly eating her insides.

'I didn't tell him anything was wrong with Harry! Do you really think I would fake my own child being injured just for attention? You psycho druggy! I wish it was you in that accident rather than him!' Harriet snapped, jumping up to stand in front of Jessica, knocking the chair into Patrick as she did so.

'Me too!' Jessica snapped back, tears rolling down her face.

'You are actually vile,' Patrick added to Harriet, pushing the chair back, off his left foot.

'I...' Jessica began, before David raised his hands to the room to silence everyone.

'I don't think this is the time or the place to be doing this, do you?' he said softly. Jessica nodded in agreement and apologised, feeling embarrassed for causing a scene. She grabbed her bag and made for the door. She wiped her eyes roughly with the back of her hand, making her wince as they stung from the hand sanitiser gel she'd used before entering the room.

As she reached the door, Jessica heard David say, 'I didn't mean you needed to leave, Jessica. Please, he'd want you here.' She didn't want to look back; she just waved over her shoulder and crumbled outside the door into floods of tears. She was fully aware everyone would be able to hear her, but she didn't care anymore. The door creaked open, and Tom slipped out, slumping down next to her. He didn't say anything, just rested his head on her shoulder and put an arm round her as a sign of support.

'I still can't believe she would lie about her child being injured...' Jessica shook her head as her and Tom stood by the vending machine in the corridor. They'd hauled themselves up from the floor and Tom decided he was hungry, so they'd made a B-line for the snacks. Jessica still didn't feel up to eating anything but knew she needed to so reluctantly opted for some relatively plain, ready salted crisps.

'Really? I can,' Tom replied with a mouthful of chocolate.

'I don't know, it just seems a really low thing to do. Would a mother really do that? She swears blind she didn't say anything of the sort. You know she sold stories about me to the press too?'

Jessica added, suddenly remembering.

'I mean, I'm not surprised, but what a bitch,' Tom said. They were interrupted by Patrick racing towards them, looking anxious. Something was wrong. Jessica felt the ready salted crisps gurgling in her stomach, ready to come back up.

'There you are! Jess, he's asking for you. Come on, hurry up!' he spluttered, already heading back from where he came from, urging the pair to follow him.

Asking for her? Did this mean he was awake?

Arriving back in the room, they were met with the sight of Harriet stood over Jake, stroking his forehead, and repeatedly saying, 'Darling, I'm here. Don't worry, I'm here.' He was also surrounded by nurses who were fiddling around with machines. Jessica heard mumbling from Jake's lips as his eyes remained closed. She tried to get her ear in to figure out what he was trying to say, then clear as day, if not a bit husky and rattly, she heard him.

'I want my wife! Where's Jess?' Every muscle in Jessica's body froze and her eyes were locked with Harriet's steely glare. They both stood in silence, not really knowing what to do.

Starting to back up towards the door, Jessica could hear Harriet repeating, 'I'm here, I'm here.' She fell down onto the rigid plastic seats in the corridor and put her head in her hands. She heard footsteps then felt a hand on her shoulder, from the presence that had taken a seat next to her. She glanced at the shoes and didn't recognise them.

'You know he's always loved you, don't you,' Julie said quietly. Jessica looked up, realising who it was sitting next to her.

'I'm sorry I ran off,' she whispered through tears, wiping her eyes with her sleeve. Her eyes felt raw as the rough material contacted the delicate skin.

'Sweetheart, you know he meant you, don't you? Albeit referring to you as his wife...wishful thinking in his mind probably,' Julie joked with a small laugh. Jessica shrugged and examined her nails suddenly feeling awkward.

'But Harriet was there...' she started before Julie cut her off.

'Oh please, she's just trying to make a point. Goodness knows what she's playing at. We all know that she's been playing havoc with the divorce. I mean it Jessica, he wants you in there. Please, don't leave him in there,' she pleaded. Jessica nodded guiltily and took the hand his mum offered as they stood up, following her back towards the room. Julie ushered her towards Jake, who was now back looking peacefully asleep again, his mouth slightly open. When they were younger, Jessica used to mock him for snoring with his mouth wide open. He'd never believe her and always swore blind that he didn't snore; until one night when Jessica recorded it on her phone. With everyone's eyes on her, Jessica leant forward and gently kissed his forehead, being cautious not to kiss anywhere that was bruised or swollen. Taking a seat again and taking his hand in hers, Harriet then dropped his other hand dramatically and sighed loudly.

'You win,' she sneered.

'I don't think anyone is winning in this situation,' Jessica sniffed.

'We've got kids together, just remember that when you think you've got him all to yourself,' she hissed under her breath. Jessica fought hard to ignore her and remained solely focused on Jake.

'Maybe you should go collect said kids from Izzy,' Patrick suggested to Harriet. 'Might be nice to check in on them, you know in case one of them has been injured,' he said snidely.

'Patrick,' his dad said sternly as a signal for him to stop making the point he was trying to make. Harriet picked up her bag and coat, then made her exit, refusing to acknowledge anyone as she did so.

TWENTY NINE

Jessica spent the night alone, apart from Jake, curled up in a massive chair in the ICU room after everyone had made the decision to go home for some rest. There were still no other patients in the large room with Jake, but Jessica was woken up at about 7am by the sound of someone in the room. A nurse was looking at some of the machines and making notes as she did so. Noticing Jessica stirring, she looked over and offered her a smile with an apology for waking her.

'Is he going to be okay?' Jessica asked, skipping any pleasantries.

'If you'd have asked me that yesterday I would've said I really couldn't be sure, but his vital signs are looking good and he's responding well,' she smiled. 'His breathing is stable since we removed the additional oxygen and as you know, his voice is still there!' she smiled, referring to his brief outburst yesterday. 'We're taking him for a scan again shortly, so we'll have a better idea then. He is still extremely ill though; he's taken a real battering,' she finished.

'Yesterday, he seemed to wake up. When he was talking. It was like he was awake, then he went to sleep again. What was that about? Also, he seemed confused in what he was saying,' Jessica stuttered. The nurse smiled kindly and nodded knowingly as Jessica was talking.

'That's really common. Once patients are easily breathing on their own, they will often be stirred by something and start talking. It's just their brain waking up and trying to come to terms with everything that's happened. A bit like a kind of reset button has been pushed. It's only natural that he'd be a bit confused, he had a nasty bump to the head. Don't worry, it's all completely normal. He is doing really well. We took precautions when he came in due to the bleed on his brain but he's bravely fighting back,' she smiled before putting the charts back into the holder at the end of the bed and leaving the room. Half an hour later, hospital porters helped wheel Jake's bed for a scan. Jessica sat waiting for what seemed like hours and jumped every time she heard the doors open. Julie and David had arrived, then Patrick and Izzy, then Tom. Thankfully, Harriet was nowhere to be seen. The group had been herded into a private side room to wait for Jake and it wasn't long afterwards that the door was held open, while the same porters pushed Jake's bed back into the room. He remained asleep, looking peaceful and undisturbed.

One of the nurses hung back briefly once the bed was wheeled back into position, then went ahead to address everyone, 'I'm just going to get the doctor to come and have a chat with you all.'

With that, Julie crumbled into David, 'It's bad news, I know it! Oh god!' she spluttered, beginning to howl like an animal. Jessica sat solemnly staring at Jake, silently urging him to move or do something to show them he was okay. *The nurse earlier had told her he was doing well, how could she be so wrong?* Jessica mused. A knock on the door broke her racing thoughts and the doctor came in, greeting everyone with one of those half nod acknowledgements.

'Doctor, please just tell me. Is my son going to die?' Julie begged for an answer. The Doctor looked taken aback.

'Far from it!' he said cheerily, which stopped Julie in her tracks, minus a few sniffs. He continued, 'The scan showed that the

IV steroids have worked a treat; the bleed has stopped and it's showing very promising signs of the pressure on his brain being relieved. It's still early days of course, but all appears to be going well for his recovery.' Julie let out an enormous sigh of relief on behalf of the rest of the group and allowed David to hug her tightly. Patrick hugged Izzy. Jessica hugged her knees. Noticing this, Patrick gently let go of Izzy and came to squat in front of Jessica; taking her hands to reassure me that everything was going to be okay, despite her concerns. Izzy sat down next to her too and put her arm round her, giving her a tight squeeze. Jessica barely knew Izzy, but she thought it really was a testament to how much the Taylor family considered Jessica as extended family too.

Patrick stood up and asked his parents, 'Do they actually know what happened? How did he crash the car?' Julie explained that the police had said dash cam footage showed a car was speeding past a lorry on the A31, coming up to the M27 junction. The car tried to pull back in but lost control and ended up spinning towards Jake's car on the dual carriageway. Jake tried to slam on the breaks but ended up swerving to avoid the car which was now facing him. He ended up flipping the car onto the roof. She conceded that he was most definitely going too fast as well, resulting in the crash being more traumatic. The police had told her that the man driving the other car was on his phone at the time he was overtaking at such speed. He walked away pretty much unscathed apart from a few cuts and bruises. It always seemed to be the way with these things, Jessica thought angrily. As Julie went on to explain how Jake had to be cut free from the car and he was displaying signs of a head injury such as confusion and agitation, Jessica winced at the mental image of this.

'Why was he speeding?' Izzy asked the room, not being present for the conversation prior to this.

'Apparently he'd had a call about Harry so was in a hurry,' Julie said briefly. Jessica bit her tongue and tried to remain level headed.

'Yeah, Patrick mentioned something about Harry and then yesterday, when Jessica said Harriet had called him and he was rushing to hers,' Izzy pushed, looking confused still.

'We don't know the full details, but Harry was with you, so…' Julie paused, leaving a gap for Izzy to interject.

'I don't get it, why did Harriet ring him? Why was he rushing to see Harry if he knew we were looking after the kids? They weren't with Harriet.'

Right, that was it, Jessica thought. 'Because, he didn't know you'd got the kids. Harriet lied. She called him and told him Harry was hurt. He then rushed off to get to them. Somehow, she knew he was with me so I can only assume that she was trying to get him out of there,' Jessica brooded in her chair. She felt a little bitchy and bitter, but the love of her life was lying unconscious in ICU, so she felt she was allowed a little outburst. Before anyone else could say anything to break the wall of awkwardness encasing the room, a young healthcare assistant walked in pushing a small trolley with bowls on.

'I'm just here to give Jake a bit of a clean-up and a wash,' she gestured at the trolley.

'Let's go get a coffee,' David suggested to give his son some dignity and privacy. Jessica suddenly felt a wave of embarrassment that this poor girl was going to give Jake a bed bath; all she could think about was what they'd been doing before he dashed off. Embarrassment then turned to humour when she thought of what Jake would say if he knew. She made a mental note to tell him at a later date. She too decided to leave Jake to his bed bath and while the rest of the family went to get their coffees, she went to check on her car to see the damage. She ambled outside and tried to remember where she'd abandoned the car. She tracked it down and much to her delight, she saw no evidence of parking tickets or clamps. She was about to move the car to the actual car park, but before she could action the decision, her phone began ringing. It was her brother, Henry.

'Jess, Tom's just messaged us! What the hell happened? Are you at the Hospital? Are you okay? How's Jake?' So many questions, Jessica thought as she blinked to try and remember the first one.

'I'm fine, Jake had a bleed on the brain, but scans show he's improving...' she burst into tears before she could finish, despite the good news.

'Oh Jess, fucking hell,' Henry could only acknowledge how rubbish the situation was. 'Is there anything we can do from up here?' he offered, but she told him there was nothing they could do, and she'd just keep them posted on any changes. She agreed to call if she needed anything, and they ended the conversation. She moved her car into the multi-storey and making her way back to the entrance, Jessica suddenly heard a commotion behind her, before a small scream. It took her a second to figure out what was going on when she turned round to look. A young-ish looking girl appeared in front of her, anxiously pushing her hair behind her ears with an eager smile on her face.

'I'm so sorry to disturb you, but can I have a selfie? I'm such a huge fan!' *Jesus, talk about time and place...Jessica* thought, puffing out air.

'I'm really sorry, but it's not a good time,' Jessica admitted weakly, feeling kind of guilty. 'Oh...' the girl blushed with embarrassment, 'I'm really sorry. Of course. You're at a Hospital, I'm so sorry!' she squeaked and ran off. Jessica then felt sorry for the young girl and hoped she didn't come across as mean. A bright flash took her by surprise, then another one. *Really? Here? Now?*

'Jessica, why are at the hospital?' 'Are you visiting someone? Are you getting treatment here in the UK? Are you contributing to NHS waiting lists? Jessica!'

Really? That was a new one, she thought. She put her hood up and ran inside while the hospital security team appeared and gently escorted the photographer off the premises, explaining that it was a hospital and whilst they couldn't stop them filming on the premises, it wasn't appropriate. Jessica had been away from the hubbub of LA for so long, she forgot they even had paparazzi in the UK. Even if they were just regulars who contributed to the red tops or the local press. *How did they even get wind of where she was?* Then realisation struck her. *Surely, she wouldn't have?*

A few days had gone by, and Jake had now had all the remainder of the assorted machines and tubes removed. He was beginning to drift in and out of consciousness more often. Jessica had finally got round to booking into a hotel nearby so she could get some proper rest. She headed back for the hospital that morning and upon entering the room, she had to catch her breath when she met eyes with Jake, who was sat up in bed.

'Hi,' she gasped as he remained staring at her.

'Who are you?' he asked with a blank look on his still bruised face. Jessica gulped and took a step back, trying not to cry, to which he started laughing, 'Come here, you idiot,' he beckoned with his arm extended.

'Prick! That's not funny!' she scathed as she shot towards the bed.

'Sorry, couldn't resist!' he said, with a smile on his face, taking her hand as she sat down next to him.

'You have no idea how good it is to see you awake,' she smiled, suddenly feeling her eyes welling up, this time with happiness.

'Hey, come here,' he pulled her closer to the bed. 'Look, I'm fine. You can't get rid of me that easy,' he joked.

'Jake, you had a bleed on the brain…I thought you were going to die,' she sniffed. He didn't say anything else, he just kissed her hand and pulled her close. The door creaked open, and the usual suspects appeared.

'Ah, you've seen he's back with us in the real world,' David said, and Jessica felt Jake squeeze her hand.

'How are you feeling, sweetheart?' Julie asked.

'Starving!' Jake replied, being met with a smile from his mum.

'This one here,' she pointed at Jessica, 'has been here the entire time. When Tom called her, she dropped everything and rushed to be by your side. She even stayed when we didn't!' she chortled. Jessica felt her hand being squeezed again. A thought suddenly crossed her mind, and she looked over at Tom.

'When you called me, it came up as Jake's number. Did you use his phone?'

'Umm, yeah. It was just on the side, and I'd left mine at home when I was rushing to get here,' he replied.

Jake interjected, 'How did you unlock my phone to get into the contacts?' Tom hesitated and looked sheepish, before admitting to using Jake's fingerprint ID while he lay unconscious.

'Tom!' everyone yelled in unison, shocked and he grinned guiltily in response.

Something in Jake's demeanour suddenly appeared panicky and he spluttered, 'Wait! Shit! Are the kids okay? Where are they? Is Harry okay?'

Ah yes, the reason he was in here. Jessica adjusted her position in the chair. When no-one seemed willing to be the one to speak first, Patrick stepped up.

'The kids are fine. Harry's fine. Harriet was here, then she left. That night...' he paused, 'the kids were with me and Iz. Harriet had dropped them off.'

'I don't understand,' Jake said. 'What happened to Harry?'

'Nothing. She won't own up to it, but we think ultimately Harriet rang you to get you back over to hers, maybe she knew you were with Jess? We don't know, but the kids were with us. Nothing happened, they're fine,' Patrick said gently, desperately trying to get through to his brother. Jake took a moment to take the information in, looking round at everyone as they all tried to avoid eye contact with him.

'So, I crashed my car, because she lied about our kids being hurt?' he said, more matter of fact than a question. No-one said anything but Jessica squeezed his hand. Remembering he was holding her hand, he unlaced his fingers and practically threw her hand back onto her lap.

'Call her,' he demanded.

'Jake...' Patrick began.

'Get her here, now. I want to see her, and I want to see my kids,' he said, even more firmly. Julie reasoned with him that it might not be best for Harry and Joseph to see him in hospital, as it might be upsetting for them, to which he fortunately agreed. He remained adamant though that he wanted to see Harriet. Patrick gave in and left the room to call her. He came back in and nodded to show that he'd done his duty, and she was on her way. One of the familiar nurses came in to do some more checks on Jake, so everyone decided to use the excuse to grab another coffee, and ultimately have a collective debrief about what just happened.

'Jesus, this isn't going to end well,' Patrick admitted, rubbing his forehead.

'He's gonna have to see her at some point,' Tom pointed out.

'She obviously still cares about him, hence why she was jealous he was with me. I kind of feel sorry for her,' Jessica interjected, genuinely trying to put herself in Harriet's shoes. Everyone stared at her with gaping mouths, arguing that she should not be defending Harriet's behaviour one iota. At this point, an unfriendly presence graced the corridor like a frosty wind. Harriet. Everyone turned to see not just Harriet but her twin sister too; obviously brought along for moral support. Both were marching with purpose towards the room, blatantly ignoring the group. Patrick jumped in front of them, blocking their path and forcing them to acknowledge him.

'I'll take you,' he said, leading the way before shouting, 'Jess!' and clicking his fingers for her to follow too. Like a lap dog, she quickly ran to his side.

As they pushed the door to the room, Harriet announced, 'I'm not having everyone in here, ganging up on me!'

'Fine, everyone else leaves,' Jake said from his bed. 'Except Jess.' Jessica hesitated and told him she thought Harriet was right; it was between the two of them. Jake gave her a hard stare and she found that her lap dog persona reappeared, doing as she was told. Patrick purposefully held the door open for Harriet's sister, then let it close behind them. The two of them stood next to each other at the foot of Jake's bed, waiting for further instructions from their master. 'You can sit,' he said, unknowingly continuing the lap dog mime. 'Harriet, I don't even know where to start. What the fuck were you playing at?' He didn't give her chance to speak before going in with the ultimate question, 'Why did you lie about Harry being hurt?'

'I'm sorry,' she whispered. 'Since she's come back on the scene,' she gestured and rolled her eyes.

Jake interrupted, 'She has a name, thank you.'

'Since *Jessica*,' she overly emphasised, 'came back on the scene, it's like you're just living in this fantasy land, and you've forgotten about your family.'

'What are you talking about?' he questioned, looking genuinely baffled.

'I didn't really think we'd go through with the divorce... I thought you'd realise that it was best for the kids if we tried to work through our problems. Next thing, you're off gallivanting with your first love like some love-struck teenager.'

'Harriet,' Jake softened, 'the best thing for those kids is to have two individual parents who are happy, not living in a house where there's constant bickering and arguing. Not one where their mother has an affair,' he casually dropped out. Jessica felt her jaw drop open and her eyebrows shoot up. Her eyes shot over to Harriet, who didn't seem quite as shocked as she was, desperately trying to avoid Jessica's stare. Clearly this was the key factor in their splitting – Jake never said, Jessica thought.

'What kind of person lies about their kid being hurt though? I mean, really?' Jake pressed, raising his eyebrow.

'I'm sorry! I'd been drinking and I was angry! You were off gallivanting!' she protested. Despite it ultimately not being any of Jessica's business, she found it really hard to bite her tongue and not contribute to this conversation. She had so many words for Harriet. She felt sick just thinking what could have happened to Jake, because he was rushing to get to his kids, the doting dad that he was.

'What would you have done when I got there? The kids were with Patrick and Iz anyway,' Jake asked plainly. Whilst he was showing no emotion on his face, inside his blood was boiling. He was fighting with the urge to shout and scream at Harriet for her stupidity. He could feel his toes curling and his hands forming fists. Every ten seconds he had to mentally check himself to remind himself to remain calm and hear her out. Harriet shrugged and her casual lack of response further ignited the burning rage inside of Jessica.

'He could have died because of you!' she spat.

'Jess,' Jake tried to diffuse her anger, despite feeling exactly the same.

'No!' she shook his hand off hers and turned back to Harriet.

'What would you have told your kids if he had died? *'Oh, sorry kids, I lied to daddy about you being hurt and now you're never going to see him again!"*

'Our kids are nothing to do with you!' Harriet yelled back. Jake felt the anger inside him starting to bubble up even more, but once again he took a deep breath and forced himself to relax. Unfortunately, the deep breath was incredibly painful as he was still feeling bruised and rather fragile. He didn't let this show on his face though. He cleared his throat and said,

'Actually... they are. While I'm with Jessica, she will be their step-mum, whether you like it or not.'

Woah, Jessica thought. She loved Jake and she knew she'd love his kids, but it was a big jump to be referred to as their step-mum. She appreciated what Jake was doing and saying, but nevertheless it took her back slightly. Stupidly, she'd not really thought about how she'd fit into Jake's family life. She loved kids and most definitely wanted some of her own, but she was now wondering whether Jake would actually want any more children; he had two of his own already. It was certainly a conversation for them to have at a later date. Harriet scoffed at Jake's remark and Jessica instantly felt sorry for her again. It must be an awful situation to be in; seeing your ex with a new woman. Then she remembered the comment about Harriet having an affair and felt instantaneously disgusted by her again. Jessica took a deep breath and made a concerted effort not to raise her voice again.

'Those kids will always be yours and Jake's children, but I need you to know that whenever they would be in my care, I would look after them and love them like my own. Not because I'm trying to replace you, but because they are Jake's children and I love him. You will always be their mum and Jake will always be their dad. It doesn't matter if he's with me or anyone else. It doesn't matter if you meet someone else. Nothing will change that,' Jessica reasoned, genuinely trying to convince Harriet that she meant well. Jessica continued, 'I'm really sorry that you're hurting, and it must be shit to see someone you love with someone else. Believe me, I know! I know it's not the same, as we weren't married, but how do you think it made me feel when I saw photos of you and Jake not only loved up, but married with kids?'

'Probably the same as I felt when you abandoned me and suddenly started dating some buff American Olympian...' Jake interjected bluntly. Jessica shot him her deadliest eyes and he knew to remain silent. He had a point though, Jessica pondered, now feeling foolish and selfish for trying to make such a point. Harriet was still looking at her feet and she simply nodded along.

'You know he's always loved you,' she said, and Jessica felt a sting at the same phrase that Julie had said earlier that week. 'He's never loved me like he loved you, even when we had the kids,' Harriet admitted, only lifting her head to watch Jake take Jessica's hand in his.

'He always spoke about his ex-girlfriend but never mentioned any names, so it was always just this figure in my mind, with no name or face. His friends would talk about you, but I never made the connection; I just believed you were all good friends when we were at Sheffield. I knew his heart belonged elsewhere when he proposed. I knew he only did that as he was fed up of me constantly going on about it. He didn't have a better offer, so there was me,' she sighed. Jake looked up at Harriet and tilted his head to the side.

'Come on, that's not true. I did love you at one time. Really, I did. And thanks to you, I've got two amazing boys. I'd never change that.' Jessica then felt like apologising, but she didn't really know what for. They all sat in silence for what seemed like a lifetime. *Did she actually lure him away from his wife?* Jake looked at his ex-wife's solemn face and then over to Jessica. He sat there wondering how someone could be so beautiful but not know it. She looked up at him and at once looked away again when she saw he was staring.

'Harriet, I think we can all agree that what you did was fucking reckless, stupid and something you will definitely never do again, right?' Jake asked and Harriet nodded, wiping a tear from her eye. He continued, 'And you need to accept that whether you like it or not, Jessica is and will be a huge part of my life.' She nodded again.

Looking up, Harriet then burst into full flow tears and sobbed, 'Jake, I'm so sorry! I could have killed you! I've been so stupid!' She then looked to Jessica. 'I'm so sorry!' she heaved. Jessica resisted the urge to get up and hug her, which she truly felt like doing from both empathy but also relief that this feud was over. Instead, Jessica gently put her hand on Harriet's as a sign of solidarity.

'Thank you. I'm sorry for whatever part I played in this too. Can we please just start again...?' Jessica pleaded with emphasis.

Harriet nodded and half smiled as she blew her nose, 'Yes please.'

Jake exhaled and rested his head back into the pillow that was propping him up, 'Thank fuck for that!' Jessica decided not to question whether it was Harriet who sold photos of her to the magazines or let them know she was at the hospital. She didn't have to ask, and she didn't want to open the rift that had just been sealed.

THIRTY

Getting ready to leave the hospital after being discharged a week later, Jake felt incredibly fortunate that he only needed some physiotherapy in terms of aftercare. Jessica sat with him and his packed bags, waiting for a prescription to be signed off before they could leave. She couldn't believe so much could happen to a new couple in the space of a few weeks.

'Hey, remember when I half proposed to you in your dad's back garden?' Jake said, playing with her hand. Jessica smiled then cringed, thinking of the memory of Jake getting down on one knee to ask her to be his girlfriend.

'Vividly. What about it?'

'Can we rewind and go back to that moment?' he smiled.

'Erm, and have to go through all this again? No thanks,' she joked.

'I love you,' he pulled her closer to him and kissed her head. Just as she was nestling into him, they were interrupted by the hospital pharmacist dropping off the meds to the discharge nurse. Time to get out of here, Jake thought as everything was handed over to him. He'd been handed over a plastic bag of belongings too, which the police collected from his car at the time of the accident. As he had no transportation, Jessica drove them both back to her place back in Bournemouth. She didn't want to ask the question, but as they were driving along, she did wonder exactly where it was that Jake ran off the road. She put the thought to the back of her mind, wincing at the thought of the horrific impact.

Little did she know that Jake was having exactly the same thought. He couldn't remember exactly where he came off the road and each time they drove past certain points, he assessed the area to see if he could remember.

They pulled in through the gates that Jessica had opened with the remote in her car. She suddenly felt the same embarrassment she had when Jake first came over, when he commented on the grandeur of where she lived. Walking into the kitchen, there was a distinct smell of gone off food; she'd dropped everything when she got the call and she'd not been back since. Apologising for the mess, she ordered Jake to get comfy in front of the TV and she'd make him a cup of tea.

'Milk and one level teaspoon of sugar, no more, no less?' she checked this was still his standard order.

'The things you remember...' he smiled. Jake found himself thinking of when they were vaguely playing house at Uni. She always made him a cup of tea whenever he was ill, or hungover.

'Oh, by the way,' Jessica said, resting on the doorframe, 'I think you should send that nice healthcare assistant, Lindsay, some flowers.'

'Oh?' Jake looked up, wondering why her specifically. After all, it was a team effort to save his life.

'Yeah, the poor woman had to give you a thorough bed bath, and we both know the last thing we were doing before you rushed off...' Jessica smirked, raising her eyebrows.

'Oh my God!' Jake's face changed to a look of horror as he figured out what she was talking about. Jessica laughed and sauntered off, leaving him to stew on the embarrassment. Fortunately, apart from that one off, he'd been able to shower on his own since then. In the kitchen, Jessica could hear children's voices and knew Jake was on Facetime with his kids. She brought his tea in for him, but purposefully tried to stay out of shot.

'Daddy, when can we see you?' she heard Joseph's little voice ask.

'Ah buddy, let me think. Today is Friday, which means tomorrow is Saturday, so maybe tomorrow? I'll ask mummy. Do you want to go get her?' Jake replied. They said their goodbyes and Jake waited for Harriet to appear. 'Hey, do you think you'd be able to drop the kids here for the night tomorrow?' Jake asked casually.

Here? Jessica looked around frantically, thinking how non-child friendly her house was. After some obvious hesitation on her part too, Harriet agreed that she'd drop them round at about 10am the following morning. Jessica already felt embarrassed again that Harriet would experience the excessive grandeur of the house. Ending the call, Jake looked up and smiled, telling her nonchalantly that he couldn't wait for her to meet his kids.

'Aha, erm, what just happened?' she inquired.

'I want to see my boys,' Jake said, looking confused. 'What's the problem? I thought you'd want to meet them?' Jessica examined her patchy nail polish to delay a response.

'Of course, but to come here, to meet me? So soon? Is Harriet really okay with it? Also, my place isn't exactly child friendly, is it?' she waved her arms around frantically as a gesture to prove her point. Jake glanced around the room and frowned. '

It's fine. They aren't babies anymore. They know not to walk into the fireplace...' he said with a straight face.

'What about food? And beds?' she asked, feeling slightly panicked as she now stood there with her hands on her hips. He sighed and reached out for her hand.

'Jess, relax, you don't need to worry about this stuff,' he said while gently pulling her to sit down next to him. 'You've got four spare guest bedrooms, I think we'll be okay!' he joked, and she prodded him in the ribs, forgetting he'd just been discharged from hospital.

'Ow!' he laughed, still feeling the effects of the bruising. They sat cuddled up on the sofa for a while, but Jessica was still running through everything in her head. She was thinking about everything, from what they would eat, to wondering what the two boys would think to this random new woman that their dad was hanging out with. Almost as if he was reading her thoughts, he lifted her chin and kissed her softly. 'They're going to love you. I just hope you love them! They're nuts!' he laughed. In reality, he truly couldn't wait for her to meet his kids and he wholeheartedly knew that they'd love her; they were mini versions of him. *Well, she loves me, so what's two more miniature versions of me?* He thought to himself.

Saturday came and by 8am Jessica had cleaned the house from top to bottom. Late on Friday night, she'd ordered some random toys and some children's bed sheets on Amazon Prime; for a ridiculous price but with the convenience of next day delivery. As she was fighting to stuff a duvet into a Pokémon bed sheet, Jake told her she was being silly and there was no need for it all. She just so desperately wanted to impress. She'd already opened the gates ahead of time so Harriet could just drive in; she didn't want the grandeur embarrassment any more than possible. At pretty much 10am on the dot, the doorbell went, causing Jessica to jump out her skin. Despite it being her house, she felt it more appropriate for Jake to answer the door to his kids and ex-wife. She stood to the side as Harriet waltzed in and did a full 360-degree assessment of the house with her eyes, before landing on Jessica's.

'Lovely place you've got,' she said through what seemed like a fake, forced smile.

'Thank you,' Jessica whispered and right on cue, the oven timer began beeping, so she politely excused herself, thanked Harriet for dropping off the kids and headed for the kitchen. She switched off the timer and made a bunch of clattering noises with the pans. She hadn't got anything cooking, she'd just pre-empted wanting a getaway excuse, so she set the timer for two minutes when she heard the doorbell. She heard the front door close and suddenly the house was filled with riotous noise; there was clattering, shouting, electronic beeps, and music.

'Right, you two, settle down,' Jake said firmly. Everything quietened down a bit and he appeared in the kitchen doorway as Jessica stood holding an empty pan. 'Ready?' he said with a smile.

'What would you do if I said no?'

'Carry you in there anyway?' he replied with a flirtatious smirk.

'Fine. We'll save that for later though,' she winked. As Jake hobbled through into the living room, with Jessica in tow, she felt more anxious in her stomach than she did when she was about to go on stage.

'Okay guys, I want you to meet someone really special...' Jake started, as they stood in the doorway. He went ahead to beckon Jessica into her own living room. 'I want you to say hello to Jessica,' Jake said purposefully. Both of them stared up at her with blank looks on their faces. Oh god, she'd failed at the first hurdle, she thought as her heart fell.

'My mummy says you're famous. She says you're more like Joe Bean than Dolly,' Joseph said as he stared blankly at her.

'Jolene!' Jake muttered under his breath with a snort, ruffling his son's hair in amusement. Jessica felt her cheeks going red, not knowing how to respond to that.

Brilliant, she thought.

Part of Jake was furious with his ex-wife for making such a comment at all, let alone to the kids. However, part of him was also trying not to laugh at his son's innocence and unawareness.

'But I don't know who those people are,' Joseph continued, shrugging.

While Jake stood there still trying not to laugh, Jessica gulped and said, 'Well, I'm a singer. I sing songs and play music. Do you like singing?'

'No.'

Bugger, she thought.

'I like playing drums instead,' Joseph went on.

Okay, okay. Let's find some common ground, she mused.

'I like my daddy's music too.'

Bingo!

'Ah yes, is daddy teaching you how to play music? I like his music too. He helped me make music when we were younger,' she smiled at Jake for reassurance. Suddenly, Joseph burst into life and began jumping round the room pretending to drum, dramatically. Harry joined in, then Jessica, then Jake. Joseph then stopped as abruptly as he had started.

'I like you,' he said as he looked Jessica straight in the eyes.

'Thank you. I like you too!' she said cheerily.

'Do you want to have a baby with my daddy so we can have another brother?'

Woah. She almost had to steady herself at the swift topic change.

'Ermm...' Jessica spluttered, desperately trying to think of an answer. Before she could continue, Jake scooped Joseph up and starting tickling him, causing him to screech with laughter and giggles.

Good distraction technique noted, she contemplated.

THIRTY ONE

Jessica was used to eating dinner at about 8pm so having to sit down for a full meal at 5pm was a bit of a shock to the system. After much deliberation last night, her and Jake settled on roast chicken, potatoes, and vegetables; it was easy and something that everyone would eat. The only downside was that Harry had to sit on Jake's lap at the table; as Jessica's stupidly expensive but lovely John Lewis chairs were too low down for him to reach his food. Each time Harry wriggled, she saw Jake wince slightly. She kept forgetting he had only just got back from hospital and was still recovering. She made a mental note to herself: Buy some kind of booster cushion for Harry and remind Jake to take his pain killers. Jessica remembered having to be practically forced to eat her broccoli and carrots when she was their age, but Joseph and Harry actually asked for more. She couldn't quite believe it. As Joseph and Harry were chattering away to each other, about things Jessica didn't understand, Jake met her eyes and gave her a loving smile before taking a gulp of wine. They'd decided that after the week they'd had, a large glass of wine with their meal was pretty reasonable. After eating, it was playtime again for the boys. Jessica showed them the toys she'd bought which they looked thrilled with and instantly began playing with, so she took that as a positive that she'd done a decent job.

'What on earth is that smell?!' Jake burst into the room,

causing Jessica to look around and even try to subtly sniff her own armpit. 'I can smell two very stinky little boys who need a bath!'

Oh, I see, she thought.

This was met by both boys in unison shouting 'No!' and sulking.

'Come on you two, you can play with the toys tomorrow. Bath, story, and bed.' They both started to look as if they might go into a full blown temper tantrum but Jake quickly raised his finger to silence them. 'Now, please.' It was weird seeing Jake be so firm. Jessica had never really imagined what kind of parent he was; and while he was by no means strict, they knew to do exactly as he said without questioning. Jake ran the bath about a quarter of the way full and then asked for Jessica's help to rally boys both up and strip them off. They took responsibility for one each and much to her dismay, Jessica got stuck with Harry. Despite being younger and therefore smaller, he seemed to go at double the speed of Joseph. Just as she managed to get his tiny underpants off, he scarpered and started running round one of the rooms in the buff, giggling as he did so. It was like trying to round up an excited Labrador. He kept changing direction to avoid her grasp, still giggling away as he swerved his way round the room to avoid her. Jessica tried not to focus too much on the fact that she was being out-smarted by a child.

'Are you coming?' she heard Jake shout from the bathroom.

'I'm trying to wrangle a cheeky little naked monkey!' she yelled back, grinning at Harry. She needed a new approach, so she stood still, pretended to look the other way then lunged forward and managed to scoop him up. She thought the children would settle down once they were in the bath. Alas, they did not. Bubbles were flying everywhere, crayons being used to scribble on Jessica's lovely white tiles. Jake obviously saw Jessica wince at this and quickly reassured her that it all washed off very easily and not to worry. She also saw that the bubbles were as a result of her expensive bath liquid, which was £35 a bottle. It was a bit of an impulse purchase at the time, but something she had treated herself to. She tried her best not to stare at the half empty bottle that had been glugged into the toddler's bath.

Both the boy's hair all soaped up and each styled into a dramatic quiff, Jake then filled a play watering can and instructed, 'Eyes closed!' before pouring clean water over their little heads to wash the soap out. She'd never really thought about it, but seeing Jake as a doting dad was incredibly sexy. She admitted it felt weird to think that, but it was clear how much he loved his kids and they hung on his every word. Pyjamas on, they headed downstairs to watch the allotted half an hour of TV before bed. Watching a bedtime story on CBeebies, Jessica suddenly became interested in being a parent. She didn't realise they had well-known, handsome actors from Netflix period dramas reading the bedtime stories. Hell, I didn't need kids for this, she thought. She'd happily watch this on her own with a glass of wine.

Both Harry and Joseph were sleepily rubbing their eyes which meant it was bedtime. 'Do you mind?' Jake gestured towards Harry as he picked Joseph up. Jessica nodded and lifted Harry's sleepy body into her arms. By the time they'd got up the stairs, he was already fast asleep. Jessica gently placed him down into his bed and tucked him in. Without thinking, she gave him a gentle kiss on his forehead then paused, thinking how natural it felt. She heard Jake saying goodnight to Joseph who was in a separate room before meeting him on the landing. He pointed towards her bedroom and mouthed the words, 'Shall we?' to which she nodded. She flopped down on the bed and exhaled; she felt exhausted. She had a new found respect for parents who did this day in, day out. Jake joined her, in a slightly less dramatic way as he gently eased his body onto the bed so as not to cause himself any pain. His hands started to wander and explore her body, trying to find an access point under her clothes. Jessica slapped his hand away playfully.

'You must be joking! I'm knackered!' she laughed, running her fingers through her hair.

Jake laughed, 'Welcome to parenting! We've got to do it all

EMMA DUNNILL

again tomorrow!'

THIRTY TWO

One year later

It had been just over a year since Jake's accident, and you wouldn't have known anything had happened to him. Him and Jessica often reflected on the last year and spoke about just how lucky he was. Things could have been hugely different. Every time they spoke about it, Jessica got chills just thinking of Jake lying there in ICU, lifeless and gone to the world. She still couldn't forgive Harriet for the part she played in it, but Jessica kept that grudge very much hidden, for everyone's sake. The pair were as inseparable now as they were back at Uni; Jake had moved in with Jessica and they were already looking at moving and getting a place of their own. They'd been looking at something smaller and more homely. Jessica knew she didn't need all that space and all those things; she had everything she wanted. The last year had taught her what was profoundly important. She'd been taking a break from writing and recording too. Her earlier catalogue had been all about drug abuse, depression, and heartbreak. She conceded that she didn't have anything to write about at the moment. Harriet had finally signed the divorce papers and the legal admin was nearly complete. Jake had been sharing custody of the children and they seemed to be getting on better than when they were married. Joseph and Harry would come over to Jessica's every other weekend, and they spent increasingly more time there during the school holidays. Jessica knew Jake wishes he saw more of them, but while they were in school it was difficult logistically. Despite her grudge holding, Jessica did have a better relationship with Harriet these days; she'd even sometimes stop for a coffee when she dropped them off. She'd confided in Jessica that she'd actually met someone, but she'd sworn her to secrecy until anything was 'official.' Jessica was genuinely happy for her; because despite it not being factually correct in the slightest, a part of her did always feel like a home-wrecker. Jessica did of course tell Jake about Harriet's new man, but she swore him to secrecy too, which he agreed to.

Jessica and Jake had driven to a hotel not too far from her dad's house; they decided it best to stay in a hotel with a king-size bed and breakfast, rather than enduring the rickety double bed in her old room and her dad's standard porridge breakfast. They were heading over for the annual family get together that her dad had organised. Jessica had missed so many in the last ten years that after attending last year, she felt she still needed to make amends. Leaving the hotel just before noon, Jake drove them to her dad's house. As they pulled into the drive and onto the crunchy gravel, Jessica could already see silhouettes of people in the kitchen window. Stepping out of the car into the warm sunshine, she watched Jake lock the car and march towards her. He didn't notice Jessica ogling because of her mirrored sunglasses but he was dressed in a pair of dark denim jeans with a white shirt unbuttoned at the top. His styled dark hair was pushed back off his face. She couldn't help herself thinking just how handsome he looked. Jessica had always been so incredibly self-conscious, but since she'd got back with Jake, she had this new found confidence, similar to the self-assurance she had back at university. She felt she was reprising her role. With the sun shining bright and warm, she opted for a casual, dark floral dress, with sandal heels which she already couldn't wait to take off. They locked hands and strode towards the door, which Jessica knocked at melodiously.

'How many times? You don't have to knock, you dafty!' her dad exclaimed as he opened the large wooden door to greet them. They were swiftly ushered in, and Jessica saw the familiar faces of her brothers. She hastily kicked off her ludicrously uncomfortable heels and ran towards them, squealing like an excited toddler. She hugged them all one by one, along with their respective partners too. She felt something grab at her leg and nearly screamed, until she looked down and saw a mass of blonde curly hair.

'Oh my God, no way! Is that Ava?' Jessica exclaimed as she lifted her up.

'Do you remember your Auntie Jessica?' Ollie said to her, enunciating every syllable, obviously trying to encourage her to speak. She gurgled something incomprehensible in response. Jessica cooed over her just like she had a year prior, marvelling at her gorgeous white blonde tight curls. Jake shook hands with her brothers and politely embraced their partners. Some hadn't seen him since the accident so most of them were in awe of how well he looked, considering. As she was catching up with Ollie about everything Ava related, Jessica noticed that Jake was chatting quietly to her dad and Henry in the corner. They all looked deep in private conversation. She fondly remembered the first time she brought him home to meet everyone; he was so nervous. He was convinced that her brothers would be super protective of her, which of course they played up to and threatened all sorts. Needless to say, they couldn't keep up the charade and quickly eased up on him, allowing him to relax. Seen as Henry was in a band at university too, they instantly bonded over similar music taste. Ollie was telling Jessica all about how him and Lisa were already thinking of having more children.

'I just want Ava to have lots of brothers and sisters, like us!' Ollie grinned as he stroked Ava's cheek as she sat comfortably perched in Jessica's arms. She began to get fidgety and fussy, so Jessica passed her back to Ollie. After a cuddle and kiss from her dad, Ava was fine again and wanted to be put down to run around and wreak havoc for the audience.

'How are you getting on with Jake's brood?' Ollie asked. Jessica admitted it was tough at times, feeling like the step-mother with no authority, but on the whole that she felt she had a good relationship with them. She was still leaving any disciplining to Jake; she was still wary of how Harriet would respond if she knew Jessica had shouted at her children.

Then again, she pretended one of them was injured just to get Jake away from her...no...stop! She thought. *Water under the bridge. Kind of.*

Their chat was interrupted by their dad tapping a knife on a glass, ready to make a speech. Their dad loved a speech; any opportunity he was making profound statements about looking to the future, usually quoting some ancient orator or poet. As everyone quietened down, Jake joined Jessica and put his arm round her.

'Well, another year and here we are again. Yet again, I can't believe so much can change in a year; we've had divorces, car accidents, stays in ICU, new relationships... and that's just Jake!' dad joked. As everyone laughed, Jake raised his glass and mock bowed. 'But...I actually wanted to use this opportunity to introduce you to someone,' he paused as everyone froze and looked at each other, confused. They all frowned at each other, wondering what was happening. Henry looked at Jessica and mouthed *'what the fuck?'* to which Jessica shrugged and pulled a face, equally as bemused. 'Caroline, will you come out please?' their dad said loudly as if announcing to the entire room. An elegantly dressed, tall, grey haired lady walked in from the garage. 'Everyone, this is Caroline and...well...it feels very teenage of me to say this, but she's my girlfriend,' he said with slight hesitation in his voice. No-one said anything for about ten seconds until Henry piped up, breaking the silence.

'Dad, did you really make the poor woman wait in the garage for the last hour?' Everyone laughed as their dad looked incredibly sheepish.

'Well, we didn't know how you'd react, so I had to bide my time when it was best to announce,' he confessed. Jessica had never seen her dad so coy about anything. He explained to everyone that they met about eight months ago at a local walking group. He admitted that he was concerned about how the siblings would react, assuring them that it didn't mean that he'd forgotten about their mum. He also added that their mum's random Aunt that was usually invited to these family do's, actually asked him why she was always invited. It therefore transpired that she didn't really want to keep attending such events, so invites had now ceased. Jessica started welling up at the mention of their mum. She had to quickly explain that they were happy tears, as she dramatically flapped her arms aimlessly near her face to fan her eyes.

'Sorry! I'm just pleased for you. We all know you loved and still love mum, but you're allowed to find happiness again!' Jessica said, wiping her eyes and hugging her dad. Her brothers all agreed in unison and hugged their dad in turn.

'Love you, kiddo,' Jessica's dad whispered to her over Ollie's shoulder. The siblings all individually went to personally greet Caroline who was equally as nervous about the introduction; explaining she was having to calm herself down while hanging out in the garage.

Henry clapped his hands together and exclaimed, 'Champagne!' before popping the bottle and pouring everyone a glass.

'Too early for me, thanks,' Jessica said, putting her hand over the glass, swerving the alcohol. 'I'm fine with my Diet Coke for now,' she confirmed.

Everyone raised their champagne flute and toasted, 'To us!' They all started mingling again and asking each other how work was going, speaking of old friends; the usual general catch up topics. Jessica nudged Jake.

'Hey, come with me. I want to show you something.' He obliged, intrigued, and followed her upstairs. She ushered him into her old bedroom, and he raised his eyebrows at her suggestively.

'Right, on the bed, the floor or the chair?' he joked, grabbing her overly dramatically.

'Get off!' she laughed. Instead, she nodded towards the photo frames on display and his face lit up.

'Oh wow...we look so young!' He leant forward to examine the photos more closely, smiling as he did so. His eyes flicked around them all. 'Look at Tom on that one!' he laughed and snapped a photo on his phone, ready to send to their group chat. 'Who would've thought those kids would go through so much and then end up back together again?' He stood up and put his arms round Jessica, thinking about how beautiful she looked. He couldn't remember a time when he genuinely didn't think she looked beautiful. Even when she was in her loungewear, hair scraped up and no make up on; he was besotted. He didn't say anything, he just delicately pushed her hair behind her ear and kissed her gently on the lips. Jessica took a deep breath and stood back from him, suddenly feeling dizzy and anxious.

'Jake, I need to tell you something...'

'What...?' His face dropped at the serious manner she'd said it in.

'Please don't get mad, okay...' Jessica started before he interrupted her.

'What?' he repeated with a stern look on his face, jaw then clenched tightly shut again.

'I'm pregnant,' she whispered, taking his hands. His eyes widened and he took a step back himself, dropping her hands and taking time to compose himself through a deep exhale. He felt dizzy and disorientated as he tried to process what Jessica had just said.

Did I just hear her right? He thought as he remained staring at her, only blinking.

'I'm sorry?' he managed to find his voice. Jessica found herself garbling as she repeated what she'd said.

'I'm...I'm pregnant. I missed a period a while ago but thought nothing of it; sometimes that happens for all sorts of reasons, like stress. Then the next month, still no period and I was feeling a bit sick too. Again, I just assumed stress or anxiety from all these changes going on. Anyway, I took a test, then when it came back positive, I panicked and rang Izzy...'

'Patrick's Izzy?' he asked, interrupting her once again.

'Yep. She came with me to the doctors who arranged an ultrasound, and they confirmed I was pregnant. I didn't want to say anything because I didn't know how you'd react, but I already knew I wanted to keep it and so I kept quiet. I had my twelve week scan the other week. I'm so sorry I didn't tell you!' Jessica realised she was still garbling at speed and looked at Jake for some kind of response. He just looked at her blankly then rubbed the back of his neck. Uh oh, she thought, noticing his telltale signal for *'I am uncomfortable!'*

'So, how many weeks are you?'

'Fourteen.' He took a deep breath, held it, and exhaled loudly again. Jessica's fears had been confirmed; he didn't want this baby. He had two already and didn't want another one, especially to a different woman, even if that woman was Jessica. She felt her heart sink into her stomach. She'd been expecting this response. Izzy assured her that he'd be pleased but Jessica knew. She thought of how quickly he'd brushed off the question from his son when they first met.

'You've got a scan photo?'

'Yep, it's somewhere here in my bag,' she said while rummaging in the pockets to find the folded piece of photo paper. Jessica handed over the scan picture with a neat fold in it, which he examined in detail. Her throat was burning as she tried to fight back tears of disappointment and anger.

'I'm sorry I went to the scan without you. I'm sorry that this happened. I know we were being careful, but I guess it does still happen,' she said, trying so desperately not to cry.

'And why didn't you want to tell me?'

'Because I know it wasn't planned, you've already got two kids and we've only been together a year, but I wanted to keep it! I know that might change things for me and you but there's no way I was going to get rid of it,' she said as she gently stroked her non-existent bump. Jake looked at her, confused by her angry outburst. The room had stopped spinning, and he was able to clearly see her again.

'Jess...' he hesitated before smiling.

'What?' she looked at him quizzically, wondering why he was smiling all of a sudden. He pulled her close and kissed her, still smiling.

'I can't believe we're going to have a baby!' he whispered, grinning.

'So, you're not mad?'

'Mad? Jess, you, and your brain. It was a bit of a shock, that's all! I'm sorry,' he laughed, cradling her face in his hands. Jessica fake sulked and he pulled her in for a long hug, kissing her cheek gently. He thought he loved her as much as he possibly could, but he suddenly felt a new wave of adoration for her. He held her close into his chest, gently swaying as he couldn't keep still.

I can't believe I'm going to be a dad again, he thought. His mental picture of his future and family always involved Jessica and now it was all coming together. He found himself wondering already if it would be a boy or a girl. *Would it be another mini me or would it be a beautiful mini Jess?* He pondered the possibilities.

'I love you so much,' Jessica said as she buried her face into his chest, feeling safer and more loved than she ever had before. He shook his head as they stood apart.

'I can't believe you didn't feel you could tell me. I'm so sorry if I made you feel like that,' he said, suddenly feeling dreadful that he'd given her that impression. He had to bury the thought of how she may have chosen to end the pregnancy if she honestly thought he didn't want it. He felt sick even thinking about that potential outcome, then thought about how actually Jessica would never realistically do that. She always wanted to be a mother; the thought probably didn't even cross her mind, he decided.

'No, it wasn't you. I just had no idea if you'd be happy or not.'

'Remind me to thank Izzy for looking after you. On that train of thought; if Izzy knows, does that mean Patrick knows?' he asked.

'No, she swore she would keep it between me and her until I told you,' Jessica smiled.

'Could you really not tell just by looking at me?' she went on to ask, prodding her flat belly. Despite there clearly being nothing obviously protruding about her stomach, Jessica felt ginormous. She's been constantly looking in the full length mirror, assessing her stomach and whether it was obvious or not. She concluded that it most definitely was obvious, and she was the size of a whale. That was her body dysmorphia kicking in again.

'No!' Jake said, astonished and they both laughed.

'I'm not sure if that means you think I've just gotten chubby or if you're just thick...' Jessica put her hands on her hips and pulled a face at him.

'I'd be inclined to go with the latter,' he laughed. 'Today of all days...' he muttered under his breath, rubbing the back of his neck again.

'Huh?' Jessica grunted.

'Come on, let's go back down,' Jake said. They then spent the next ten minutes at the top of the stairs, deliberated whether they should tell Jessica's family here and now. It would certainly be easier to make an announcement rather than having to ring each of them individually. Jessica then thought about how Ollie never told her about Ava until that home visit. She quickly did the adding up and realised that they would have found out while she was in rehab, so she could let that one slide.

Jake felt so eager to tell everyone the happy news. He wanted to shout it from the rooftops. *But then, what if something happened and they lost the baby? Was it too soon to share? She'd had the twelve week scan and all was okay there. Also, if anything was to sadly happen, they'd both want family support anyway.* Jake found himself musing over the pros and cons then shook the nerves from his body as Jessica looked at him longingly for confirmation of a decision. 'Okay, let's do it,' Jake said, and Jessica nodded, beaming. 'You lead the way!' he said, gently tapping her bum cheekily with his hand as she passed him. Back downstairs they joined the rest of the group and it seemed that no-one had even realised they'd disappeared. This time, it was Jessica tapping a champagne glass with a knife. Unfortunately, she did so a little too vigorously and the glass smashed over the counter. *Brilliant*, she thought as met Jake's eye. He was stifling a laugh with an amused expression as he shook his head.

'Well, at least I've got your attention…works the same way!' Jessica laughed, looking at everyone's shocked faces. 'So, we've got some news…' she continued as she looked over at Jake. He came to stand next to her, resting his hand on the small of her back.

'We're having a baby!' they said in harmony. Then came a plethora of gasps, hands smacked to mouths, smiles, and cheers. The kitchen became a hub of noise; with everyone suddenly closing in to congratulate them. Jessica received hugs and Jake received hand-shakes and pats on the back.

'My little girl…' her dad said with his eyes just about holding back the water that was gathering, as he hugged Jessica. 'Your mum would be pleased as punch,' he said with a wobble in his voice, and he quickly cleared his throat with a cough. Jessica didn't need to say anything back, even if she felt like she could. She swallowed the lump in her throat, trying not to cry. As they pulled apart, he mouthed the words, *'love you,'* again and she did the same back to him. Unlike the other hand-shakers, her dad embraced Jake and muttered something in his ear. Jake muttered something back with a smile and nodded at him, then over in Henry's direction too. Jake suddenly had a feeling of butterflies in his stomach and had to compose himself slightly.

Okay, here goes, he thought, egging himself on.

'So, erm this has kind of ruined my surprise a bit…and it may well potentially put plans on delay somewhat…' Jake announced to the room. Jessica turned to him, bewildered. As she turned, he disappeared from her eyeline.

Why was he on the floor? Oh god, he was doing that fake proposal thing again.

'Jess, will you marry me?'

Nope, actual proposal!

Her brain told her as she stood there in shock. A gorgeous emerald cut ring was glistening in the afternoon sun that shone through the windows. Jessica gulped, looking around. Everyone was waiting with bated breath, including Jake who was still on one knee and starting to look a bit worried. He shifted his weight slightly as his knee started to ache. His stomach was flipping, wondering if she was actually going to say no. He'd asked permission from her dad and even Henry, as her closest brother. They couldn't have been happier for the pair. He thought of how they were never in any doubt she'd say no.

'Really?' she asked, still unsure if this was another bit he was doing.

'Yes really, you idiot,' he laughed.

'Oi! Don't call your future wife an idiot!' she pretended to kick him.

'Is that a yes then?'

'A thousand times yes!' she grinned. He jumped up and placed the ring on her finger, rubbing his knee which had become very sore on the hard kitchen floor. Jesssica admired the beautiful ring that was glistening in the light.

'Thank god for that!' he laughed, running his fingers through his hair.

'He asked my permission and everything!' dad repeated in the same way he had with the fake proposal previously. Everyone laughed and again, they found themselves being congratulated by all. Jessica locked her arms round Jake and stood on her tiptoes to kiss him.

'I love you,' she whispered, beaming with love and joy.

'I love you too. Always have, always will,' he whispered back.

NEWSPAPER ANNOUNCEMENT
BIRTH
Taylor, Robyn Alice
Jake Taylor and Jessica Cooke are proud to announce
a little sister for Joseph and Harry.

THE END

ABOUT THE AUTHOR

Emma Dunnill

Emma lives in beautiful North Yorkshire where she works full-time as a charity fundraiser, then spends her evenings and weekends writing.

Emma openly talks about her struggles with anxiety and depression, quickly discovering that writing became a wonderful distraction and coping mechanism for her. Emma admits that completing her first book and having it published is one of her biggest achievements. Having worked many a job and met many a people, Emma gets her writing inspiration from everywhere. Even eavesdropping into conversations on public transport.

A lover of learning new things, Emma enjoys conducting research for her writing, to bring the most realistic stories to her readers.

Follow Emma on Instagram: @emma_dunnill

Printed in Great Britain
by Amazon